Re:ZeRo
-Starting Life in Another World-

"You are using too much energy. In your hands, feet, neck, hips, and in your head."

"Unah!!"

"Besides that, it's good to exchange drinks with someone of a different rank and position once in a while."

The light *clink* was accompanied by the sound of the ice shifting within... as Crusch narrowed her eyes.

Re:ZERO -Starting Life in Another World-

The only ability Subaru Natsuki gets when he's summoned to another world is
time travel via his own death. But to save her, he'll die as many times as it takes.

CONTENTS

Re:ZeRo

-Starting Life in Another World-

VOLUME 5

TAPPEI NAGATSUKI
ILLUSTRATION: SHINICHIROU OTSUKA

YEN ON

NEW YORK

RE:ZERO Vol. 5
TAPPEI NAGATSUKI

Translation by Jeremiah Bourque
Cover art by Shinichirou Otsuka

This book is a work of fiction. Names, characters, places, and incidents are the product of
the author's imagination or are used fictitiously. Any resemblance to actual events, locales,
or persons, living or dead, is coincidental.

RE:ZERO KARA HAJIMERU ISEKAI SEIKATSU
© TAPPEI NAGATSUKI / Shinichirou Otsuka 2014
First published in Japan in 2014 by KADOKAWA CORPORATION, Tokyo.
English translation rights reserved by YEN PRESS, LLC under the license from
KADOKAWA CORPORATION, Tokyo, through Tuttle-Mori Agency, Inc., Tokyo.

Yen On
1290 Avenue of the Americas
New York, NY 10104

Visit us at yenpress.com
facebook.com/yenpress
twitter.com/yenpress
yenpress.tumblr.com
instagram.com/yenpress

First Yen On Edition: October 2017

Yen On is an imprint of Yen Press, LLC.
The Yen On name and logo are trademarks of Yen Press, LLC.

The publisher is not responsible for websites (or their content) that are not owned
by the publisher.

Library of Congress Cataloging-in-Publication Data
Names: Nagatsuki, Tappei, 1987– author. | Otsuka, Shinichirou, illustrator. |
Jeremiah Bourque, translator.
Title: Re:ZERO starting life in another world / Tappei Nagatsuki ; illustration by
Shinichirou Otsuka ; translation by Jeremiah Bourque.
Other titles: Re:ZERO kara hajimeru isekai seikatsu. English
Description: First Yen On edition. | New York, NY : Yen On, 2016– |
Audience: Ages 13 & up.
Identifiers: LCCN 2016031562 | ISBN 9780316315302 (v. 1 : pbk.) |
ISBN 9780316398374 (v. 2 : pbk.) | ISBN 9780316398404 (v. 3 : pbk.) |
ISBN 9780316398428 (v. 4 : pbk.) | ISBN 9780316398459 (v. 5 : pbk.)
Subjects: | CYAC: Science fiction.
Classification: LCC PZ7.1.N34 Re 2016 | DDC [Fic]—dc23
LC record available at https://lccn.loc.gov/2016031562

ISBNs: 978-0-316-39845-9 (paperback)
978-0-316-39846-6 (ebook)

1 3 5 7 9 10 8 6 4 2

LSC-C

Printed in the United States of America

PRoLoGUE

—The man was skin and bones.

Surrounded by a darkly robed group, he was covered in a black priest's habit himself. Slightly taller than Subaru, he had deep-green hair that was long enough to catch the eye. His cheeks were gaunt; his bones seemed to have only the minimum amount of flesh necessary to maintain a humanoid physique.

Judging from such an appearance, one might think his body was devoid of vitality…save for the twinkle of madness in his eyes.

"I see… Certainly, certainly, this is of great interest."

The man leaned his body forward, bending his neck more than ninety degrees to the side as his wide-open eyes gazed unflinchingly at Subaru. Behaving in a manner that could only be described as bizarre, he nodded as if something was clear to him.

Then, still leaning at an angle, he thrust his right thumb into his mouth and crushed the tip without any hesitation.

The flesh was mashed and the bone broken; he sucked on the drops of blood as his dead eyes opened wide.

"Could you…possibly be 'Pride,' by any chance?"

The man's question was directed at Subaru, who was bound to the wall. However, the boy did not reply to the question. He only blankly stared up at the face of the man standing before him, with merely a flippant and thoroughly out-of-place smile coming over his lips.

Subaru's black eyes blinked, but just like the man behaving in deviant fashion, they were empty, devoid of sanity.

"Hmm… That doesn't seem to be a reply."

The man drew his thumb out of his lips, tapping his own head with his bleeding hand as if he had just remembered something.

"Ahh, I see. It occurs to me that I have been rude. My goodness, I have yet to introduce myself, yes?"

He acted with courtesy that seemed wholly out of place and then gave a malevolent laugh that tore the edges of his pale lips. He politely bowed at the waist as he stated his name.

"I am Petelgeuse Romanée-Conti—"

After that, he stayed bent over, twisting only his head to face forward before he stated his title.

"—Archbishop of Sin of the Witch Cult…entrusted with the duties of Slooooth!"

The man—Petelgeuse—pointed at Subaru with the fingers of both hands and laughed.

Cackle, cackle. Cackle, cackle. Cackle, cackle—

CHAPTER 1

A DECAYING MIND

1

The clear, refreshing-looking sky spread overhead, filling Subaru's vision as he lay on the ground.

Thinking back, about two months had passed since he had been summoned to this other world.

He wondered just how many times he had gazed up at the blue sky in the same way during that time.

The thick cumulonimbus clouds intercepted the sunlight, but bright, dazzling rays broke through the thick cover, pouring down to the surface.

The sun's radiance was burning the insides of Subaru's eyes when he suddenly had a thought.

Come to think of it... I haven't seen a single rainy day since I came here.

He'd experienced small sprinkles late at night and showers right around sunset several times over, but there was nothing even close to resembling a long downpour that lasted an entire day.

The temperature of Lugunica was slightly too hot for long sleeves, which felt not unlike June in Subaru's old world or perhaps the lingering effects of summer stretching into September. Maybe the lack of rain was due to his current world's dry season.

"Shall we bring this to an end?"

As Subaru lay on the ground, idly thinking, an elderly male voice suddenly called out to him.

The boy remained faceup, raising his head to peer at the older man standing there. He was a tall man dressed in a black servant's outfit. He stood perfectly straight, his extremely toned body inconsistent with his apparent age. His bountiful white hair was perfectly combed, suggesting his refinement.

The senior's peaceful face had gentle wrinkles carved into it, giving him the look of a warm, elderly gentleman, but his hand gripped a long wooden sword.

Subaru replied to the man's question.

"Nah, not yet. I was just thinking about a philosophical question."

"Ohh, how interesting. And what did you ponder?"

"Fire above and water below... So I'm caught between a rock and a hard place. Or something."

Subaru swung both legs high, and then brought them down with enough force to pull him to his feet.

The core of his body still felt heavy in some respects, but the pain of his bruises and other wounds had largely subsided. Subaru rotated his limbs a little to check before swinging the wooden sword still in his hand to the fore—thrusting it straight at Wilhelm.

"One more lesson, if you please."

"Incidentally, what was the answer to the earlier philosophical question?"

"Nothing major—just me getting pissed even though I'm the one who wet the bed."

With that nonsensical answer, he stepped forward and swung with his waster, tracing a semicircular arc from a low posture.

The tip swept through the air, the wind whipping around the full-force blunt strike.

However...

"Unah!!"

"You are using too much energy. In your hands, feet, neck, hips, and in your head."

Wilhelm parried the hard-driving blow, smoothly deflecting it away from its target. The attack, aimed at his head, sailed above it. The old man turned his body, and the sword danced in his hand to accurately and gently rap the boy's head, throat, and solar plexus—all vital points of the human body. The slight impact of Wilhelm's waster sent Subaru's body flying.

Thanks to his extreme restraint, the damage was practically nil. But even so, the shock to Subaru's vitals hindered his breathing, and his failed defense ended up making him groan audibly.

"Gwoeh!"

The hit to his back made him dizzy. He was flat on the ground with his limbs splayed out once again, the sky laughing down at him. He was starting to resent this decidedly pleasant sight for some reason.

"Shall we bring this to an end?"

Wilhelm inquired gently without the slightest hint of sarcasm or disparagement.

How many times had he already voiced that question, gauging Subaru's intent?

"It seems you are working hard."

As Subaru gazed hatefully upward, a female voice interrupted.

He lifted his head to see a woman standing at the terrace, gazing down at Subaru, limbs spread wide as he lay in the courtyard.

"I only heard your voices, but you seem to be quite worked up about this."

The beautiful green-haired woman leaned on the railing as she looked down at Subaru and Wilhelm. Her long, dark locks had a lustrous jade sheen, and she gave off the air of someone who naturally stood straight, bold, and proud. Her body, blessed with very feminine curves, was clad in a rather masculine military uniform. She was the lord of the manor as well as Wilhelm's master—Duchess Crusch Karsten.

In spite of her young age, she was a brilliant woman occupying a critical national post—making her someone extremely important to the Kingdom of Lugunica's present and future.

"My, Lady Crusch. Have we interrupted your duties?"

"No, I was just thinking of taking a break. No need for concern."

Crusch nodded amicably at Wilhelm before shifting her gaze toward Subaru, prone on the ground. She added, "Besides, I do not want to be so haughty as to stifle the earnest efforts of others. Employees need time off. By all means, make full use of yours, Wilhelm."

Wilhelm bowed deeply in thanks for Crusch granting permission in her typical manner.

"Understood. Having said that…"

Then, the old man shifted his attention toward Subaru.

"Shall we bring this to an end?"

"Even I'm smart enough to tell that you mean, 'Let's end this now.'"

Subaru pulled up his grass-stained body, moving his limbs to confirm for the third—no, tenth time—that all was well. He cracked his fingers and sighed audibly.

"I feel like getting my butt kicked while a pretty girl's watching is kinda hard to swallow as a guy… My manliness gauge is dropping fast."

Subaru made a strained smile as he tossed the wooden sword back to Wilhelm, who caught it with ease. Crusch replied, "There is no need for concern. It is hardly the first time I have seen you getting hurt."

"Urgh!"

The merciless statement had Subaru clutching his chest as he groaned.

"I only heard about what happened after the fact, but I believe your words are a little too direct, Lady Crusch."

"Is that so?"

Crusch reacted to Wilhelm's comment with an innocent rise of her eyebrows before continuing.

"It is evident when a far superior opponent is impossible to match.

But I do not think an unflinching display of determination is anything to regret or be ashamed of."

As Crusch touched her chin and expressed her thoughts, Subaru felt moderately uncomfortable.

Putting aside the unexpected appraisal of his humiliation the day before, he was reminded of everything that happened before and after that episode. The greatest failure of his life—when they had parted on the worst possible terms in the castle waiting room.

"Truly, if I were you, the events last night would have been far harder to accept. I have only hearsay to go on, but…knowing myself, I imagine I would be indignant."

Feeling Crusch's partially sympathetic gaze, Subaru scratched his cheek and laughed drily.

"…Ta-ha-ha."

It was the only reaction he could muster when thinking about what had occurred that evening, a mere half day prior: an unscheduled meeting with Reinhard, the Sword Saint, who'd gone out of his way just to visit Subaru at the Crusch residence.

Seeing the change in his expression, Crusch returned the conversation to the previous topic.

"And besides, even if it is painful to receive instruction while a woman is watching, is it not something you have already done many times over?"

She leaned halfway over the rail as her gaze, rich with meaning, crossed to the other end of the courtyard. There stood a blue-haired girl who had quietly watched everything.

Realizing that Crusch was looking at her, Subaru grimaced in embarrassment.

"…Embarrassment feels a little different when it's in front of a friend."

"I would think continuing to reveal your hand before your eventual enemy is a problem in and of itself… But the same could be directed at me for welcoming such a person to my mansion. For once, I am somewhat at a loss about my own thoughts."

Crusch nodded a few times, as if her reply led her to some internal reflection. Then, she set such thoughts aside for the time being and addressed her servant.

"Wilhelm."

"Yes."

"I feel up for a little exercise. I shall delegate the remaining affairs to others. It is earlier than scheduled, but could you give me today's lesson?"

"As you command. Please take as much time as you need."

"That is a somewhat difficult request given my current mental state..."

A wry smile came over Crusch as she moved away from the railing, standing and returning to the study. She was the picture of dignity. Her green hair fluttered and danced, softly taking in the light of the sun until it vanished from Subaru's field of vision. The boy watched her go as he released the tension inside him with a sigh.

Subaru smiled bitterly at himself when he realized the raw sense of relief he felt when she left his sight.

Put bluntly, Crusch was exactly the sort of lady he had a hard time with. Her straightforward and unyielding gaze was so sharp, it seemed to pierce straight to the heart. There had been many cases where her honest, sincere personality, and the words and deeds supporting it, left him distinctly troubled.

She lived strong and proud, full of confidence, without a single shred of hesitation about what she should do. Comparing his position to hers, Subaru seemed all the more pathetic.

"Shall we finally bring this to an end?"

As the boy shook his head to change emotional gears, Wilhelm turned back to him and asked again.

"That didn't sound like a question, so I guess that's that..."

Wilhelm gracefully shifted into position with his wooden sword, and the disappearance of the question mark at the end of his sentence told Subaru that this kind yet stern session was coming to a close. The older gentleman made a thin smile when he saw the sincere regret in Subaru's black eyes.

"Now that Lady Crusch has arrived, I must fulfill my duties as an instructor. This is half the reason the House of Karsten employs me, you see."

"Hey, I'm not gonna be selfish like a little kid. You did me a big favor, spending some of your time off with me like this."

Subaru pointed the wooden sword directly at his opponent's eyes, feeling intense loneliness as the training approached its conclusion.

He'd quit kendo in middle school, but he'd still picked up the basics of swordplay. Seeing Subaru's straight posture and quiet disposition, Wilhelm's face abandoned all trace of softness.

"—En garde."

"Any time."

Subaru replied to his tutor's declaration, leaping forward across the ground.

He didn't even try to feint. His attack was a plain downward swing, no tricks involved. From a high position, the blade sliced through the air in a helm-splitting strike, but the tip lost sight of its mark and thrust into the ground. Subaru, missing his target, found his forceful lunge turning into a forward roll.

Then, "—!"

Subaru sustained what seemed like countless sword blows.

2

It had already been three days since Subaru Natsuki had entered Crusch Karsten's manor.

The home of the duchess of Karsten was located directly in the middle of the Nobles' District within the royal capital's upper strata—a mansion that stood out even among the luxuriant dwellings alongside it. He had been told that it was a villa used only during stays in the capital, but its size and sheer extravagance rivaled that of Roswaal's primary residence.

But Crusch herself had no interest in the decor of the overly ornamented manor. No doubt she saw it as a display of consideration for the many nobles who might visit the capital.

And one of those visitors had been Reinhard van Astrea. The

incident from half a day prior was bitterly etched into Subaru's memory.

"I am truly sorry I was unable to stop the incident at the training ground. I am ashamed of myself for being unable to do anything but watch."

After calling for Subaru, the first thing Reinhard did was apologize, bowing his head under the magic lamps illuminating the Karsten residence's front gate.

It was an apology from the man so trusted and respected by his nation that he was commonly known as the Sword Saint. Subaru, who didn't think himself worthy to even face Reinhard, was taken completely by surprise.

"Wa-wait-wait-wait. Why do you have to apologize for everything? You didn't do anything wrong, did you?"

"That isn't the case at all, Subaru. I'm your friend, and Julius's as well. Not stopping my friends from making a mistake was a failure on my part."

"Fr...iends..."

Subaru's breath caught a little at the mention of the second-to-last name in the world he wanted to hear. But Reinhard bore no malice. Indeed, he was apologizing for not intervening at the time. If he'd involved himself, no doubt Subaru wouldn't have experienced a fraction of the misery he was going through now.

The "duel" between Subaru and Julius might not have qualified as the real thing, but it was not the place of others to interfere with a bout that was held to settle an issue. That much was set in stone. Therefore, Reinhard had been feeling guilt for something he shouldn't have given a second thought. The fact that he still felt compelled to apologize showed why Reinhard was the "knight among knights."

"...Well, whatever the case, I'm real happy you came all the way over to see me. You have to be busy with a million things right now?" Subaru said.

"I do not want to balance my schedule and my friendships on a set of scales. If I hadn't taken the opportunity tonight, I wouldn't have had a chance to apologize to you for some time."

"'Some time'? What, you're heading off somewhere?"

"Lady Felt will be away from the royal capital, under the care of my family. There are many things she needs to learn, and there are new recruits who require training."

Reinhard talked with a thin, wry smile at the numerous hardships he expected. But at the very least, the knight didn't harbor any unease about the rapport in his master-vassal relationship. Subaru posed a question.

"You think Felt can really pull this off?"

"—Strangely, more so than I ever did before. I'm sure her determination and talent will surprise everyone. I will be merely encouraging her to help bring that future about."

Hearing that unreserved reply, Subaru subconsciously shifted his gaze away from Reinhard.

"…Is that so? Glad to hear it."

He couldn't bear to look straight at the knight. The red-haired young man didn't worry about hardships, nor did he hold any concerns about his relationship with his master. He had not even the slightest ambivalence about doing his duty to his utmost abilities.

At that moment, the difference between him and Subaru was simply too great—

Noticing Subaru was averting his gaze, Reinhard's brows furrowed in a sympathetic look.

"Do you…have regrets?"

Regrets.

…Subaru bit his lip as the word floated inside his head.

He'd always had regrets. Yesterday, he felt remorse for the day before that. Today, he was bitter about yesterday. Tomorrow, he'd no doubt be anguished about the present day, too.

The choices made over the course of his life amounted to a never-ending trail of regrets. It was impossible not to yearn for the world he'd missed due to choices he hadn't made.

With Subaru silent, Reinhard lowered his eyes.

"I will not say anything as flippant as, 'I understand how you feel.' But I am equally ashamed of what transpired. Perhaps it is the first time I've said such a thing, but I regret what happened."

The words seemed not quite apropos to the chagrin that enveloped Subaru, but that was only natural. Their positions were different, so their points of view were different. The two didn't see events the same way. That was why Subaru braced his heart for what Reinhard might say next. And yet—

"The duel that day between you and Julius…was a meaningless battle. I knew, but I did nothing, and as a result, you were unjustly hurt. It has pained me ever since how I simply stood back and watched."

"_____"

But his meager resolve didn't prepare him to hear *that*.

"—No meaning at all?"

"Yes, that's right. What happened because you and Julius clashed there? You were injured, and Julius has a black mark on his record, nothing more. Are you aware that he was placed under house arrest afterward? I'm sure Julius is regretting his own actions this very moment."

Julius's punishment was news to Subaru, and it actually surprised him. So many knights watching the spectacle had been in Julius's corner. Subaru had been convinced his opponent had made arrangements to avoid trouble afterward. And yet, he had been disciplined.

—But Subaru didn't think the knight felt any regret at all. He had crossed swords with him, albeit wooden ones, more than enough to understand that loud and clear.

Unaware of what was in Subaru's heart, Reinhard said with sincerity in his eyes, "If you had both had more time, you could have calmly discussed the matter. I should have ensured you had it… Things could have been resolved peacefully with no ill feelings instead of with a duel."

"…So there'd have been no fight at all?"

"Correct. This may seem somewhat hard to believe, but normally

Julius is a man who sincerely listens. If you'd fully aired your differences, the misunderstanding could have been immediately—"

"Reinhard."

With an earnest voice, Subaru interrupted him.

The red-haired young man closed his mouth, looking back at Subaru with an unclouded gaze. Not a single negative emotion resided in his azure eyes.

In other words, Reinhard had been completely serious.

He truly believed that duel held no meaning.

—He couldn't understand that it was a matter of pride, with neither side able to pull back from the brink.

"I understand how you feel, and I'm glad. You're…a really good guy."

"Then…"

"But I won't accept what you said. I can't accept what you said… This conversation's over."

The sight of Subaru breaking off the discussion and turning his back left Reinhard beyond surprised. When the boy passed through the gates to return to the mansion, the knight instantly began to reach out to him.

"Reinhard. You're a super-good guy. I totally understand that everything you said just now was out of pure goodwill, and you meant no harm at all… I get that."

The remark stopped Reinhard mid-motion. Sensing it behind him, Subaru didn't turn back as he passed through the gate.

"But…just don't. I won't let you rob that duel of its meaning. Anything…but that."

Subaru didn't want that, and neither did Julius or the knights who had seen the duel to the end.

Their fight had to be worth something. It had concrete, definite value, even if Reinhard, the Sword Saint, couldn't understand it.

While Subaru distanced himself, Reinhard attempted to bridge the gap.

"Even if that is so… What did you gain from that duel? You've only lost things, haven't you?" But the words he chose for that purpose provided the last nail in the coffin. "You've even lost Lady Emilia."

The very last name in the world Subaru wanted to hear at that moment had materialized. He replied to the Sword Saint indifferently.

"Go home, Reinhard. Before your master gets lonely and starts yelling."

With a loud noise, the gate closed between them. And so they parted ways.

"...He didn't need to bother, geez."

Subaru gritted his teeth at the memory of the previous night as curses he couldn't bring himself to say to Reinhard's face spilled out.

His lips twisted as he tore at his head, as though brushing away the still-raw memory.

"Do not be like that, Subaru. You've been hit on the head, so behave while I tend to it."

As Subaru lay there, a voice full of affection gently brushed his eardrums.

When he glanced up, he saw the blue-haired girl smiling down at him pleasantly. She was wearing a rather short black-motif apron dress. The maid with the adorable face—Rem—was kneeling on the green grass with Subaru's head on her lap in the venerable "lap pillow" position.

Rem, appointed as Subaru's maid, ran a finger through his hair as she whispered softly.

"You've worked hard in special training. Please, relax and rest on my lap for a while."

"Doesn't really deserve to be called 'special training'... Just simple sword practice. Must've been boring to watch, huh?"

"It was not boring at all. Just spending time with you makes me very happy, Subaru."

Everything pouring out of Rem was positive, but in his current state, Subaru couldn't accept any of it. He covered his face with a hand, averting his gaze from her, who saw even his most unsightly moments in a positive light. She'd watched the sword practice, hardly anything more than playing around, from beginning to bitter end without complaint.

Even despite Subaru concealing his emotions, Rem didn't speak a single cross word.

She silently waited out his attempt to hide his true feelings and affectionately supported his weight, softly running her finger through his hair as if to simply remind him that time hadn't stopped.

Unable to bear the silence any longer, Subaru spoke first.

"…Hey…Rem."

His halting voice brought Rem's finger to a standstill. As she indulgently waited for him to talk, Subaru took a fair bit of time before continuing to speak.

"Do you…think I'm pathetic?"

It had come from his own mouth, but he genuinely wondered what answer he was hoping to hear. Did he want her to say yes? Did he want her to say no? What exactly did he want her to appraise about him? Did he mean right then, or three days prior, or perhaps long before that…?

"I do."

Rem easily answered, interrupting Subaru's rumination.

As his concerns unraveled, Subaru glared at Rem from below in protest.

"So you think that, too? Why are you sticking with me if I'm pathetic, then? 'Cause you were told to?"

Rem, upside down in his field of vision, gently shook her head at Subaru's acerbic reaction.

"Thinking you are pathetic and being with you is not a contradiction. Even without a command, I believe I would have stayed with you regardless, Subaru."

"…Why's that?"

"Because I want to."

Her reply was brief.

The matter-of-fact delivery left Subaru speechless. He had no idea what to say, although the words made his chest feel light.

It was as if his incomprehensible self-examination had received an equally baffling answer.

"Rem… You're really something else."

"I am. But Sister is even more incredible."

"I still don't understand why you put your sister on a pedestal, but you're incredible."

Subaru raised a hand in surrender, letting his entire body relax as he sank into Rem's lap fully. He closed his eyes, leaving her to stroke his forelocks with her finger once more as she said, "I am here because I believe you want me to be here, Subaru."

"So I want you to watch me get beaten up and then act pathetic and embarrassing after? That makes me sound like some kind of masochist…"

Rem curiously inclined her head, asking with a completely innocent look, "You aren't?"

Subaru could only exhale deeply through his nostrils in a wordless reply.

Time continued in a quiet, lazy fashion, without any intrusions. Finally she asked, "Perhaps we should head back in? Any longer and we might be in the way of Lady Crusch's sword practice."

When Rem's thighs seemed about to move, Subaru grabbed hold of them, his cheek savoring the feeling.

"Just a little longer. I've been hit on the head. Might be dangerous to move this soon?"

Rem let her legs relax as she acceded to Subaru's suggestion.

"Yes… If that is what you desire, Subaru."

Thanks to her unlimited kindness, he didn't have to think about the things he didn't want to. He let his body sink deeper and deeper into that gentle quicksand.

—It had been three days since the declaration of the royal selection. Three days since Subaru and Emilia had parted ways.

Subaru Natsuki was steadily rotting away.

3

I must've done something wrong, Subaru thought once he had time to reflect.

He knew it was an unpleasant memory, but before he realized, he was going back over and over to that evening and the sight of a silver-haired girl turning from him and walking away.

As the sound of a closing door echoed, Subaru thought, *I must've come up short somewhere.*

He was well aware that his words had gone too far.

The fact that it had come right after receiving a beating had been part of it. When Emilia's words forced him into a corner, he'd ended up blurting out a lot of really unacceptable things.

As a result, Subaru and Emilia had ended up separating.

Did the suddenness of his words mean that they were just jumbled half thoughts? Or did it mean that they had been dwelling in his heart all along?

He cared for her, and he wanted her to acknowledge that; both feelings were true.

But how much he meant the rest of what he'd said... Even he wasn't sure anymore.

"—Hey, kid. Kid!!"

Subaru was submerged in a sea of self-doubt when a throaty voice from nearby reeled him back to reality.

When he blinked, the man standing right in front of him slumped his shoulders, lamenting as he creased his brow.

"Come on, kid. Don't be glaring like that in front of a man's shop. You'll scare off the customers," he lamented with a frown on his stern face, marked by an attention-grabbing vertical scar.

Subaru, back in the present, gently rubbed his eyelids, quickly recovering from the impact of the man's fierce countenance.

"Hey, Pops. I think it's your glaring at customers that scares 'em off."

"I'm not glaring! I'm worrying about you, damn it! You come here with some weirdo in tow, and then when Old Man Rom hears your message, I can't get in touch with him anymore. I should be giving you an earful for all the trouble you put me through!"

The shopkeeper raised his voice in anger and pounded the counter with one of his thick arms.

As he did, the slam caused a basket with fruit on display to tilt, threatening to send his produce tumbling. However, with a flutter of the hem of her skirt, Rem landed in the space right in front of the shop.

"That is no way to handle food."

Her fingers gripped the basket on the counter, gently catching it before it could fall along with all the fruit within.

"Ohh, thanks a lot, miss."

The man—Cadmon—sighed with admiration at her skillful move, taking the basket back from Rem with visible relief.

Then he lowered his voice as he directed a look back at Subaru. "So take my advice. Get away from this mean-mug guy. It won't end well."

"Hey, what are you talkin' about here? Don't go around spreading unfounded rumors, geez," Subaru countered.

"It's not unfounded at all. You were here with a girl not long ago, and now you've got a different one, don't you? The earlier girl… Ah, I can't remember clearly, but that just means this young lady is prettier. Two-timers can go to hell."

"Do I look like I can handle two-timing girls? In the first place, how did you…?"

Forget about Emilia, Subaru had been going to say. But Cadmon's lack of memory was an effect of the anti-recognition magic she used to conceal her identity.

Recalling that brought her face to the forefront of his thoughts, accompanied by a painful throb in his chest.

As Subaru fell into silence, Cadmon gave him a suspicious look before resuming his speech to Rem.

"You see? Incorrigible. You'll end up with nothing but hardship no matter how hard you try."

"Thank you very much for your consideration… However, I am doing this because I want to." Rem's cheeks reddened as she glanced at Subaru to gauge his reaction. Cadmon's look, even sourer than before, made plain that he thought her unfortunate.

"I have to say, though, the feel on the street's different today. There aren't more people than usual, but… It's like there's a stir in the air. Maybe more people are…stopping and standing than usual?"

Subaru gazed at the hustle and bustle, changing the topic to distract them from how he hadn't finished his previous sentence.

"Surprisingly sharp eye. Well, that's how it is. When big stuff's going on, it's time for merchants to make some money. Right now, everyone's hungry for the next rumor."

Cadmon nodded at Subaru's musings as he grabbed one of the fruits lined up in front of his shop and took a bite.

Subaru gawked at the owner holding fruit with teeth marks. "That's your merchandise…," he remarked before he continued. "Well, I'm not sure what business opportunities the royal selection has for a fruit vendor, but I'm impressed you weren't left behind when it started. Guess you're a natural genius at this, Pops."

"Oh, shut your mouth. At any rate, it's because there're more people rubbing shoulders and whispering to one another. Everyone's talking to everyone else right now. See, look over there."

Cadmon forcefully pointed with the core of his fruit, indicating a sign at the edge of the street. Even among the signs desperately competing to stand out along Market Street, this one stood taller than all the rest.

"Well, if it's anything but I-script, I can't read it."

"What? How uneducated. You can read my store's sign, then?"

"I feel like the characters are close to I-script, but they're so bad that I can't read them."

Cadmon was taken aback at Subaru's ill-natured attempt to cover up his own lack of education.

"So what is written on that sign, anyway?"

"The same thing we've been talking about. 'The Royal Selection Has Commenced.'" Subaru frowned, unsure what Cadmon's point was, so the shopkeeper roughly scratched at his head and added, "All right. Let me spell it out to you. Miss, take care of the store for a bit."

"As you request."

The way Cadmon abandoned his station as if it was nothing, and the way Rem followed up without the slightest hesitation, left Subaru simply uneasy as he slouched.

"Don't let amateurs run your shop just like that, geez. And Rem, don't make promises you can't keep."

"All she has to do is exchange merchandise for coin according to the prices listed. It's not like I'm getting customers anyway."

"So you finally admit it?!"

Subaru wore a defiant look as Cadmon led him away. Rem waved after them as she headed toward the counter.

"I have to say, though—young or old, everyone seems super interested in the royal selection. What do you think, Pops?"

Cadmon scowled bitterly at Subaru's words and replied.

"Hmm. Well, there's a lot of hot air about who'll become the next ruler, but it's not as if they can leave the throne empty forever. I wish they'd just hurry up and decide already."

"This is only what I've been told, but doesn't the Council of Elders handle running the country? How badly does not having a king affect the people?"

"Hey, if that's a joke, it's in bad taste. Now, some people snub the king as a figurehead when it comes to administration but... The Covenant with the Dragon is made with the royal family generation after generation. We have the Dragon protecting Lugunica to thank for the clashes with Volakia down south not turning into anything besides skirmishes."

Gusteko to the north, Lugunica to the east, Kararagi to the west, and Volakia to the south—those were the names of the great nations that ruled this world. Subaru had heard that smaller nations existed, too, but they were treated as client states of the great four.

Subaru asked another question.

"Volakia, huh... What, you think if the Dragon's gone, they'll invade?"

"Their imperial motto is, 'Many troops, strong nation, eat the weak, grow strong.' They say Lugunica was in the middle of a war with them four hundred years ago right before the Covenant with the Dragon was first made. Some say they're still sore about the Dragon butting in."

"So that's how the people feel about not having a king, huh…"

"Even if it wasn't for that, a country without a ruler's in as much of a bind as a beast without a head. The last king wasn't a wise one, but he wasn't bad, either. That's what I think, anyway."

Cadmon cut through the throng of various races before standing in front of a sign that towered above the already tall man. He blended in with the people looking up at it with the same objective, craning his neck to read the characters that Subaru could not.

"It's an announcement that the royal selection has begun, and a summary. The king will be determined three years hence before the Dragonfriend Ceremony, who shall conduct the ceremony thereafter, et cetera. Then it lists the candidates."

Cadmon, reading the details in Subaru's place, relayed things the latter already knew. Subaru's interest had begun to fade, but the last word, *candidates*, put a stop to that. Cadmon, watching from the side as Subaru licked his parched lips, nodded appreciatively.

"The candidates are on your mind, huh? There're five royal selection candidates in total. The best-known are Duchess Crusch Karsten and the Hoshin company president, a girl named Anastasia."

"Is that Duchess Crusch famous?"

"Well, she's a duchess. It'd be pretty bad if people living in the capital didn't know her name. She's still young, but as duchess and heir to her household, she's already considered one of the most brilliant women in national history. The tales of her first sortie in the duchy of Karsten, the reason she inherited the title, are common even here in the capital."

"First sortie…?"

"The duke of Karsten at the time—her immediate predecessor—was injured by a horde of nasty monsters that appeared in the duchy of Karsten. So she took over command for him and brought things under control in the blink of an eye, and then everyone knew her name. There'd always been rumors that she was brilliant, but she was

so good that her father had his seventeen-year-old daughter take over for him."

Listening to someone outside Crusch's sphere of influence evaluate her made Subaru's shoulders feel tighter and tighter.

Not noticing Subaru's internal turmoil, Cadmon traced the scar on his face with a finger as he went on.

"And there's not a merchant around who hasn't heard about how much progress the Hoshin Company has made these past few years, even for them. That young lady at the helm—Anastasia—she's even taken down major companies and brought them under hers. Just like that old legend, Hoshin of the Wastes. It's like she's a reincarnation of the man."

Subaru wondered if the proud way Cadmon spoke of Anastasia was due to his identifying with her as a fellow merchant. Going from a mere trader to a royal candidate was a real Cinderella story.

On the one hand, there was Crusch, a woman with an inspired demeanor, pursuing her beliefs with an iron will. On the other was Anastasia, the girl with light-purple hair, standing out due to her Kansai accent.

The details on the sign before them had no discrepancies from what he'd heard in the royal selection conference. The contents were conveyed to the populace with thoroughness and sincerity and no unfairness whatsoever.

Cadmon resumed.

"So rumor has it that those two are the leaders for the royal selection. Personally, I think Lady Crusch, in a crucial position in the kingdom, has more weight than a merchant born in another country."

"So both are leading the pack, huh."

No doubt Cadmon's words were colored by personal opinion he'd ventured at the end. Even so, it was without doubt that Crusch's position and family name constituted powerful backing. To the people, unaware of her speech, it was most natural to assume that Crusch would inherit the throne.

"So Crusch is the favorite, and Anastasia is the runner-up... So who's the dark horse?"

After Subaru's comment, Cadmon read the names of the three remaining candidates, crossing his arms with a conflicted look on his face.

"It's hard to talk about dark horses. Putting those two aside, the three others are basically unknown. I've lived in the capital for a long time and even I don't know them. This Priscilla seems to have a noble's name, but I don't even see family names for the other two. Given how the president of the Hoshin Company became one, I really have to wonder how they're picking these candidates."

On that point, Subaru imagined he'd be in perfect agreement if he didn't personally know the details. You had the current heiress of a hereditary duchy, the young president of a foreign trading company, an unknown bearing a family name of noble pedigree, and two remaining candidates with no family name and uncertain origins. Withholding information about the basics of how they'd been selected was unfair to the general populace. Even Subaru, who knew that the crests with the Dragon motifs had been used to select the candidates, had no idea what the Dragon's motives were in choosing the girls.

But just when Subaru was about to burst into laughter at all the idle speculation, Cadmon narrowed his eyes, twisted his lips in disgust, and spat his opinion.

"But I'm hopping mad they included a half-elf. I can't help it. It lists some basics about each royal candidate, but this Emilia... Apparently they made a half-demon a candidate. I tell you, it's stupid any way you slice it."

"Half-demon...huh?"

"It's what we call people who look like witch accomplices. What the hell are the high and mighty thinking...?"

Cadmon glared up at the tall sign that was a full two heads above him, his eyes filled with disgust. Subaru couldn't immediately react.

"..."

He had a not-insignificant amount of goodwill toward the scarred shopkeeper. This was the first man he'd spoken to in this other world, and when reunited with him later, he'd grown to view the man as someone he could trust. In contrast to his stern appearance, his personality and character were amiable, and he was full of love for his wife and child. At the very least, Subaru didn't doubt that he was a benevolent person.

The boy couldn't help but be surprised to hear such a man speak such slander about another as if it were a matter of course. Besides, to Subaru, it couldn't be casually dismissed. And so, his lips blurted out a denial.

"...It doesn't mean everyone who looks like that is involved with the Witch, does it?"

"Hah?"

Under Cadmon's curious gaze, Subaru's emotions got the better of him as he pushed on.

"D-don't go judging her just because she's a half-elf. That 'Emilia' girl, she's incre... She might be doing this for the sake of the country. She might be a good, incredible girl for all you know."

"Hold on. I don't know why you're trying so hard, but stop covering for a half-demon. If someone else overhears, they ain't gonna understand."

"Yeah, I suppose so. And you wouldn't want the pretty girl doing on-the-job training to see a grown man making a scary face, talking trash about someone he doesn't even know."

Subaru's large helping of invective mixed with sarcasm made Cadmon put a hand to his forehead.

"I get it, give me a break. I said too much. I apologize, okay?"

"...Tch."

Though it was an apology he was pushed into, Cadmon's mature reaction made Subaru back down.

Yet as Subaru relented, Cadmon carried on.

"You're free to think what you like. But it's not possible for a half-elf to become king."

"You're still...! Why not? Because of the Witch of Jealousy? What, because the Witch was a half-elf, that means all half-elves are dangerous?!"

"—That's right."

To Subaru, worked up again as their argument resumed, Cadmon's voice had a shockingly cold ring to it.

"There you go again…!"

Subaru was about to make a rebuttal when his voice caught in his throat, because he saw the look of fear in Cadmon's eyes.

"The Witch is scary. That goes without saying. It's a feeling everyone shares. I don't know how you grew up not knowing this, but at the very least, the vast majority of people avoid half-demons for the same reason."

"…"

"Look. They say the Witch…the Witch of Jealousy…is a monster completely off the charts. Four hundred years ago, her shadow swallowed up half the continent. Famed heroes and dragons succumbed one after another before that. If it wasn't for the Holy Dragon's power, the Sage's knowledge, and the Sword Saint of the day, the world would've been destroyed for sure."

Subaru had never heard this before, and he was unable to avert his eyes from Cadmon's deadly serious expression as he heard the details he couldn't dismiss.

"But in spite of all that the Witch of Jealousy has done, we know next to nothing about her. What we do know is that she's a half-elf with silver hair. That, and the fact she can't be reasoned with, can't understand how others think, and she seems to rampage around out of a hatred for everything in the whole world."

The wave of surging emotion behind Cadmon's trembling pupils conveyed the raw emotions of every person living in the world in a way dry sentences alone never could.

Like the picture book Subaru had seen, the story of the Witch was passed down orally and through the printed word. Depending on the storyteller, the means and the amount of repetition varied, but the final result was always the same: absolute terror that the people born in that world would never shake, as if it were a nail driven through their very hearts.

"The Witch is a symbol of terror. Everyone's afraid of things they don't understand. So people want to use the few details they do know to keep as far away from them as possible."

"…And that justifies discriminating against half-elves?"

"At the very least, a lot of half-demons having twisted personalities is the literal truth. I will admit that I don't know if it's just their natures or if it's the circumstances that make them like that."

Cadmon was grimacing as if chewing on a bitter insect, likely because Subaru's words had backed him into an uncomfortable corner. The man seemed well aware that what he was saying was irrational. But the emotions about the Witch welling up inside dimmed his view of any rebuttal of that logic.

Moreover, that thinking may well have been a universally held opinion in their world, from the lowest rungs to up on high.

When Subaru realized that, only then did he truly appreciate the meaning of the plea Emilia had made at the royal selection conference.

"—"

She was a half-elf. Her destiny was something she could not divorce herself from no matter how hard she tried. She wore an iron shackle that others starting in the same position did not, one she could never remove.

Cadmon crossed his arms and spoke sullenly.

"And since that's what people think, she has no chance of winning at all. Someone being fond of that half-demon and promoting her like this… It's a bad joke, I tell you."

The object of his argument, and his anger, seemed to have shifted from the candidate herself, Emilia, to whoever had hoisted her onto a palanquin when she had no chance of victory.

It was a benevolent concession on Cadmon's part, but it was small comfort given the thoroughly negative image of half-elves.

The girl Emilia first needed to overcome the obstacle of prejudice.

To the uninformed Subaru—ignorant of the tyrannical history of half-elves and why people feared the Witch as a result—Cadmon asked, "Why put her through it if she has to carry a handicap like that?"

Certainly, Subaru was completely inexperienced where the history of that world was concerned. He couldn't know about the wicked deeds of the Witch beyond the details written on a page. It was hard for him to imagine just how much people feared half-elves, how deep their aversion ran, and for that matter, what half-elves living in such an environment thought of other people.

But he'd heard the girl's words, spoken with a voice clear as a bell…

"—Hold it right there, evildoers!"

She had saved Subaru, who had been crawling on the ground in pain and humiliation.

Where were the expectations and calculations behind her actions back then?

Subaru didn't know their world's history, about the Witch or half-elves. But he knew Emilia.

"My name is Emilia. Just Emilia. Thank you, Subaru."

He understood that the girl with silver hair and stubborn benevolence who always acted with no regard for her own loss or gain might resemble the Witch of Jealousy, but that had absolutely nothing to do with her.

He knew that she, who had lived in a world that showed no kindness to her whatsoever, possessed heartfelt good will toward others even so.

No matter how badly the world might treat her, at least Subaru would—

Suddenly, a chill ran up his spine as a frosty voice interrupted his thoughts.

"—It was all for your own benefit, wasn't it?"

In the back of his mind, her lovely, charming smile transformed into a sharp gaze and a stern voice.

"I wanted to believe you…but you're the one who stopped me, Subaru!"

He had trampled her trust underfoot, and her pained voice reverberated inside his cramped skull.

He tried to understand. He thought he got it. He'd acted as if he did. And he'd frivolously broken and tossed aside the promise he'd made to her. The blame impaled his chest once again.

"—*If you don't say it, I can't understand, Subaru.*"

In his memories, Emilia berated him for his actions on that day over and over.

He felt agony as if pieces of his chest had been ripped off, and sadness bore down on him to crush him, but Subaru's anger toward the girl glaring at him also surfaced.

He'd worked so hard. He'd helped her so much. He'd been hurt so much. What was wrong with hoping for a reward? What was wrong with wanting her to respond?

—*If I don't say it, you can't understand? I could say the same to you.*

Emilia hadn't told him anything about the royal selection, discrimination, or her feelings on that day. She'd shunned Subaru, pushed him away from her goal, treated him like he was barely a side character.

Of course Subaru didn't know anything about Emilia. She wouldn't tell him anything.

He didn't know how she had lived up until then, how she felt as she aimed for the royal throne, what she thought about the world seeing her as the Witch herself...

And as for what Emilia thought about Subaru, he didn't want to know.

"—Kid. You all right? Hey!"

"...Eh?"

Subaru, realizing that Cadmon's face was leaning in extremely close, recoiled with a start.

"Waah! Pops, don't do that! Your face could kill someone like that, damn it!"

"That's a horrible thing to say! You were staring into space again, just like earlier. You got some chronic illness?"

"W-well, if the passionate feelings burning in my chest are a disease, I might have been infected with something. It's a feverish, nasty illness that seduces mankind, sometimes gently and sometimes severely..."

Cadmon, unable to keep up with Subaru's joking attempt to hide his empty, wounded heart, shook his head.

"Yes, yes, you're afflicted with poor character is what it is. Fine, let's head back to the shop."

Subaru, following him on the way back, came to realize that his entire body was drenched in a cold sweat. Perhaps it was due to the roiling emotions inside him, but each step felt very heavy.

His head drooped as Cadmon abruptly murmured, his back still turned, "And this might be sticking my nose in, but stop talking about the Witch out in the open. If anyone hears you, they're not gonna be understanding...me included."

It didn't seem like an effort to revive the earlier debate. Sensing the seriousness in Cadmon's voice, Subaru silently indicated his acceptance.

With such thorough prejudice, there was no telling whose ire he would earn by running his mouth. At the very least, he had no desire for any more trouble in the royal capital.

Cadmon ignored Subaru's agreement and repeated himself for emphasis.

"—You never know who's listening."

As they cut through the throng and made their way back to the shop, the air between them seemed weighty somehow. Subaru hadn't managed to sort through his feelings, and Cadmon seemed annoyed and embarrassed about the dispute. There was barely a word spoken between them as they returned to the shop.

However...

"Welcome back. The final customer was just departing."

Cadmon's mouth dropped open, and he stared agape at the sight of Rem exchanging merchandise for money and seeing off a customer with a polite bow.

Dumbfounded, he peered at the empty display cases on the counter. For a moment, perhaps he thought that he'd abandoned his shop, trusting it to Rem only to have her sell his merchandise at fire-sale prices, but the store's till filled with coin showed that wasn't true. In other words, she'd sold it all.

Cadmon sank to his knees, covering his face with his palms, his pride as a merchant apparently wounded.

"I-in that short time, you sold more than my shop normally sells in an entire day…"

With no regard for the store owner's dignity, Rem smoothly slipped around the counter and rushed to Subaru's side. She glanced expectantly toward the boy, and it seemed like an invisible tail was swaying behind her.

"How did I do, Subaru? I heard he helped you in the past, so I worked my very best to at least be of assistance. You can praise me if you like?"

The rare sight of Rem going, *Praise me, praise me!* made Subaru realize his heart felt just a little lighter.

"…You really are incredible, Rem."

"I am. But Sister is even more incredible."

Subaru forced a smile and, following Rem's lead as she offered her head, gently petted it. He savored the totally familiar texture of her hair, and Rem's throat let out a small sound from Subaru's soft touch.

"I still don't get how that logic of yours works, you know…"

Watching the interaction between the two from behind, Cadmon stroked his own scar with a finger and slumped his shoulders. He murmured, "I guess appearance does matter…"

The reason for his shop's slow sales was now all too clear.

4

"Interesting. So that's why he gave mew these abbles for your troubles."

Cat ears twitching, the speaker thrust a fork into a mountain of sliced red fruit and raised a juicy morsel to smiling lips with perfect grace.

Those short feline ears were the same color as the shoulder-length flaxen hair below them, and the white ribbon adorning those locks joined large, round, teasing eyes to complete the picture of a pretty girl—who was actually a boy.

Subaru replied, "Well, I already taste tested them, so all I had to do was hand them to the kitchen. Setting that aside, don't give me sidelong glances and lick your lips. It's giving me chills."

No, knowing both his external appearance and his actual gender, the proper term was definitely *pretty boy*.

It was in between meals, some time prior to supper, and abbles had been brought in as a light snack. Cadmon had given them the fruit as a souvenir, looking both grateful and deeply burned at how Rem had broken his store's sales record in a short span of time. She had returned to her quarters for a change of clothes, intending to rendezvous with him later in his room as the daily ritual during Subaru's stay in the capital continued until suppertime.

Subaru remarked, "That said—man, returning to my room only to find a pretty boy sneaking into it ahead of me... I was careless for not leaving the door locked, but isn't that, you know, impolite for a knight?"

"Aww, it's fine, no, isn't it? It's just proof how much Ferri can relax around you. Besides, Lady Crusch could never see Ferri act so lazy, even by accident."

The pretty boy—Ferris—flopped right down next to Subaru's flank. As Subaru felt the bed bounce against his rear, Ferris looked up meaningfully from his position on his belly.

"Did your heart flutter just now?"

"It skipped a beat. I don't think anything bad about you, but I just don't have those kinds of interests at all. I like girls, as ordinary and regular as they come." No matter how adorable he might look, the fact they were the same gender was a barrier that Subaru had no intention of crossing. He shook his head in exasperation at Ferris's shocked expression. "In the first place, I have no idea what your reason is for being so relaxed around me. I mean, it's not like I remember getting along especially well with you before. I'm not giving off some kind of pheromones I should be worried about, am I...?"

Ferris put his chin on his palms and responded blithely.

"Ah, that's pretty simple, actually. It's because there's no doubt meowtsoever that you're weaker than Ferri, Subawu. You're a weakling, so no worries."

Subaru blinked once and murmured, "You have a really bad personality, geez."

"Wooow, what a surprise! Ferri was sooo sure mew were going to blow your lid there…"

"Hey, facts are facts. I'm not gonna get bent out of shape over that."

Subaru had learned many times over just how feeble he was. Since being summoned from his own world, he'd had his powerlessness repeatedly pounded into him. If the day of the clash with Julius at the parade square was the greatest example in terms of quality, the number of times Wilhelm had smacked him to the ground there at the mansion provided quantity. Besides, that sense of powerlessness wasn't particular to his new world, either.

The pain of his own frailty was something he'd experienced everywhere he had ever lived.

"Well, you can keep saying I'm weak, but how about you? I mean, since you're a part of the Knights of the Royal Guard, you've probably been trained some, but…"

"Mm, me? Ferri doesn't have any skill with a sword at all. Knights' swords are heavy, so Ferri doesn't carry one—just the dagger from Lady Crusch. Nothing good will come of waving it around, so Ferri doesn't."

Ferris's cackling laugh and kicking feet embarrassed Subaru. The sight of the cat-eared boy so casually admitting his own shortcomings made his chest burn, plain and simple. His attitude—not thinking of weakness as a failure—was not one Subaru could dismiss so easily in his current state.

Ferris seemed to see right through the silent Subaru's inner thoughts as he made an addendum.

"But Ferri has other redeeming features, mew know? That's why being completely mewseless as a knight isn't upsetting at all."

"Good save. Well, if you accept it then that's totally fine… Totally fine."

Ferris's confident declaration was no doubt built on a very strong foundation. Subaru, with no such footholds, averted his gaze in distinct discomfort.

Perhaps because Subaru turned his back doing so, Ferris sat up from where he lay on the bed and nestled into Subaru's shoulder, letting it support his weight. Then he asked a question.

"Nervous?"

"On the first day I was, but not anymore. If you're gonna do it, please, go ahead."

"Boooooring."

Pouting, Ferris sat Subaru up and put his hands on both of his shoulders. It was a shoulder rub posture, but Ferris held still in that position, silently closing his eyes.

—The warmth passing from Ferris's palms began to circulate from Subaru's shoulders into his whole body. The power of the water mana in his hands met the magical mechanism inside Subaru's body called a gate, rising and flowing through it.

Ferris spoke again.

"Gently, slowly, softly. Ah, found a split end. It feels like you've been working unusually hard, Subawu. Ah, a gray hair, too. Yanking that…"

"Ow! And could you not babble when you're working? All this mana sloshing around in my body feels pretty icky. If you aren't careful, you're gonna make me dizzy."

His head felt a little heavy, and his limbs were sluggish. His body felt like it was reacting poorly to the attempted treatment.

Ferris was the preeminent water magic user in the royal capital—real name Felix Argyle. The reason Subaru was lodging at the Crusch villa was so that he could take advantage of the healing magic to heal his damaged gate.

The idea of healing via water magic might have called to mind something cool and refreshing, but in practice, it was nothing that simple. A gate was the means by which one used magic. The direct cause of the damage to Subaru's gate was repeated overuse, as well as doping when his mana was depleted.

Thanks to that continual abuse, just bringing his gate back to a normal state required rather rough measures.

Subaru offered a comment.

"So this healing technique is like taking a hose that water only trickles out of, plugging the leak and pushing out all the mold and junk that's built up inside…"

"What? From the way you're speaking, it feels like mew aren't very happy about this, *meow*?"

"I'm just beating myself up. Don't worry about it. Ugh, this feels gross."

Subaru shook his head, enduring the sensation while trying to placate Ferris, whose mood had worsened.

It was the third day he had been living at Crusch's mansion—in other words, the third day of Ferris's treatment—so perhaps he had begun to grow a little accustomed to that part, too. On the first day, he'd groaned out loud from the very start, unable to silently endure the urge to vomit.

It was Ferris's turn to speak up.

"Well, that first day couldn't be helped. Ferri had to pump this directly through the worst, ickiest part. That's what happens when you're a living corpse with wounds all over your mind and body, *meow*?"

"You don't go halfway when you poke at uncomfortable stuff, do you?"

Subaru hated how Ferris, who should have been unable to see the look on his face, seemed able to read his thoughts through his body. One might say that the way he unflinchingly dug at Subaru's scars was far craftier than how Reinhard unconsciously peeled the scabs off his heart without even realizing.

"Oh, Subawu, it feels like mew really are thinking of getting payback. The training you're doing with Grandpa Wil isn't unrelated to that, is it?"

"Can you stop jabbing at a guy where it hurts? I'm sure even you understand how I feel… Wait, do you?!"

"Of course. Ferri's been like, 'I wanna be strong!' too… Well, Ferri's given up on doing anything reckless like that, though."

Ferris's tone sounded slightly more serious as he used his pretty-boy speaking style to dance around the matter.

Subaru was a little surprised, sensing Ferris's reaction contained his real feelings on the matter. Even someone as unflinching as that had had moments in the past when he was uncertain or lost. But eventually, he had realized his potential for magic and gave up the path of the warrior.

What about Subaru, then? Did he have anything he could boast of to others? And if he could find such a thing, would it be able to drive away the miserable aching in his chest...?

"Point being, you should give up on dark thoughts like getting payback, okay? It's a little hard to say, but... If there is a next time, you might die, mew know?"

With a sulky look, Subaru closed one eye, his reply a barely spoken murmur.

"...Even I know that."

The earlier battle with Julius had ended with Subaru being pummeled beyond description. And in spite of the pounding he had received, he understood that the knight had gone easy on him.

There was no other way to explain how he had been struck so many times yet had not suffered any lasting effects. That wasn't due to Ferris's skill as a healer alone. The difference between Subaru and Julius had simply been that overwhelming.

Fully aware of this, Subaru had asked Wilhelm to teach him. He wasn't dreaming of becoming exponentially stronger in a mere several days of training. It was just...

"Can't you just let yourself be lazy? Your body's in bad shape, Subawu. No one would blame mew for sleeping the day away in recovery. Who would complain if mew take it easy and give your mind and body a rest?"

Ferris's words came out in a rush, not giving Subaru any time to make excuses. The way he said it grated on Subaru's nerves a little, but the message was extremely seductive given his current state of mind. For some reason, his heart wavered at that moment, though normally he would feel indignant. But...

The sound of a gentle voice pulled him back from his chaotic emotional state.

"—Master Felix, please do not toy with Subaru too much."

Rem was standing at the doorway of the room with a neutral expression on her face. She had supposedly returned to her room for a change of clothes, but her outward appearance was not visibly different from when she had been sightseeing with Subaru in the royal capital.

Noticing the questioning rise of Subaru's eyebrows, Rem grasped the hem of her skirt and twirled around as she said, "I changed out of my maid-uniform-for-errands into my maid-uniform-for-visiting."

"R-right, is that so. You always seem to know what I'm thinking, Rem."

"Yes. I always want you to see me fresh."

"I'm happy you feel that way, but your phrasing makes you sound like fresh vegetables…"

Subaru answered Rem's apparent request to evaluate her freshness, and the maid did not follow up. Rather, she shifted her gaze toward Ferris.

"I am grateful for the treatment you conduct for Subaru day after day. However, please desist from using that as an opportunity to lure him into temptation."

Ferris made a suspicious-sounding laugh and nestled into Subaru's back once more.

"'Luring into temptation' sounds so bad, *meow*. Ferri is only saying these things out of concern for his well-being."

The flow of power from his palms, coursing in via Subaru's shoulders, suddenly flooded through his back and into his entire body.

The influx of mana beyond Subaru's capacity to bear distracted him for a moment.

However, a soft impact against his head brought his wandering mind fluttering back into place.

"Master Felix. Please give these pranks a rest. There are some things I cannot let pass as a joke."

When Subaru gasped and regained his senses, white fabric covered his face. Straining his eyes, he realized that his face was pressed into a very familiar apron dress and that Rem was caressing his head.

"Hey, um, Rem, this is a little embarrassing to do in front of someone else…!"

Subaru tried to cover up his bashfulness with his usual jokes as Rem embraced him even tighter.

"Subaru, be quiet for a moment—Master Felix?"

Her tongue formed polite words, but they carried cold emotion.

Ferris traced little patterns on Subaru's back like a child whose prank had been figured out.

"Oh. They did say you can use a few water arts, Rem. Guess that would make you object to what Ferri has been doing…"

"Hey, Ferris. Having a pretty boy do weird finger stuff like that doesn't make me happy one little b… Er, wait, Rem? My head, ah, feels good, but don't…hug…so…strong—l… Gyah!!"

"Ahh, Subaru, I'm so sorry. Master Felix just wouldn't pull back… I thought, if someone was going to take you from me, it was better that I…"

"That statement's going dangerous places!!"

Feeling like his skull was creaking, Subaru rolled to the floor to escape from both Ferris and Rem. He warily glared at the other two from the corner of the room, while Rem visibly lamented as she shook her head.

"Subaru, you poor thing. You've gone through quite an ordeal, haven't you?"

"What you were saying at the end was the scariest of all, Rem! There's a crazy little *yandere* in you, isn't there?!"

Ignoring Subaru's objections, Rem faced off against Ferris across the bed. She gazed emotionlessly as the cat boy twirled his finger around his flaxen hair with a mischievous expression.

"You have a reason to be angry, Rem, but it wasn't all some scheme by Ferri, mew know? It was for Subawu's sake, just a teeny widdle bit."

"And everything besides that 'little bit'?"

"The rest was for my friend's feelings, and everything else was for Lady Crusch. That's natural for a retainer, isn't it? It's no different for you, is it, Rem?"

"It is not. Accordingly, you must understand what my reply must be, Master Felix."

Ferris must have sensed something in Rem's stare, because he soon raised both hands in surrender.

"Okay, *okaaaay*. Ferri will stop using the treatment to brainwash him."

"From here on, I shall be present for all treatments."

"*Meow*, no trust at all. Well, that's fine, really."

Ferris glanced sideways at Subaru. When Rem shifted, as if protecting Subaru from that gaze, Ferris stretched up and looked down at him over Rem's shoulder.

"So that's enough lecturing from Rem for today. Our next date will be somewhere she won't find us, meowkay?"

"I don't remember dating you, and you just said 'brainwash,' didn't you?! I'm not meeting up alone with a guy who'll say something freaky like that!"

"Okay, okay, that sounds like a yes."

"No doesn't mean yes, geez!!"

Ferris, waving as if the matter were settled, hopped off the bed and stretched as he headed toward the door. He stopped right before putting his hand on the doorknob as he looked back.

"Rem."

"Yes?"

"You might not believe this, but... The part about this being for Subaru's sake, it wasn't a complete lie, mew know?"

"...I...understand."

Since Subaru was standing behind Rem, he couldn't see her expression. But he sensed that her brief reply held just a slight bit of hesitation.

"Ah. Well, that's good. Bye-bye, then!"

With a smile, Ferris gave his carefree salutation and finally left the guest room.

Subaru, feeling utterly exhausted for some reason, flopped down from the sudden rush of lethargy.

"I'm supposed to be getting treatment. Why do I have to feel this tired from it?"

"Are you all right, Subaru?"

"Mmm… I'm all right…I think. I don't really get it, but you saved me from something?"

"That is unclear. Master Felix does not appear to hold any ill will toward you, so… I do not know the true motives behind his previous behavior."

Seeing Rem ponder the matter, Subaru turned his head, perplexed.

"Errr, so what state was I in earlier, anyway?"

"Until just now, Master Felix was interfering with all the mana in your body, Subaru."

"That so? Just figured healing required it. It's not a good feeling, and it's pretty awful, to be honest, but somehow I put up with it…"

"Having another person's mana in you like that is the same as taking that person inside you. That made Master Felix's words much easier for you to accept, you see."

"The way you said that sounds pretty bad, you know?!"

Subaru stood up in a hurry, patting his body down to check things out.

"Am I all right? There's nothing weird going on? My heart isn't becoming more womanly or my speech having more feminine twists to it or something?!"

"It is all right, Subaru. You are quite splendid. I am always watching you, so please believe me."

Subaru thought for a moment that he couldn't allow the peculiarities of her statement, but instead, he let it roll over him as he patted his chest down in relief. He also gained a new appreciation for just what position he was in.

"Now that I think of it, this is, like, one of the enemy's main headquarters. I've been relaxing and letting my guard down a lot, though…"

"Please be at ease. It is true that you are incorrigibly laid-back and slow to catch on, but I am keeping guard, so there is nothing for you to be concerned about."

"You couldn't leave out the 'incorrigibly laid-back' part?!"

That moment, the truth struck him clear as day. Just imagining how much Rem had been waging a one-woman war while he was idly whiling away his time made him want to run out the door.

"I'll try to be a bit more careful from now on. Everyone here is an enemy, after all."

"…An enemy, you say?"

He was trying to pull himself together after having been so focused on one thing. But in his determination, Subaru didn't notice that Rem was murmuring something.

After ensuring his body was safe and sound, Subaru gazed at the magic crystal on a wall of the room to check the time.

"Oh, time's a-wasting. How about you help me study until we get called for dinner, Professor Rem?"

Subaru headed to a desk in the room. The remaining abbles were on top of the desk, sitting alongside study material he had brought with him from Roswaal's mansion.

In other words, it was study time for Subaru, who had not yet mastered the language of this other world.

"I really cannot get accustomed to being addressed like that."

"Well, I think it's all right, since you're the one doing the teaching… If you don't like it, I can stop, Professor."

"No! Please continue! It is something you call only me by! So Subaru may not call anyone else that! If you do, I will be upset!"

"Well, if you're gonna be like that, I'll be relentless, too! Nggggh, you won't outdo me…!"

Subaru chose an odd point to make a show of stubbornness, fiercely turning toward the table. Rem stood behind Subaru, watching him affectionately. But from time to time, she would stare into the distance, her mind wandering as her face showed faint signs of strain.

"Professor, I don't understand this part very well…"

But all traces of that look vanished the instant she heard Subaru's voice.

"Oh Subaru, you are helpless. You could not get anything done if I were not here with you. I would not mind if you demonstrated your gratitude from time to time...?"

5

"Excellent timing. Subaru Natsuki, would you come with me for a while?"

Subaru had finished bathing and was on his way back to his room when someone addressed him in the lobby on the second floor of the Crusch residence. The long-haired woman was ascending the stairs and carrying a tray when she called out to him.

For a moment, he wasn't sure who it was, since the outfit and aura she gave off were completely different from usual.

Subaru's only reaction was to raise his brows.

"...Miss Crusch?"

"It is. Is there something odd about...? Ah, I see, this is the first time you have seen me in an outfit unrelated to my duties. I imagine it has startled you."

Crusch seemed to realize what had unsettled him. The outfit she normally wore that resembled an army uniform was gone; in its place, she wore a nightgown with thin, dark fabric and a cape over the shoulders. Unlike the scrupulously buttoned-up military uniform, the nightgown showed off her very feminine physique with every step, greatly altering the aura she projected.

Subaru was averting his eyes, feeling vaguely embarrassed, but Crusch apparently hadn't noticed. She continued, "Either way, it is fortunate that question has been resolved. To return to the original question, do you have some spare time? If it pleases you, I would like to have a drink with you this night."

"...I don't drink alcohol, though."

"You may sip water if you wish. I do not intend to drink enough to become inebriated."

Crusch smiled a little as she rose farther up the stairs. Subaru was a little thrown off but, finding no reason to court her displeasure, made a short run to catch up.

She led Subaru to a balcony on the third floor of the mansion. A white table and chairs had been placed in one corner of the terrace. Crusch sat down first and indicated the opposing chair with her gaze, so Subaru meekly complied.

"The breeze is very refreshing tonight. It's the perfect weather, since I like to drink my liquor while watching the night sky."

"I'm wondering why you invited me today, though. You could have invited Ferris or someone?"

"Of course, normally I would have Ferris with me... However, he must work late this evening." Crusch must have been referring to Ferris's work as a healer, in great demand even in the royal capital. Just as Ferris had done for Subaru in the evening, he treated numerous people on a daily basis. It was a packed schedule that made almost no allowance for free time. "Besides that, it's good to exchange drinks with someone of a different rank and position once in a while."

"I said it once already, but I don't drink alcohol, you know?"

"You can simply add plenty of ice. You may even fill it with cold water if you wish. Now, then?"

The tray on the table had a pair of wineglasses on it. In one, she poured amber-colored alcohol; in the other, she poured clear water. Subaru accepted the water, reluctantly touching his glass to Crusch's.

The light *clink* was accompanied by the sound of the ice shifting within it as Crusch narrowed her eyes.

"It seems you are anxious about a number of things, but please be at ease. I have not brought you here out of any desire to interrogate you. I swear that it is no such petty trick."

"Ah, no... I wasn't worried about that."

"There is no need to try to hide it. I can see anxiety and doubt in the night breeze around you. As we belong to rival camps, I am actually relieved by your wariness. That way, I do not forget my own principles."

Crusch made a show of enjoying her half-filled glass, savoring it with her red tongue. Subaru, desperate to wash away the sense that she could see right into his mind, poured the cold water down his throat.

"So these last few days, you've been pretty busy... Is it related to the royal selection?"

"—Ha-ha-ha! As soon as I tell you caution is unnecessary, you plunge straight into the heart of the matter. I certainly did not expect that. I do think that is exactly how rival camps should be, however."

"Not knowing my place and not reading the mood are kind of my defining characteristics."

"I would add spinning your own vices into virtues to the list. Certainly, it is the royal selection that has kept me occupied these last few days. It has added to Ferris's and Wilhelm's labors as well."

Her wineglass held at an angle, Crusch spoke smoothly and in good humor. She seemed even more attractive than usual to Subaru's eyes, so he shifted his attention to the courtyard, which was in sight of the balcony.

"And it's related to all the stuff you've been hauling into the mansion and the people coming and going?"

"A sharper eye than I expected... Or rather, the scale was large enough that you could not fail to notice." With no sign that her good mood was waning, Crusch loosened her lips and replied to Subaru's question. "It's not unrelated at all. My house is currently assembling all the men and materiel possible for a particular task. It may cause you and Rem some trouble in the coming days."

"I feel like it's us who are causing you a lot of trouble, but... What's this particular task?"

"—Have you heard the details of how Wilhelm came to enter my service?"

After his question was answered with another question, Subaru couldn't say anything. He understood only that the "particular task" Crusch had mentioned concerned Wilhelm—and that the details were not a topic he could broach without the old man's permission.

"You are free to speculate... It seems I have said too much. Wilhelm might well scold me for this."

"Wilhelm doesn't look like someone who'd talk to his master like that, though..."

"He is a man without mercy. You should watch him instruct me in the sword at least once. He must think of our first meeting as a rather embarrassing one himself."

Crusch made a wry smile, savoring the wine with the colorful tip of her tongue as she switched subjects. Subaru also sought a change in subject to reset his mind.

"So you have sword lessons every day, too, huh?"

"Surely you are not saying I should not wield one because I am merely a woman?"

Subaru instinctively responded with embarrassment, but Crusch winked at him.

"I jest. It is merely something I am accustomed to hearing since my youth—that the little Karsten princess is both a maiden as well as a crazed fencer. I was considered the fool of the duke's house for my love of getting my hands dirty more than flowers."

"...That's pretty different from the rumors I've been hearing. In public, all the common folk are praising you, saying you'll leave your mark on the kingdom's history."

"The people changed their appraisal when they learned of my exploits. The sudden shift was rather calculating of them in my opinion, but it is my own fault for not having produced results in all that time. I do not intend to blame lords for altering their public stances. As for the rumors in the city, I can only call them embarrassing."

She was apparently a big enough person to accept whatever people said about her deeds, for good or ill. Crusch never averted her eyes from discussion about being "merely a woman." Public opinion had dramatically changed because of her exploits—which jogged Subaru's memory about something.

"So that famous first battle was what changed how everyone thought of you?"

"Mm..."

As Subaru pursued the topic, Crusch rested her lips on her wine-glass as she let out a small sound. Her amber eyes narrowed.

"It is embarrassing."

She turned her head with an uncharacteristic pout on her face. Subaru countered, "How can it be embarrassing? I heard demon beasts attacked your land, and you handled it great in your father's place. That's pretty cool for a first battle, isn't it?"

"Of course not. Let me correct one misperception. I did not fell the demon beasts. I merely drove them off. I was a princess hastily and impudently taking command in place of her injured father."

"But it worked, didn't it?"

"Of course it did. I could not allow my first sortie to end in failure after I brushed aside my father's objections. However, the problem is the extent of the results. To me, my naïveté at the time is a shame most difficult to bear."

Her mood had not fallen, but Crusch wasn't sugarcoating anything, either. She didn't think it was worthy of heroic tales. The topic Subaru had chosen was, from her perspective, a sore point of sorts.

Thus, Crusch concluded the topic, shooting Subaru a jovial look.

"You are rather fond of needling people yourself. As expected of a political rival, I suppose?"

Subaru was completely unaware that he was such a person, but she'd given him no room to argue. He brought the ice-cold glass to his lips and tried to change the topic in an attempt to smooth over the awkwardness.

"S-so incidentally, what else has changed besides that?"

"—Let me see. Since word of the royal selection spread, the number of proposals has increased by leaps and bounds. Though such talk comes with the territory of being a duchess to begin with."

"Pfft!"

Subaru spewed out water without thinking when his probing of a rival's internal circumstances took an unexpected turn.

"P-proposals, as in, proposals for marriage?"

"I will soon be twenty years of age... Marrying then is not uncommon. It is awkward due to my gender and position, so I have deftly evaded such talk until now."

"Ahh, the...duchess thing must really intimidate the men..."

"A rather blunt way to put it. But that is indeed the case. A few have come forward to take my hand, each trying to make me his, but... That was then, and this is now."

Crusch closed her eyes as a larger sip of wine flowed across her tongue.

Her position as a royal candidate made her an especially pivotal person for the nation. No doubt there was a horde of potential suitors coming out of the woodwork who'd never made an attempt for her hand.

"Miss Crusch, you're pretty optimistic about this proposal talk. Are you looking to get married?"

"I wonder. It is a topic I have pondered myself. If I were to marry someone, he might be of great assistance to me in many situations, including ascendance in the royal selection. But all the candidates are single women, so the conditions are the same for all. I suppose matters are slightly different for Priscilla Bariel, who is a widow."

Hearing Crusch's opinion, a wave of anxiety pressed against Subaru's innards.

"I-I see... Everyone's single. Similar conditions... Marriage, huh..."

Marrying someone of high status meant bringing that person into one's political camp. If Crusch had received marriage proposals, the other candidates probably had, too.

Naturally, the same could be said for the young Emilia.

"Forgive me, Subaru Natsuki. I have been somewhat mean to you in revenge."

"...Eh?"

Subaru, distracted by the possibility of Emilia marrying, was slow to react to the apology.

"All individuals chosen as candidates for the Dragonfriend Ceremony are forbidden to marry during the royal selection period. Nominally, it is because one should put the kingdom before the self, but in reality, it is more of a desperate measure to prevent marriage ties from exacerbating political conflict."

"Th-then all these marriage proposals you've been getting?"

"I will assess them all after the royal selection is complete. Making the proposals beforehand rather than after the fact is more acceptable, I suppose. I will not make empty promises only to revoke them later, however."

Subaru sighed with relief. If marriage arrangements were prohibited, there was no danger of Emilia being married off to someone behind his back.

"But one can hammer out all the details while leaving the actual marriage for later."

Subaru sullenly complained, "…Miss Crusch, do you enjoy toying with the hearts of men?"

"You prodded at my own source of shame first. The least I could do was to return the favor." Crusch tilted her glass without a single hint of guilt. "Besides, people are usually too conscious about differences in rank to be honest with their own hearts. I have a rather deep interest in how such affairs will be settled."

"Worry about your own love life before someone else's, sheesh. If you're pushing twenty, you must have one?"

Since she'd been toying with him, Subaru tried to counterattack, but the reply he received was unexpected.

"Unfortunately, having been born a Karsten means I cannot hope for freedom in marriage. I am still a woman, however much I may deviate from the conventional norms."

In contrast to Subaru's romantic fantasies, Crusch had already given up on her own freedom to decide her relationships. It was a natural view of marriage in a world where status and family determined partners regardless of personal interest.

As Crusch's eyes gazed at the melting ice in her glass, they quietly held unshakable will and resolve. Subaru took his time trying to form a rebuttal, but he was unable to speak a word.

With the night breeze blowing across the balcony, Crusch ran a hand through her fluttering hair.

She had pale skin. Almond eyes. Beautiful green hair, and a profile filled with such beauty and elegance as to shake others to the core.

As much as she said that she deviated from the norm, Crusch was a beautiful woman. That fact did nothing to detract from the sublime nobility of her beliefs.

Unable to bear the silence, Subaru chose a topic that might have been overly vague.

"Miss Crusch... What do you think of the royal selection?"

"Mm," she began in response, closing her eyes as she thought it over. "I spoke of it at the royal selection conference, but I harbor misgivings about the state of this country."

"...You did say that, yeah."

"If I take the throne, my policies will be as I stated. In spite of that, the Dragon Tablet selected me as a candidate, someone who would surely reject the Covenant. This is either the Dragon's will or that of some divine being. Do you not think so, Subaru Natsuki?"

As Crusch posed her question, Subaru fell silent. Since he was unable to immediately give her a reply, she continued.

"I do not overestimate or underestimate my own abilities and position. Reputation comes not from within but from others. That is especially so for one who rose to the status of candidate as I did, judged by those who thought nothing of me. It's not how I have lived until now that should be judged but how I live from now on."

"It sounds like you want to make people pay for judging you like that."

"Quite the contrary. Reputation is something granted by others, but I believe it should be granted after the fact, not before. If someone has a certain level of ability, judge her once you have seen the results. And yet the Dragon Tablet brought me, one convinced of these things, within reach of the throne... Perhaps that was a smart thing to do."

Crusch's amber eyes narrowed slightly as they gazed at the ice in her glass. Subaru couldn't think of a response. He felt like she viewed the world in a very different way than he did.

Unable to bear his silence, Subaru tossed the ice in his glass into his mouth and crunched it down.

Just as he tried to use the sound of crushing ice to break the silence, a scornful voice suddenly interrupted him.

"Aaah! Why is Subawu here with mew, *meow*?!"

In the direction of the cry, he could see Ferris rushing onto the balcony, his shoulders heaving. He hurried to the table and banged a hand on it, shaking the glass bottles as Crusch thanked him for his labors.

"Thank you for your hard work, Ferris. I'm sorry, I thought you would be back much later, so I had a drink with Subaru Natsuki as an appetizer."

"Did you just call me an appetizer?!"

"Goodness, Ferri can't leave you alone for one second, *meow*! Ah? And Lady Crusch, you've had much more wine than mewsual, haven't mew?!" Ferris looked at how much liquid remained in the bottle as he spoke. "Being all friendly with Subawu... Having such a fun conversation... Aaaagh, so jealous!"

"It is true I've enjoyed more wine than usual. He is a rare conversation partner, and we leaped from topic to topic. Some of it was rather embarrassing, however."

"People are gonna get the wrong idea if you put it like that!"

"Grrrrr! What is this?! And Lady Crusch, you're wearing such a defenseless outfit!!"

When Ferris pointed it out, Crusch looked down at her mere nightgown. She inclined her head slightly, raising her glass a little.

"What of it? Do I not always dress like this when I have drinks with you in the evening, Ferris?"

"That! Is! The! Problem! Mew can't compare your time with Ferri to a ravenous beast of a man like this! Men are wolves, *meow*!"

As Ferris admonished Crusch like an aggrieved parent, Subaru yelled back.

"Hey, don't single me out here! You're a man, too, aren't you?!"

Subaru had not forgotten about how Ferris's gender had thrown his heart for a loop.

"That's because Ferri would never cast a lascivious gaze upon Lady

Crusch! But the way Subaru wanders this way and that, he can't be trusted, *meow*."

"That's enough toying around, Ferris. All at the royal selection conference know who Subaru Natsuki cares for. He would not set his sights upon a woman as lacking in charm as myself."

When Crusch eyed Subaru in search of agreement, he hesitated for a moment.

"Err… Well, that's true…I suppose?"

Ferris instantly cut in.

"Haahh? What? You're disappointed with Lady Crusch in some way…? Do you want Ferri to kill mew?"

"Why do I need your approval for my answers?!"

Crusch interrupted.

"Wait. Why did a wind of hesitation and deception flow from your direction just now…? What does this…? Ah, I see. You have Rem as well. Certainly my words were not adequate."

"And now she really has the wrong idea!"

Crusch wore a very accepting expression while Ferris glared frostily at Subaru. The conclusion she had come to was trouble enough, but the usually adorable cat boy was quite intimidating when his expression was serious.

Subaru desperately tried to explain and clear up the misunderstanding as the night breeze again washed over the three on the balcony.

In front of Subaru, who was taking little sips of his water, Crusch and Ferris filled their glasses to the brim with wine. As he watched them, he abruptly voiced something that had been nagging at him.

"You two get along really well. Been with each other a long time?"

"Hmph. Continuing to gather intelligence on the enemy?" Ferris asked.

"Not at all. You just look so close, I wanted to come out and ask."

Ferris sat alongside Crusch, glancing at his master while enjoying the same wine. Subaru didn't think feelings that ran as deep as Ferris's were formed in a short period of time.

"You are right. Ferris and I have been together for a long time… Ten years now, is it?"

"Ten years, one hundred twenty-two days, six hours. Give or take, *meow*."

"That's so specific it's scary, you know."

Ferris glared at him. Subaru regretted his comment as the pretty boy put a hand to his own cheek.

"Even now, Ferri can't forget that first glimpse of Lady Crusch. It's engraved in my meowmery. Since that day, Ferri has been Lady Crusch's eternal servant."

Crusch commented, "You make too much of it, Ferris. I did no more than what was required of me. The fact that doing so earned me your loyalty is what I would call the most fortuitous event of my life."

There was no distance between them. From a simple crossing of paths, they had become so incredibly close. Their relationship as master and servant surely made them the pair with the strongest foundation out of everyone vying for the royal throne.

"We get along fabulously, right? Unlike some other pairs I could meowntion?" Ferris said.

"—!"

"Goodness, Subawu, you're too easy to see through!"

Ferris smiled, having bluntly revealed the thoughts currently rising to the surface in the back of Subaru's mind. His cheek twitched as he glared at Ferris, but the feline eyes watched him innocently as their owner tilted his wineglass.

Crusch took up the topic instead, closing one eye and giving Subaru a stern look.

"I presume that what has brought you to a standstill is your relationship with Emilia as lord and vassal." Crusch drew her chin in a little, gently licking her alcohol-drenched lips. "You cannot use my relationship with Ferris as a reference for resolving that stalemate. The issues between Ferris and me were resolved an entire decade ago."

"…My 'stalemate'?"

"Perhaps I should call it a rite of passage... Something that must be overcome by people before they can become lord and vassal in a true sense. Now that I think of it, right after Ferris decided to serve me, he explored what he could do through pure trial and error."

Like a child being teased, Ferris's face turned red at having his past abruptly revealed.

"W-wait, Lady Crusch! Please don't talk ameowt that. It's embarrassing!"

Crusch watched Ferris and shook her head.

"It is nothing to blush over. How could the sight of one doing his best to locate his place and appropriately serve another be shameful? Impressed by your resolve, I went to equal lengths to be a master who would not bring you disgrace. Even now, I do not know if I have achieved such a thing."

"Ferri will never harbor dissatisfaction toward his lady Crusch, not in an entire lifetime!"

"You spoil me. You would say the same thing if I spent all my days in complete idleness. This is why I must have a strong character: to resist the temptations of depravity."

It was a very humble-sounding statement, and Crusch seemed to be earnestly speaking from the bottom of her own heart. Ferris sent her an even more passionate look, but Subaru simply wanted to run away.

Seeing their relationship, and the absolute, unshakable trust between them, tore at his heart.

Crusch said to Subaru in a sharp voice, "—Do not lower your eyes, Subaru Natsuki."

"...Eh?"

"If your eyes become clouded, your soul will go astray. That will mean your future is closed and you have lost your purpose for living."

"—"

"When you follow your own sense of justice, you can do any number of things if you just look at the ground. Lift your face, look forward, reach out your hand. Even when doing something for others, you must be able to see them for your feelings to get across."

Subaru's throat caught. Every drop of blood in his body froze. For a moment, Crusch's words drove a nail into his heart.

Still, she didn't look at the frozen boy, but at the wine in her inclined glass.

Subaru wondered: if those eyes pierced him at that very moment, what would have happened?

—Perhaps, at that instant, he would have fallen on his hands and knees without a single moment's hesitation.

Subaru was not only surprised at her seeing right through him, but he also had to take his hat off to her skill as a great stateswoman. Still, he was able to avoid kneeling before her because Ferris was the first to respond to her words.

"Ahh, Lady Crusch... I swear again to exhaust my life in service of my master."

"Then I can only respond to your loyalty with the entirety of my spirit— Subaru Natsuki, strive to do nothing that would diminish yourself. I do not want to think of you as an insignificant foe."

Ferris's loyalty, Crusch's nobility—both stirred Subaru's heart deeply. He wet his parched tongue, failing to form words several times before he managed to speak.

"Lending an enemy a hand, huh... It's awfully nice of you to give your opponents a fighting chance."

"This matter is important enough to decide the future of the entire nation. This may be highly impudent of me to say, but if I must struggle for the throne, I wish for it to be against worthy rivals. A crown earned by defeating weaklings will do nothing to impress the lords of the land."

"...Wanting strong opponents means you're confident about beating them, huh?"

"I have no such confidence whatsoever. What I have is will, and I have poured effort into achieving optimal results so that I can do what I must. Furthermore, I hope that my rivals do the same."

This was the individual named Crusch Karsten, her every thought humble until the bitter end.

Having exchanged drinks with her like this, the impressions he held of her—"sincere," "high-class"—changed. This was a woman like a sword, fierce as a firestorm, pitiless as a naked blade.

Ferris relaxed his voice, clapping his hands together as he dissolved the tense atmosphere.

"Somemeow, the conversation became so formal. Let's unwind now."

Bathed in a cool breeze, Subaru realized that his brow was covered with sweat.

Crusch replied, "I am sorry for speaking so stiffly. I mustn't get carried away with entertainment or my drinks."

"No, no, mew needn't apologize for anything, Lady Crusch! Subawu understands what he needs to do meow."

Ferris's words, summarizing the earlier conversation, sounded very hollow to Subaru's ears.

"What I…need to do now…?"

Surely he understands had been the implication, but Subaru couldn't put his finger on it. The only things he'd picked up during the evening spent over drinks were that Crusch and Ferris shared an unshakable bond and that he was small and confused.

Subaru didn't see anything about what was to come or what he needed to do.

Yet in spite of that, what could Subaru tell them that he now understood?

"—"

"As far as Ferri is concerned, having Lady Emilia and Subawu all split up is kinda fun, but that's not what Lady Crusch wants at all. Sooooo you need to make up with Lady Emilia as soon as meowssible. And do what mew can do to make that happen."

"What I can do?"

Could he really accomplish anything, worn to the bone as he was?

"Yes. A long time ago, back when Ferri became Lady Crusch's

knight, he thought very, very hard about what he could accomplish."

Ferris put a hand to his chest as he returned to that time in his memories. Crusch's lips slackened slightly as she glanced over at him like that. For a moment, Subaru heart beat faster in his chest.

—*Something only Subaru Natsuki could do?*

He realized it, as if it had come down to him like a revelation from the heavens itself.

"There…is something I can do."

Both of the others glanced at him as he continued, "There's something only I can do—Yeah, that's right. No one should've had to tell me that."

Now he knew. No, he'd always known.

He'd been reminded when he had been on the verge of forgetting.

Truly, Crusch and Ferris were benevolent people. They were providing aid to the enemy with everything they had, like the famous Kenshin Uesugi.

—They had reminded Subaru of exactly what he could do for Emilia's sake.

"Yeah… I have something. I've always had it."

It had nothing to do with power, or knowledge, or rank, or status. It didn't need to.

For, just as Ferris had said, Subaru possessed a single, ultimate weapon.

It had been in him from the beginning. But everything that had happened to him had shoved it into a dark corner of his mind.

Images of Julius, Reinhard, and Emilia came to him, one after another. All of them looked at Subaru with contempt sharp enough to cut his soul.

—These were the people Subaru Natsuki had to prove himself to.

"I just need a chance. If I can get that… I can make all my problems go away."

Subaru felt like a dark cloud had lifted as doubt left his heart and he gained confidence in its place.

He clenched a strong, tight fist, picturing a silver-haired girl in the back of his mind.

Crusch gently turned her wineglass around in her hand as she murmured offhandedly.

"The wind blows stronger. It would seem tomorrow's weather will be somewhat stormy."

Then, with a small sound, the melting ice cube within her glass neatly split in two.

CHAPTER 2

EVENTS IN MOTION, AND REM'S DECISION

1

The tip of the wooden sword made contact with Subaru's forehead. The next instant, centrifugal force immediately blew him away. He felt like the sky and the ground had been swapped as he wrapped his arms around himself, cushioning the blow as he made a well-formed roll. Having neutralized the damage from the tumble, he proudly licked his lips at his own mastery.

"Geh, there's dirt on it. Ptoo, ptoo, ptoo. Tastes like grass. Ptoo, ptoo!"

"Shall we bring this to an end?"

"Surely you jest. You saw my expert falling technique, didn't you? My genius has finally blossomed!"

Saying the words almost broke Subaru's heart. He had mastered the skill in the course of being pounded day after day.

The boy had sparred with Wilhelm every day during his stay at the Crusch villa. He still couldn't land even one attack, but his ability to improve his falling technique suggested that Wilhelm wasn't simply smacking him around without a purpose.

The older man presented a rebuttal, though.

"However, it is a useless technique for a duel with real swords."

"You didn't need to point that out!! The pine tree of my heart has a lot of cracks right now!!"

Certainly, in a bout that could end in a single sword stroke, a martial arts skill for properly receiving a blow and falling was not very useful. Improving a skill used solely for practicing was a misplaced priority, but it was still well worth it during sword training.

"I must say, you seem to be more spirited this morning somehow."

"Last night, I had a little discussion with Miss Crusch about my concerns— Thanks to that, all my hesitation's disappeared. I feel pretty good at the moment."

"In a book I read yesterday, a character who was only beginning to become accustomed to the battlefield spoke much like you are now. He lost his life because he took his fight for granted, Sir Subaru."

"So there's death flags even in other worlds?!"

Apparently even in a small corner across the cosmos, there were lines that marked you for death, just like back home.

But Subaru had been anxiously awaiting Wilhelm's words of concern.

The older man raised his eyebrows in a questioning expression.

"Sir Subaru?"

A smile came over the boy as he shook his head.

"...Nothing. Really, nothing at all."

—At that moment, "the field of battle" and "death" were things he could welcome with open arms. Those were opportunities for Subaru Natsuki to establish his worth in an undeniable way.

"So much waste."

"Ugah!"

When sword practice resumed, Wilhelm exploited the opening created by Subaru's wandering thoughts, using a minimal motion to strike with his sword. He took advantage of all the boy's excess power and unnecessary momentum and easily sent Subaru's body dancing into the air with no visible power behind the sword attack.

"I can handle this!"

Subaru, desperate to keep from falling on his head and causing serious damage, instantly shifted his head and curled up, adopting an ironclad fall-breaking posture that could let him land anywhere without major injury. However…

"Do you really think that is the last of it?"

With one smooth motion, Wilhelm inserted his wooden sword through a gap in Subaru's curled-up limbs, wrecking his posture. The boy's arms and legs spread out wide, and unable to grasp what was happening, he slammed into the ground, limbs splayed.

"Gyah!"

Subaru rubbed his still-smarting nose and shot an objecting glare at Wilhelm. His sword-fighting tutor responded by thrusting his wooden weapon straight down into the grass. Subaru's breath caught in his throat under the calm gaze.

"Adopting a position to break your fall and prepare for whatever might come next is the first meaningful progress you have made. But more important, I refuse to accept the premise of teaching you to fight in a manner that assumes defeat from the very beginning."

"Uhh…"

"If I may, before teaching you how to swing a sword and techniques to break a fall, I shall tell you how to prepare in a more fundamental manner."

As Subaru grunted, showing Wilhelm had hit the mark, the tutor raised a finger.

"—If you have decided to fight, fight with all your body and soul. Forget all pretty words that lead to defeat. Hunger and thirst for victory using any means necessary. If you can still stand, if you can still move a single finger, if your fangs have not yet been broken, stand. Stand. Get up, get up, and attack. So long as you live, fight. Fight, fight, fight!"

"_____"

"That is what it means to do battle."

Wilhelm's visible pause lifted the tense air that had come to dominate the courtyard. Only then did Subaru realize just how loudly his own heart had been beating. At the same time, each deafening throb drove home the fact that he was alive.

—Living had never felt better.

The feelings that had made him welcome the prospect of death until mere moments before had suddenly flown away.

The instant Wilhelm began to speak of preparing for battle, the air around him completely changed. He might have looked like a mild-mannered gentleman, but Subaru felt a sword-wielding demon within him. Perhaps that was the true nature behind the old man named Wilhelm.

The one who wielded such strength that he was employed as the personal sword instructor of Crusch Karsten, favorite to win the royal election—the aged swordsman, Wilhelm Trias.

"So fight to win, even if you know…you're gonna lose… It's a little inconsistent, but I understand what you mean. It's not logic; it's a matter of emotion. Then…"

Subaru, still in awe of the elderly man, felt the fighting spirit in him rekindled as he replied.

I can handle this, said his stubbornness.

He couldn't let that breakthrough to his doubts, that ray of hope come apart in such a short time.

The feelings of Subaru Natsuki were not that cheap. He couldn't let them be.

"—If I can do that, can I get a little stronger?"

"That is a different matter. The desire to be stronger and actually doing so are separate matters altogether."

"So now you deny me?! Don't you think saying yes would make for a more beautiful tale?!"

"…I have learned the cruelty of lies through bitter experience. I could not forgive myself for telling one."

Subaru did not notice how the other man's eyes momentarily fell as he spoke.

"I believe sometimes the truth is crueler than a lie, just so you know…"

Subaru felt like Wilhelm was dodging the question, so he re-gripped his wooden sword and abruptly murmured, "Do you see any sword talent inside me?"

"From where I stand, unfortunately, you have none. Your aptitude for the blade goes no further than the common man's—the same place as mine."

The strained, self-deprecating smile that came over Wilhelm made Subaru raise an eyebrow in surprise.

"That's pretty humble coming from you, saying you have no talent with a sword."

"It is the truth. I have no gift for it. If I did, I surely would not have had to wield one nearly as much. Therefore, it is possible for you to arrive at the same level as I."

"...Incidentally, how long would I have to work at it?"

"Nothing so great. You would only need to devote half your natural life to it."

"Only, he says."

It was often said that continually striving to improve was true talent. In actuality, even with Wilhelm telling him that he could arrive at the same level, Subaru couldn't fathom the drive to devote as much time to the sword as the old man, or a reason to do so.

In the first place, the reason Subaru had Wilhelm teach him like this was—

"I thought, like, pouring myself into the sword without worldly thoughts might let me find enlightenment for the first time..."

"I wonder now. Whatever you might grasp will not make you suddenly stronger, after all, and I do not think a clear mind or lack thereof determines who will win and who will fall in the end."

Wilhelm drily conveyed his opinion. "Besides," he continued, "if I must say so, I have rarely wielded my blade with a clear mind. Particularly when I first began, I had very few thoughts about the way of the sword."

"So what did you think of?"

"My wife, and my wife alone."

"Sheesh, Wilhelm! Sometimes you really go on about that wife of yours."

Subaru remembered how he had spoken of his beloved wife when they had first met, but Wilhelm had also praised his bride to high heaven during Subaru's stay at the mansion. It must have been a harmonious marriage.

Seeing Subaru break out in a strained smile at the latest episode of this behavior, Wilhelm rubbed his chin.

"Someday, you will reach a point where such preparedness is necessary to become stronger. Well, it's nothing you need to worry about at present, Sir Subaru."

"What do you mean?"

Subaru tilted his head slightly. Wilhelm shook his head a tiny bit at the gesture.

"I simply mean that there is little point in lecturing someone about what it takes to become stronger when he has already abandoned the choice to do so."

"—"

For a moment, Subaru's face froze over, unable to comprehend what he was being told. However, the breakdown was momentary. He immediately shrugged, as if dismissing it as a joke.

"Hey now, what are you saying all of a sudden, Wilhelm? I'm as surprised as a burglar who gets stopped before he actually steals anything. I've done what now?"

"If you are aware of it yourself, it would be inelegant to speak further of it. I have said what I wished to say. It would have been difficult to tell you had I let this opportunity slip by."

Wilhelm, speaking as if he understood everything, left no room for Subaru to pursue the matter.

Unease smoldered in Subaru's chest. Wilhelm's words had left him with an undeniable sense of nervousness. And Wilhelm could tell exactly what that feeling meant.

Instantly, that truth tore unbearably and mercilessly at the boy's heart.

Subaru, sweating in the throes of a phantom chill, raised his head when Wilhelm looked toward the mansion and spoke.

"Sir Subaru. It seems that this morning's practice is at an end."

"—Ah?"

When Subaru followed his gaze, he noticed a small silhouette racing into the courtyard—Rem.

Normally, she was not one to show emotion on her face, but he could see a sense of quiet tension on her as she ran.

Had something…happened?

For Subaru, at that moment in time, it was fortuitous salvation, a golden opportunity to forget his conversation with Wilhelm. He looked at Rem's haste and agitation with relief.

Or maybe that was because Subaru had suspected where things had been headed.

"Subaru— We need to talk."

When Rem stood right before him, her serious expression made his heart tremble.

—But Subaru would never speak to another about the anticipation he felt in that moment.

2

Lady Crusch, waiting in the reception room, gave a knowing nod as she saw Subaru approach.

"It would appear that you have already heard."

Crusch and Ferris were together in the reception room, waiting for Subaru and Rem as master and vassal. Subaru, last to enter the room, couldn't deny he felt late to the party as he shook his head a little.

"I haven't heard the details yet. Seems like Rem only has a vague idea, too."

When Subaru's eyes shifted to indicate Rem beside him, she dipped her head with a tense expression and said, "What I have felt is only a result of the consciousness I share with Sister. Sister's clairvoyance would be able to gather more details about the situation, but…"

Rem lowered her eyes as her words trailed off, looking dismayed at her own powerlessness.

Rem's reply caused Crusch to exhale in apparent admiration.

"Shared consciousness—I have heard of this, that close relations from a select few humanoid species, such as twins and blood relatives, can understand each other's thoughts without requiring words… And you can do this from the royal capital to a place as far removed as the Mathers dominion?"

"As already stated, it is a vague thing. Powerful emotions and words that one wishes to convey very strongly can be related. However…"

As Crusch sat, Ferris adopted a casual posture behind her, his kitty ears quivering.

"From how mew put that, mew must have felt something pretty unsettling over that telepathy, right?"

Subaru, put off by Ferris's demeanor, shifted to stand in front of Rem.

"Don't keep us in suspense here. If you know anything about this, say something. Don't just leave Rem twisting in the wind like that. Spill the beans already."

"Ooh, mew don't like me now? Besides, intelligence doesn't come for free. You're just a patient and a guest, Subawu. Why should we tell you anything?"

"You…!"

Properly speaking, Ferris was right. Even if he was a guest on the surface, Subaru's position was that of a patient and an outsider. He could insist it concerned him all he liked, but since he was part of a political faction, only a fool would toss him a bone just because he'd begged for it.

But as Subaru cursed his own shallowness, it was Crusch who rebuked Ferris.

"Ferris. Do not be unkind. There is no reason for you to play the villain here. All toying with Subaru Natsuki will earn you is an angry glare from Rem."

"Fiiiine."

Crusch, still seated alone on the sofa, motioned for Subaru to sit in the chair opposite her.

"Self-reflection leads to personal progress. But that depends on the time and situation. I would like to prioritize trading opinions here and now. How about it?"

"...Sure thing. Hate to take a free ride, but I really want to hear what you have to say."

Subaru accepted her offer and sat with Rem standing at his side.

Crusch began.

"In the Mathers dominion—that is, in the fiefdom of Marquis Roswaal—dangerous activities have apparently been reported around his manor. Part of the domain has already been placed under lockdown at the marquis's command."

Subaru's brows rose at the unsettling language.

"Dangerous activities? Lockdown?"

The fact Rem's telepathic connection had been triggered had prepared him for bad news, but even hearing the details made unease churn within him.

"We do not actually know what is occurring within the Mathers dominion. But I can hazard a guess, given that the marquis's support for Emilia—in other words, a half-elf—as a royal candidate has come to light."

"What, you mean the serfs are on stri— They're complaining left and right?"

When Subaru voiced the first misgivings that came to mind, Crusch easily agreed with them.

"That is quite possible, of course. The infamy of the Witch of Jealousy makes prejudice against half-elves a battle she cannot avoid."

Once again, Subaru couldn't allow the circumstances of her birth to be her shackles. He was growing to hate the faceless mob that talked trash about Emilia without knowing anything about her as a person.

"Your rage is surely misplaced. She chose this path, knowing what she would face."

"Misplaced? You mean me or those people? ...So what, they're kicking up trouble in Roswaal's fiefdom for a stupid reason like that?

Are these little brush fires that'll burn out, or is it going to turn into a massive firestorm?"

"Setting aside whether the reasons are petty or not, the summary is sound. This also explains Rem's telepathic reaction." Crusch turned to Rem as she spoke, drawing all eyes to the previously silent girl.

"The feelings I am picking up from Sister are partly unease and largely...anger. I believe she did not mean to convey these things but did so subconsciously."

"Do these shared sensations between you occur with great frequency?"

"No, it is quite rare. We are always controlling our thoughts to a certain extent. I believe that in this case, Sister transferred these things to me in spite of self-restraint."

When Rem reached the latter half of her explanation, she could not conceal the anxiety coloring her words. It was not an exaggeration to say that Ram had the most mental strength of anyone at Roswaal Manor. A crisis that could shake even her restraint was clearly no small matter.

And yet, beyond what Ram had let slip telepathically, she had made no effort to call for Rem's aid.

Subaru murmured to himself alone as his conclusion burned him up inside.

"It's like she's...trying to keep us from getting involved..."

The only explanation he could come up with was that Ram had told Rem of the danger over their mutual link without calling her sister back, because she intended to convey that information to Rem...and avoid letting Subaru know.

—Did *she* want to keep Subaru out of her problems to that extent?

"But she's in trouble, isn't she...?"

The situation was bad enough that it had reached Crusch's ears, there camped in the capital.

As was typical, there were few that Emilia could count on, and she had enemies numbering beyond reason. In such circumstances, who would take her side without some kind of ulterior motive?

The answer was no one. After all, there was nobody currently at her side who would be her staunch ally.

She had left behind the one who would have.

No doubt, when Emilia realized that, she would regret what she had done. That was why—

Subaru lifted his head and murmured with determination, "I've... got to go save her, don't I?"

This time, all gazes fell upon him. Crusch raised one eyebrow, and Ferris softly closed his teasing lips. Then Rem tugged on Subaru's sleeve with a nervous look.

"N-no, Subaru, you mustn't...!"

The anxiety and mournful pleading in Rem's eyes startled him.

She continued, "You must do as Lady Emilia and Master Roswaal have told you and concentrate on your own treatment. I, personally, agree with them. You must focus on healing your body for the time be—"

"If I do that, stuff will happen that can never be undone. Rem, it's like that time back when we talked before going into the demon beast forest. We've...got to do something."

"...!"

Rem's expression stiffened in pain at Subaru's words.

They had spoken like this in the past, just before entering the demon beast forest to rescue the abducted children. Subaru had said the same things to Rem when she'd tried to stop him.

Those actions had consequences. As a result of his decision, the children had been rescued safe and sound. That was why Rem knew very well what was behind Subaru's resolve now.

Keeping Rem at bay as she clung to him, he shifted to look straight at Crusch, seated before him.

"It's as you heard, Crusch. Rem and I will go back to the ma... To where Emilia is. Until things are settled, I'll have to put off the treatm—"

Subaru was delivering his verdict as a member of his political camp when Crusch curtly interrupted him by calling out his name.

"Subaru Natsuki."

Subaru's breath caught under Crusch's penetrating gaze. His heart beat much harder; he had the sinking feeling that he'd forgotten who he was dealing with. Then she coldly stated...

"—If you leave this place, it means that you have become my enemy."

Subaru felt those words as keenly as a blade slicing into his flesh.

Then, when the meaning began to dawn on him, like a laceration just beginning to ache...

"Wh-what do you mean by...?"

"Let me correct your misunderstanding. My treatment of you as a guest and Ferris's healing you is the result of a contract."

"Contract...?"

"Yes, a contract for your care between Emilia and me. My house has received collateral in exchange for treating you as a guest. However..."

As her words trailed off, Crusch put a hand to her chest to indicate herself.

"The circumstances before the royal selection, when the contract was formed, and now are different. Now that we are publicly political enemies, I must take great care in any negotiation with Emilia's camp. It is the same for the contract governing your treatment. If there is any violation of its terms, I have no obligation to uphold an agreement formed before the commencement of the royal selection now that it has begun in earnest."

To Subaru's ears, the word *contract* that she kept repeating sounded like *promise*. It sat very poorly in his chest, mingling with his memories of parting ways with Emilia.

Crusch pressed on.

"In these circumstances, your departing from my residence would be a violation, a unilateral abridging of the contract midway. After all, though there is no enmity attached, Emilia and I *are* enemies."

Subaru's mind couldn't catch up with Crusch's blunt declaration of war.

He understood that the duchess and her people were "enemies" on paper. He'd barely finished saying to Rem that he was sorry for leaving himself defenseless in the manor and would adopt the right mindset going forward. And yet, Subaru had yet to fully grasp what that meant.

The person standing before him was the greatest enemy standing in his and Emilia's way.

"I did have it all wrong... I thought for a little bit that we might be able to be friends or something."

"—"

"That was just dumb talk over drinks. 'If you can do something, do it...'? I was a fool to take an enemy's words at face value. I'm being petty. Tripping up your opponent is the right thing to do."

The same hazy sense of alienation that he'd felt at the royal selection conference seeped into his chest.

Subaru saw his memory of their conversation over drinks the night before in a new light and felt betrayed, since it was Crusch herself who had told him to do whatever he could.

To stand in his way despite those words: Was that not a betrayal?

Ferris, silent to that point, spoke as if he couldn't stand to watch.

"...Don't misunderstand, *meow*!" His sharp look made Subaru bite his tongue and swallow his words. "Lady Crusch isn't acting out of malice but kindness. It wouldn't hurt her at all if mew left to return and try to help Lady Emilia—"

Crusch interrupted.

"Ferris, stop."

But Ferris brushed off Crusch's rebuke and glared at Subaru.

"No, I will say it. For such a minor meowsunderstanding, it's far too cruel, so someone has to say it... Subawu, going will do nothing to change things. It's pointless to go. On top of that, you'd be wasting Lady Emeowlia's contract, which she paid for with a fair sum. After the humiliation you went through at the royal palace and what happened with Julius at the parade square, you still don't get it? Staying put, hoping for the best, and focusing on healing your body is the far better choice."

—Subaru heard something.

The sound of something snapping inside himself.

He'd been stuffing his anger into a sack within him, and when he realized it was now open, Subaru was seized by such a rage at the humiliation inflicted on him that his teeth cut into his lip.

Those provocations were more than enough to harden his resolve.

"I've decided—I'm returning to the mansion where Emilia is. It's been a short time, but thanks for your hospitality."

As Subaru spoke his farewells, Rem shouted to hold him back.

"Subaru!"

But he held up a hand to Rem as he rose from his seat, looking down at Crusch.

Crusch folded her arms and closed her eyes. He had no idea what was inside her heart. Ferris, seated beside her, let out a long sigh, his face making his sullen mood clear as he said, "No respect for others' feelings... Shouldn't a good man take warnings at face value?"

"Your warning let me make my decision. Thanks."

Ferris apparently gave up on discussing the matter after Subaru returned his sarcasm. Instead, Crusch unfolded her arms before looking at him and resuming the conversation.

"Subaru Natsuki. Unfortunately, all of this house's dragon carriages for long-distance transportation are already assigned to other tasks. All that I can lend you is a slower freight carriage or a mid-range carriage that would require you to dismount and go part of the way on foot."

"...Er?"

Subaru's eyes widened. He'd expected her to berate him for unilaterally breaking the contract, but Crusch...almost sounded like she agreed with Subaru's decision. The unexpected reply made Subaru's eyes nearly bulge out of their sockets.

She raised an eyebrow with a questioning look before turning toward Ferris.

"Ferris. Did I say something odd?"

Ferris put his hands to his cheeks and squirmed as he replied.

"Even Ferri's dazzled at how incredibly you can adapt, Lady

Crusch. But, ah, you aren't actually going to lend Subawu a dragon carriage, are you?"

Crusch nodded in the affirmative.

"It is as I said. I respect the decisions of others. No matter what the decision, it is very important to take responsibility for it. And no matter what burden you bear, you must work to achieve what you want to achieve and bring no dishonor to your soul— Is it not so?"

"…Yeah, it is. That's exactly it. I don't want my soul to become shameless. If that girl's in trouble, there's no way I can stay here as a patient and spend my days without a care in the world."

Crusch's affirmation made Subaru uncomfortable, as if he had been gearing up to fight an opponent that didn't plan on doing battle.

Perhaps Subaru had conveyed his resolve, because Rem closed her eyes, seemingly berating herself for a single moment. When she opened them again, she had returned to her normal neutral expression.

"In place of my master, let me extend my deepest thanks for everything you have done to date."

"I don't mind. There is benefit to us as well. However, I would like to speak to you concerning the last leg of the journey…"

Rem lowered her head, treating Crusch's offer with great courtesy.

"If I may be so bold, we would be grateful for the help. We wish to confirm that the dominion is safe without a moment to spare. However, time is short. It will no doubt take two and a half days to reach the Mathers lands from the royal capital."

Subaru exclaimed, "Over two days?! Why? When we came it didn't even take half of one day to get here!"

If his memory was correct, the dragon carriage left Roswaal Manor in the morning, arriving at the royal capital just past noon. Even without a long-distance carriage, the disparity in the lengths of the journeys was too extreme.

"That's impossible now. The Liphas Highway we used to get here cannot be used currently. The season is poor, and fog is covering the road… Therefore, we must take a detour around it."

"So what if there's fog on it? If we just cut right through that—"

Ferris interrupted, swatting Subaru's opinion down with what was apparently public knowledge.

"It's the White Whale that makes the fog, mew know? If mew stumble across it inside the fog, your life is gone. That's just commeown sense, right?"

Subaru scowled at the unfamiliar term *White Whale*. But Rem set aside the fact that Subaru didn't understand and proceeded with the larger discussion.

As a result of her negotiations, they came to the following terms: Subaru and Rem would borrow a medium-range dragon carriage from the House of Karsten and then board some other dragon carriage at a village along the way to return home as fast as possible.

Subaru gritted his teeth over the inconvenient lack of a dragon carriage that could go the whole way without stopping. It was times like this that he painfully missed cars, something that needed only fuel to make it run farther.

It was a bad situation that made him want to hurry, but hurry he could not. The fog that covered the highway seemed like a manifestation of the worry spreading before his eyes.

The sense that this was a looming bad omen wouldn't stop pricking at Subaru's heart.

3

Once the plan had been hashed out, things moved quickly.

In short order, Subaru and Rem were headed toward the front gate of the Crusch villa with their luggage, yet there was already a vehicle awaiting them, stripped of all ornamentation to lighten it, with a single red-skinned land dragon drawing it.

Wilhelm was holding the beast's reins as he awaited their arrival. When he noticed Subaru and Rem rushing over, the aged man bowed deeply.

"This is the fastest land dragon that this house is able to lend under these circumstances. Even so, I dearly regret that it is inferior to the long-range dragons employed by the marquis…"

With Rem taking the reins, Subaru stood beside her and looked at Wilhelm.

"I'm immensely grateful you're lending me anything at all… I'd love to say I'll return it for sure, but…"

His tone dropped at the end.

Wilhelm was the only one to see off Subaru and Rem at the front gate. They had said their farewells to Crusch and Ferris at the entry hall of the mansion. The least he could do was politely return the dragon carriage later as a final parting of ways.

"In my position, I can but obey Lady Crusch's decision. Once you depart from the mansion, my master and your master will no doubt become mutual enemies— This dragon carriage will serve as a parting gift for the half-fulfilled treatment and sword instruction."

"But that's… I don't think they said one word about that when we left the mansion."

At the very least, the farewell from master and vassal suited them almost too well.

"I pray your efforts shall be valiant, and that you will strive to make your choices proudly, without shame to your soul."

"With Lady Crusch being this nice to mew, you'd better make up with Lady Emilia in a hurry. Now get going already!"

That last sentence probably left the strongest impression. There hadn't been any hint of the kind of consideration he felt from Wilhelm, but…

"I, too, serve Lady Crusch, so I am somewhat familiar with my master's way of thinking."

"Incidentally, when did you start working for her?"

"I believe it is just over half a year now…"

"Hey, that's way shorter than I thought!! From how you talked about it, I thought you'd been master and servant for years and years!!"

Rem was piling luggage onto the dragon carriage while Subaru and Wilhelm traded words in that manner. Rem took the reins again and gave the land dragon's snout a gentle stroke.

"—Understand? Then do as I say. That's it, good boy, good boy."

"Rem, how's it looking?"

"He seems to have a slightly wild disposition, but I have just instructed him who is on top, so there shall be no trouble. I believe he will obey my commands."

"R-right… Gotta establish the hierarchy. You really know how to crack the whip, huh?"

As a result of Rem's "conversation" with the land dragon, they seemed to be getting along. Given the fact they'd be racing together for over a day's worth of time, the relationship between driver and land dragon was crucial.

Rem discussed their plan.

"Taking a detour across the plains to avoid the fog, we should pass through two villages on our way to the marquis's lands. We can likely procure and switch to another dragon carriage at a village named Hanumas near the border."

"Incidentally, how long till we get to Hanumas?"

"It will likely take fourteen to fifteen hours. If we run the dragon carriage into the ground after we switch, we might be able to arrive at the fiefdom in another half a day…"

Subaru scratched at his head, biting back his words of dismay before bowing his head to Wilhelm.

"Thanks for everything. It's a shame to leave practice half-finished like this…"

"I believe I have taught you the most important things. Beyond this, if you desire to increase your skill at the sword, there is no better way than to continue swinging one. May you stay in good health."

Wilhelm offered his hand, Subaru accepted it, and the two exchanged a good, hard shake.

Rem took over the driver's seat as Subaru entered the small carriage. Poking his head out of the window, he gave one last wave to Wilhelm, who was seeing them off from the front gate.

"Well, we're heading out. If fate allows, I'd love to spend some time together again."

"If you enjoy being welcomed with blows from a wooden sword, come back anytime."

Wilhelm gave a gentlemanly smile as he saw off Subaru and Rem with a very fitting joke.

The land dragon neighed and began gently picking up speed. The carriage accelerated further, leaving the Crusch villa farther and farther behind them. The figure at the front gate kept his head bowed until Subaru could no longer see him.

They headed downhill, passing the guardhouse that formed the entrance to the Nobles' District, heading straight down the main street to the gate that linked the royal capital to the highway outside that was their destination.

Thanks to the land dragon's blessing, the vibrations in Subaru's rear were exceedingly soft. He nervously looked out the small window, unable to bear the sense of urgency inside him.

Leaving the streets of the royal capital behind, his field of vision was dominated by green grassland and blue sky and nothing else. Since Rem was concentrating on driving, he couldn't speak to her, so there was nothing for him to do while in transit. Inside the carriage, Subaru sank into a sea of thought.

Crusch had declared that they could not lend a dragon carriage for long-range use. Accordingly, the feel of the passenger seat was much shoddier. It was probably for rushing servants from place to place.

He'd entered and left the Crusch residence in the blink of an eye. The fact that the duchess had kindly lent him a single dragon carriage upon his departure left Subaru in a tangle of complicated thoughts that were difficult to put into words. Only the night before, he'd judged her as strict but not indifferent. The back-and-forth before his departure had only added to the complexity.

What he did understand was why many people wanted to converse with her. No doubt Emilia would have to work hard to build up a network of personal connections as Crusch had. That was a necessary hardship for her. Yet unnecessary ones burdened Emilia as well.

"That's why…I need to get over there, and fast…"

Of course, these were political questions and a matter of connections between people of privilege. Subaru did not have such an inflated view of himself as to think he would be of help with those issues. He knew there would be difficult problems where he would be nothing but dead weight. But it wasn't in him to use his power-lessness as a reason to cast aside someone he cared about when she was in trouble.

If he poured his heart and soul into it, he was certain that he could overcome these obstacles.

Subaru Natsuki possessed that power.

"Nothing will work unless I'm with her... Now she'll understand that."

It was unfounded certainty—no, it was nothing but hope.

Emilia had fallen into peril. If he was there, galloping to her res-cue, somehow everything would work out. That was his slender, flickering hope, in danger of being snuffed out by the wind.

He wanted to prove his worth. He needed to.

If Emilia was in distress, Subaru would save her.

No, that's how it had to be. Subaru needed Emilia to fall into peril so that he could discover his own value—and show others that he had worth.

"That's right... It's no good if I'm not with her. For sure...!"

In the back of his mind was the incredibly lovely girl with silver hair. Her smiling face was enveloped by an amorphous darkness, buried by malice attempting to quench her sublime spirit.

"—"

With that vision in his mind, Subaru closed his eyes and bit his lip.

In the carriage, he silently let the time pass, alone.

With the exception of Rem in the driver's seat, he was isolated in that place, unable to sense the presence of any other.

—And he never noticed the faint twisting of his lips.

4

Late that day, instead of Hanumas, where they had planned to switch carriages, they rested at a stopover town ahead of it named Fleur.

Rem had suggested it as the sun was setting, just before night began to fall.

"Traveling by night will increase the probability of encountering bandits and demon beasts. I am also concerned about passing close to the fog, so I believe it's best to lodge at a nearby inn tonight."

"How long is it to the halfway point at Hanumas? We can't just rush the rest of the way there?"

"It would take until midnight to arrive at Hanumas from here. We might not be able to get an inn, and procuring a dragon carriage is difficult in the middle of the night, so…"

"Ugh… That's true. So it's not like we can just get there and everything will work out, then."

Rem had been thinking while Subaru was mulling things over. Naturally, she had made her proposal with much deeper consideration than Subaru's. Though he was irritated at having to stop, he accepted Rem's suggestion.

"So let's get an inn here in Fleur and head out first thing in the morning. That'll give the land dragon some rest and maybe cut down on the time needed to find a carriage in Hanumas?"

"Yes. If we leave early in the morning and things go well in Hanumas midway, we just might be able to make it to the mansion before nightfall tomorrow."

As Rem replied, her voice was filled with relief that Subaru had accepted her proposal without complaint.

Fortunately, their hope of finding an inn upon arrival in Fleur was granted. They entrusted the land dragon to the stable adjoining the inn, filled their bellies with an exceedingly crude evening meal, bathed briefly, and dove into bed so that they could rise immediately at daybreak.

But when Subaru thought of Emilia, his sense of urgency and impatience drove off all drowsiness.

"Can't sleep…"

Desperately trying to doze off, all he ended up doing was blindly changing positions in bed over and over. After all, he'd spent quite some time at Roswaal's mansion and Crusch's villa, the finest laps of luxury that world had to offer; the hard bed of a backwater inn made it hard for him to sleep.

Of course, given that he wanted to wake up as early in the morning as possible, curses for time and his own body welled up his chest. He didn't need more time to think. What he needed was an opportunity to link the conclusions drawn in his mind to tangible actions. Thus, all he yearned for was the morning sun.

How many times had he glared at the ceiling and at the backs of his eyelids? How many times had he turned in bed?

A sound slid into his eardrums; a knock at the doorway, then someone hesitantly opened the door.

"...Subaru, may I come in?"

When he lifted his head and looked over, he saw Rem's upper body leaning into the room. She'd slipped out of the servant's outfit he was used to and had changed into a thin blue nightgown he'd seen at some point before.

Rem, realizing Subaru was awake, looked relieved as she headed toward the bed. Subaru asked her, "What's wrong? If you're here to say you feel lonely and can't sleep by yourself, it's a hard day for it. If I was a little calmer, I'd have a really good laugh at that, but right now..."

"That proposal makes my heart flutter, but no. I could not sleep, so I wanted to talk a little."

"I see... You, too, then. Well, nothing we can do about that, huh?"

Subaru crawled out of bed as Rem timidly sat down by his side. Feeling like their shoulders were close enough to touch, he turned his attention to her pale face and opened his mouth.

"I feel bad that you've had to take care of me ever since we left the mansion, Rem."

"Please do not apologize for that. I do not think of anything as hardship if it is for your sake."

Her strong shake of her head pricked at Subaru's conscience. He knew that was what Rem would say. Ever since the demon beast uproar, she had been his ally through thick and thin.

Ironically, she was probably the one who most understood his worth.

"…Finding out by telepathy must've made you way more worried about the mansion than me. And here you are worrying about me on top of that— We still don't know that anything's happened, right?"

Rem nodded stiffly in reply to his question and lowered her eyes.

"—Don't worry about it. I'm sure something rough has happened, but she's not cute enough to fold that easily. We'll get back soon. I'll manage to take care of it somehow."

Subaru smiled with unwarranted cheerfulness, trying to lessen even a little the burden weighing Rem down. He wanted to make her feel at ease.

As was typical for him, Subaru's claims were baseless. It wasn't as if he had some brilliant, tangible plan to overcome difficult obstacles. Anyone ought to have doubted a declaration like that.

And yet…

"—Yes. I believe you, Subaru."

Rem smiled pleasantly at him with relief, as if ten thousand cavalrymen had come galloping to her aid.

"—!"

Realizing that her smile had captivated him, Subaru's face reddened as he averted his gaze.

He'd said something embarrassing, and her acceptance of it had been equally shameless. Subaru immediately turned his back to her without continuing. He didn't know what Rem must have thought of him.

—His breath caught when he suddenly felt the weight and warmth of her body against him.

"M-Miss Rem? Er… I wonder, why are you hugging me like this?"

The soft sensation against his back and her breath made Subaru unconsciously slip into a more formal form of address.

"…Because I want to."

The answer she gave in response, rich with meaning, carried a warmth that set off alarm bells in his heart.

Behind Subaru, still sitting on the bed, Rem had her arms around him, as if to cover him up. Her feminine softness, sweet scent, and arms around him drenched Subaru's entire body in warmth.

"Er, ah… This feeling is…"

Subaru, sensing it from head to toe, tilted his head when he suddenly realized that the "warmth" Rem was imparting was something apart from body heat—greatly resembling something he had felt over the past several days.

In reply to Subaru's misgivings, Rem maintained the contact and opened her mouth.

"I am healing your gate, the same as Master Felix did for you, Subaru. After all, I had several opportunities to watch while standing right beside you. Compared to Master Felix, perhaps I cannot do much more than put you at ease a little, but…"

"R-right, treatment! Treatment, yes! I see, I see. Yes, yes. E-exactly, huh. Ha-ha."

Feeling embarrassed at his impure delusions, Subaru glossed things over with a hollow laugh. He felt Rem smile slightly behind him as the strength of the mana flowing into him increased.

"Whoa, incredible… This feels way better than Ferris's stuff ramming into me."

"Thank you very much. But that assessment is unfair to Master Felix."

"Not at all. I'm totally serious. It feels good and…makes me feel… sleepy…"

Maybe the effect of the treatment was inferior to Ferris's, but Rem had far greater consideration for her patient. He felt like he was immersed in warm water, wrapped in softness.

He felt comfortable, relaxed, and drowsy, so he did not catch Rem's faint whisper.

"That is most likely…the difference between our feelings toward you, Subaru." His head was slipping down when Rem brought her lips close to his ear. "It's all right to fall asleep. I'll lay you down in bed properly, cover you with blankets, and leave after I've had my fill of watching you sleep."

"I wasn't worried about my belly being out in the open, and that's quite a line at the end… But when you're working so hard, how can I fall asleep in the middle of it, Rem?"

It was petty stubbornness, but he didn't want to come off as rude after everything she'd done.

He sensed Rem beaming as he felt her hands touch his head. The warmth coming from her palms increased, making his eyelids even heavier.

"Aww, crap… Why am I…? I mean, it's…hard for you, too, but… Rem, why are you…doing this for me…?" He rubbed his eyes, irrationally resisting the drowsiness, continuing to speak to hold on to his consciousness. "Rem, why…so much…for me…?"

"Because I want to… I do not need any other reason."

He let go of his mind before her words really sank in. Even so, he heard Rem reply, "I want." That part was important.

That was probably the starting point for all the thoughts enveloping Subaru—

What would happen when he returned to the mansion and reunited with Emilia? He was full of anxiety.

"She'll…yell at me at first, won't she…?"

Subaru's eyes fell as he shook his head.

As he wobbled, Rem's arms gently embraced him to provide support. "It'll be all right, Subaru. You're a wonderful person. With time and a proper meeting, if you tell her how you feel, I'm sure she will understand."

"Is that…so. Guess…I am, for you to think…like this about me…"

Sound grew distant. No, his mind had begun to withdraw from reality.

The comfortable drowsiness coursed through him like a curse, his eyes closing to become a cage around his mind.

Just before his consciousness completely slipped away from reality, Subaru thought he felt the faint touch of Rem's lips against his neck as she said, "So please keep me in a little corner of your thoughts, and don't go anywhere else, Subaru…"

Subaru no longer had the mental strength to reply to the seemingly pleading whisper as his mind gently sank into the darkness.

5

—What woke Subaru up was the feeling of hot sunrays burning his eyelids.

He remained lying in the bed as he absentmindedly lifted a hand to block out the sun. The light entering through the room's large window was strong; with him covered in bed up to his shoulders, they made him so hot that it was hard to sleep.

He indulged in that feeling for several long seconds before enough blood flowed into his half-asleep head for him to realize…

"The…sun's up?!"

Subaru threw off his blankets, leaped off the bed, and sprinted to the window. When he pushed it open, a cool breeze flowed into the room, and he gazed dumbfounded at the sun watching him from high in the sky.

That sight struck him with the terrible truth.

"No way… At a time like this… Am I an idiot?!"

Having arrived at the despairing conclusion he'd overslept, he rushed with all haste to Rem's bedroom next door in the inn. Subaru knocked furiously on the door before throwing it open.

"Rem! Wake up! We massively overslept!"

Cursing the fact that he'd slept nearly half the day away, he scanned the room in desperation. Anyway, he had to get Rem up so that they could resume their march— Or so he had thought.

"…Rem?"

The room was completely empty.

There was no bulge on the bed. The sheets were untouched. Subaru had a bad feeling about the lack of evidence that anyone had been in the bed at all. The room held no warmth from a human presence.

Unable to even see any luggage, he ran out of the room to the inn's front desk. The innkeeper who had greeted him and Rem the previous evening was sitting at the desk, smiling sociably when he noticed the boy.

"My, my, good morning. It would seem you slept very well last night…"

Subaru did not return the innkeeper's courtesy, slamming his fist on the desk to drive his question home.

"What happened to the blue-haired girl who came here with me?!"

The innkeeper reacted with surprise. Seeing Subaru's expression, he raised his hands in an attempt to mollify him.

"D-dear guest... Please calm down; you will disturb the other patrons..."

"Answer me! Where is she...? Where did Rem go?!"

"Y-your companion... Who came with you on...the dragon carriage late last night...?"

"That's not an answer!"

Cowed by Subaru's threatening demeanor, the innkeeper practically shouted his reply.

"Hear me out!! She left during the night! She left on the same dragon carriage you came in on! She paid for your stay and left a bag for you on the way out! She actually paid enough for you to lodge here for several days, so there is no problem whatsoe—"

"No...problem...you say?"

The innkeeper had tried to take care not to provoke Subaru, but the words he chose enraged him further.

"There damn well...*is* a problem!!"

Raising an angry voice, Subaru slammed his arm against the bag on top of the counter and clutched his head.

Welling up inside him was distrust. Doubt. Anger. Sadness. The irrational feelings wrestled with one another in his head as Subaru tore at his black hair and looked up to the sky.

"Rem... What... What the hell are you thinking...?!"

The fact that even the person who knew him best had failed to understand him weighed down on him as he wailed in despair.

6

To Subaru.

By the time you read this letter, you will no doubt be quite angry with me.

*　　*　　*

I will not ask you to forgive me for leaving you to head for the manor. However, please understand.

It is dangerous to bring you to the mansion as you are now. I am thinking not only of the state of the mansion but the state of your body, Subaru.

Therefore, please wait for me here in Fleur village. I will be back for you when everything is taken care of.

I have left behind all the money. I have already paid the innkeeper thoroughly, so you can stay for several days without any trouble.

Please take care of yourself, and please wait until I return—I beg you.

—From, Your Rem

CHAPTER 3
A DISEASE CALLED DESPAIR

1

—He'd been betrayed. Betrayed. Betrayed. Betrayed.

"Rem, you idiot…!"

When Subaru read the letter accompanying the bag left for him, he spat in irrepressible rage.

He was sitting on a hard sofa in a lounge on the first floor of the inn. No one else was around. The reason for that was his prolonged, violent behavior. The innkeeper who'd led him to the lounge hadn't even been able to look him in the eye when answering his questions.

A wise decision. That moment, anyone who appeared in Subaru's line of sight was his enemy.

"And I thought…at least you understood me…!"

The letter was written completely in carefully penned I-script. Subaru, who was still learning the written language, couldn't read anything except I-script characters. Rem had been considerate in that sense, but in light of her abandonment of him, that only shoved Subaru's heart deeper into darkness.

The letter overflowed with concern for Subaru's well-being, but so much sadness filled his head that he had no chance to realize that. He gleaned only one thought from reading the letter.

"Even you think I'm useless and powerless, Rem…"

His conversations at the Crusch residence, his dialogue with Rem the previous night, and Emilia's lecture in the royal capital came rushing back to him. Words upon words piled on him in their voices, berating Subaru for his helplessness and incompetence. He'd brushed them all aside and seized the perfect opportunity to prove to them Subaru Natsuki's value—or so he had thought. He'd thought that at least Rem believed he was worth something, yet…

"Yeah, I get it…! You're tellin' me that I'm dead weight, so you're cutting me loose… And if I don't believe you, you want me to look at how much I've been relying on you…!" Subaru spat, clenching his teeth as he rose to his feet.

The luggage and the allowance Rem had left were lined up on the table in the lounge. There was quite a lot of money in the sack. Apparently Roswaal had left a small fortune in Rem's hands. With that much money at his disposal, Subaru wouldn't have any trouble with daily necessities for quite some time. He knew that was exactly what Rem had in mind when she left it with him.

She underestimated him. Did she really think she could betray his trust, leave him with nothing but money, and expect him to meekly kneel and submit? There was no way he'd do as she pleased.

No, Subaru was coming up with all kinds of ways he could use money to break the stalemate.

"If I hire a dragon carriage and driver, I might be able to get to the mansion… That said…"

Rem had made careful preparations to trip up any such plans Subaru might have. According to the innkeeper, that village didn't have any establishment that could lend a dragon coach. In addition, the appearance of the "fog" had thrown off the schedules of carriages that regularly connected the various villages.

There was no dragon coach at any price. No doubt Rem had begun planning everything out as soon as they'd lodged at that village inn the night before. It was as if she was laughing at Subaru's paper-thin knowledge, politely smashing his options flat one by one…all to strand him in that village and stop him from returning to the mansion.

"Then I'll just have to hoof it… That's stupid. I don't have a map, and I can't deal with monsters."

If bandits or demon beasts appeared, that chapter would be over. He'd seen world maps several times over, but he didn't know the local lay of the land. Wandering around aimlessly would reduce his chances of arriving at the mansion to practically zero.

It was all a result of his own ignorance. Subaru's lack of education and strength kept letting him down.

He had never anticipated having to deal with bandits and demon beasts to begin with.

The fact that he'd never carried even a single sword on him was proof of that. He'd had Wilhelm instruct him in the art, but he could do nothing with that training if he set out empty-handed.

Subaru hadn't taken such normal, prudent measures because he was relying on Rem.

The price of an overnight stay at an inn was far less than the fare for a dragon carriage. Even if he had a small fortune, his inability to procure something of value made it worthless.

It was the cost of his lack of education, which was the direct result of Subaru's letting numerous opportunities to study slip away.

"Well, I can't help that now. I've gotta do what I can with what I have."

Subaru himself was the root cause of the stalemate keeping him penned in. His knees bounced in annoyance as he tried to pretend he wasn't well aware of that fact.

"So no hoofing it. I have to get a dragon carriage… There's gotta be a way. Think."

Subaru put a hand to his forehead, desperately reviewing everything he'd seen and heard in that world and everything he'd learned from the people in his original world, trying to come up with a plan.

"—"

He ran through every memory and shred of knowledge in his

head, focusing all his body's resources above his neckline. Then he looked at the possibilities that might exist for breaking out of his cage.

"This village…has no establishment that can lend a dragon carriage. The regularly scheduled carriages aren't available…meaning…"

The village was now occupied by its original residents, travelers who'd arrived by regular carriage, and—

"Maybe there's someone who came in on their own dragon carriage, like Rem and I did, who stopped over?"

If anyone were to enter and leave the village freely, they would have to have their own means of transportation. That very inn had stables for the use of its guests; his thought couldn't be far off the mark.

"To have a dragon carriage you'd have to be rich… No, a merchant would be perfect. A merchant who hasn't settled down is either working for someone else or a peddler going around with a horse-drawn wagon. That's just basic."

The lantern light of Subaru's extinguished hopes began to flicker once more.

To find the right person, Subaru immediately went to the innkeeper and explained. At first, the innkeeper was reluctant, but he introduced several merchants, albeit with a strained expression.

"But most traveling merchants will be intent on shipping goods to their destination. I don't know if any would be willing to take on someone as a passenger…"

"Well, I'll give it a try anyway. Thank you very much for telling me about them."

Thanking the considerate innkeeper, Subaru visited the traveling merchants one by one.

—But in line with the innkeeper's concerns, negotiations proved very difficult. Just as he had claimed, they had little inclination to alter their travel routes, but the situation was far direr than that. Each and every one responded to Subaru's suggestion the same way, shaking their heads.

"The Mathers dominion? Sorry, but I can't go there now," said a very scrawny man as he ended negotiations with Subaru.

He stood with his canopied dragon coach as his eyes lingered on Subaru with some sympathy.

"I hate to say this, but I don't think I'll be the only one saying no. In my case, though, it has to do with the cargo I'm carrying."

"Cargo?"

"I'm transporting weapons, armor, and other metal wares. Rumor has it prices in the royal capital for this stuff are through the roof, so tomorrow I'm rushing there with my dragon carriage. My profits are on the line."

The man patted the cargo in his dragon carriage as he spoke, gazing distantly in the direction of the setting sun. Then, when he saw the slump of Subaru's shoulders, he adjusted the position of his bandanna and said, "There're a lot of people who use this as a stopover to the royal capital like I do. That's why this village is pretty well-off for its size. So there're merchants who come in twos and threes but… They'll probably all turn you down."

"…Yeah. You're the sixth one to say no."

"That's because every decent merchant is rushing to the royal capital with revenues on the mind. No way around it. After all, there's the uproar over the royal selection. Everyone's caught the scent of gold."

"So that's how it is, huh…"

The man's reply and sober expression made Subaru frown as he surmised the reason for his successive failures—namely, he'd misread the merchants from a business perspective. It wasn't the prospect of a temporary payday that was luring them to the royal capital but the sight of bigger, longer-term profits. For a trader to abandon such plans to accommodate Subaru would be nothing short of madness.

The merchant continued.

"On top of that, there're all kinds of fishy rumors about the Mathers dominion flying around. Even if you find someone who's not heading to the capital for profit, they probably still won't go."

"Fishy rumors...? Related to the royal selection, by any chance?"

"Groundless speculation, I think. There's talk that one of the candidates is a half-demon and the lord of those lands is supporting her... But I haven't heard the details of the election yet. Do you know anything?"

"...No, I don't know much about it."

Subaru lied on the spot because he didn't want to be exposed as a related party, which would only make negotiations harder. But covering for Emilia's lineage still left a strange feeling in his heart.

As Subaru grimaced like he'd swallowed a bitter pill, the man suddenly clapped his hands together.

"Oh, that's right. I just remembered someone who might accept your proposal."

"Seriously?! I was pretty much at the point of giving up and falling to the dark side here!"

"I'm not sure what you just said, but it's true. Come on, I'll introduce you."

The man patted Subaru's shoulder with an easygoing look and beckoned him forward. Subaru followed a little behind him until he pointed to a building across the road.

"I'm pretty sure he's been there since last night. Wait here, I'll call him over for you."

The man left through the wide-open double doors as Subaru watched him go, looking up at the sign.

"...I feel like it probably says 'Tavern' or something..."

He had only moderate confidence, since the sign he was looking at was written in Ro-script, which he had only just begun to learn. The faint whiff of alcohol wafting from the entrance made Subaru about 89 percent sure he was right.

The energetic way the man headed in suggested the people inside would be troublesome.

"What is this person doing, glugging alcohol when he's traveling...? Doesn't this world have laws against steering dragon carriages while under the influence...? Back in my world, you'd lose your license with one violation."

Not that he was sure there were dragon carriage licenses to begin with. If the newcomer in question showed up looking drunk and dangerous, Subaru resolved to make a run for it and spend as much money as he needed to do so.

And just as Subaru hardened such tragic resolve, the man came back outside.

"Sorry for the wait. Here he is. Hey, Otto, introduce yourself."

The man roughly dragged along a young man, practically tossing him forward as they approached. He had gray-colored hair and looked no more than a year or two older than Subaru, though he was a fair bit shorter. He had a slender and fairly symmetrical face.

Subaru deemed that, at the very least, this was not the drunkard he had feared.

"My name's Subaru Natsuki. Sorry to drag you out here. I heard that you just might accept my request, so… Ughh! You stink! You totally reek of booze!"

His efforts to get negotiations started on the right foot were immediately short-circuited by the scent of alcohol wafting from the other party. The young man before him glowered sullenly, giving off a stench so strong that Subaru's stomach was on the verge of emptying itself.

He might not look scary or dangerous, but he was a tottering drunkard nonetheless.

"Why hello, *hic*. Let me introduce myself. My name, *hic*, is Otto, *hic*."

He hiccupped three times during his brief greeting.

His face red from drunkenness, the young man named Otto looked between Subaru and the other man.

"So what is it that y'wanted? Business? Was it business, *hic*? My business is, *hic*, ah-ha-ha-ha, *hic*. It's kind of a joke right now, *hic*."

Finally, Otto squatted down and suddenly burst into laughter.

Subaru, sensing that was the sound of his hopes grinding to a halt, shot a hard glare toward the man who'd introduced them. On the receiving end of that gaze, the man quickly pointed back at Otto.

"Wait, wait! I didn't deceive you!"

"If you actually meant for this to be an introduction, I'm seriously doubting your head's screwed on straight. It's not fun getting arrested for drunk driving. A student would get sent to the principal just for being in this state."

Subaru had salivated at the prospect of finding a solution, and yet the man introduced to him was a drunkard.

The man sighed at Subaru's words and roughly shook the squatting Otto's shoulders.

"Otto! Hey, get up, damn you! You're the one who told me to introduce you to anyone who could turn your situation around! What, you're going to let booze ruin it all?!"

"A way to turn things around—?!"

Otto's ears quivered, while his eyes, dead until that point, completely changed. With the support of the man's hand, he rose to his feet, as if his drunken state had never been.

"I have been most impolite. My name is Otto Suwen. I am a humble independent merchant, making his way in life as a traveling peddler."

Otto faced Subaru and assumed an expression so crisp one could almost hear the *snap* to attention.

While Subaru was speechless at the instant turnaround, Otto examined him from head to toe.

"I see. It seems that he has a certain degree of status. He certainly has the makings of a good customer. Mr. Kety, thank you very much for introducing us."

"Sure thing. You'll be all right from here out, yes? I'll get going, then. Don't forget to keep your chin up. And you owe me one, Otto."

Otto had brightened to the point one would doubt he'd ever been in his drinks, so Mr. Kety patted his chest with relief and departed.

Subaru watched the man who'd made the friendly gesture leave before turning back toward Otto. The young man had scrutinized him and acknowledged him as someone he could do business with.

Otto clapped his hands together, smiling broadly, and began, "Well then, let us talk business... What is it that my customer desires?"

Subaru's breath caught, knowing he could not let him or that chance escape, and he got down to brass tacks.

"This is a bit of a far-out request to make, but…"

With that preamble, Subaru explained the situation, careful about what not to say. If Otto said no, he was finished. He spoke as naturally as he could despite his tension as he talked business. And then…

After Subaru gave him a simplified explanation of events, Otto thought about it a little, then nodded.

"Mm, I do not mind accepting that at all."

Hearing his well-formed reply, seemingly coming from an entirely different person than the one brought before him, Subaru grabbed him with both hands in surprise and gave him a good, hard shake.

"Th-thank you! I see, you'll do it! That would be a huge help! Seriously, a huge help!"

"Oww! Ow, ow, ow! D-don't squeeze so hard! P-please wait, I'm glad that you are satisfied, but I have conditions, too!"

Otto freed his captured arms from the shaking and retreated a step from Subaru as he spoke.

The word *conditions* made Subaru tilt his head. Now that his hands were free, Otto gave a light wave.

"My dragon carriage is a resource for my business… Or rather, my lifeline. I cannot part with it lightly. Of course, this will be lending aid rather than formally loaning the carriage, particularly because there are many disquieting things happening in the Mathers lands at the moment."

"That's only natural. I won't go as far as to say you can jack up the price, though."

Subaru was a little worried that he'd be subject to price gouging. All he could offer was what he had on hand. If that wasn't enough, he'd have to get the price cut somehow.

Seeing Subaru's wariness, Otto gently loosened the corners of his mouth.

"I suppose not. Then for all the money you have here…yes?"

And so, Otto struck first in the negotiations, seizing the initiative as he thrust his conditions to the fore. No doubt he'd already deduced from Subaru's demeanor how much money was in the bag. He pressed his strategy, firmly controlling the pace of negotiations to enhance his own profits even a little, just like a textbook merchant.

It was mouth versus mouth, tongue versus tongue. The battle had begun, a verbal clash pitting the speech and business acumen of both parties against each other—

Well, not quite.

"Is that okay? All right. I'll hand this bag to you, then. Can we leave right away?"

Shock overcame Otto as Subaru readily handed him the whole bag. The weight of the purse made Otto swallow as he nervously looked at Subaru.

"Wha...? This isn't how it goes!! Normally, both people lay out their demands and then start the negotiations to find common ground, don't they?! It's never this eas—"

"It'd be a waste of time, and I'm not going to win any verbal sparring matches anyway. There's no meaning in fighting a pointless battle, and if what's in that bag is enough, you'll be granting my request regardless."

If all the money he had on hand resolved everything, it was a bargain as far as Subaru was concerned.

Otto scowled at Subaru's calm demeanor, probably wondering if he'd been too hasty.

"This is... Perchance I've been introduced to a very troublesome individual."

"Relax. I don't intend to cause you any trouble. Not on purpose, anyway."

"Are you aware that the way you phrased that only makes me even more concerned?!"

Even Otto, a man he'd just met, was indignant at his exceedingly unconvincing statements. However, he sighed in apparent resignation and adjusted his grip on the bag in his hands.

"Understood. I presented my condition and you immediately accepted. I do have pride as a merchant, after all. Just allow me to see exactly how much money this… Ehh?! Wh-what is this fortune here?! What are you doing handing off something like this so ea…? Uaaagh."

Checking the contents of the bag, Otto was so surprised at the amount of money that his nausea returned. As Otto squatted, Subaru stood behind him, clutching a fist as if he finally had hope in his hand.

So many obstacles had been placed in his path, but he'd overcome them all somehow. He still didn't know the true nature of the obstacle blocking Emilia's path, but if he stood at her side, he'd no doubt find out. And that was the kind of problem only Subaru could solve.

"Just wait. Soon…soon."

The twisted smile on Subaru's lips was plain for anyone to see.

That smile might have come over him from the thought of fulfilling his objective of saving Emilia. Perhaps it had another cause. Even he didn't know, since he didn't even realize he was smiling at all.

2

Subaru enjoyed the gentle rocking as he gazed at the rolling landscape.

The sky, on the verge of evening, was dyed orange; soon, night would fall. Normal travelers would be preparing to camp or lodge at a nearby village at that time of day.

It seemed that only the likes of Subaru and Otto would choose to set out when they did.

Otto said, "So the destination is in the Mathers domain, the marquis's own mansion, on the condition that we ride right through half the night to shorten time as much as possible… I accepted it because a fee is a fee, but this is reckless, you understand?"

"I don't wanna hear it from a guy who instantly changes his mind at the sight of money. Please. My future's riding on this."

"I'll do my best. My own future is riding on this, too, after all."

As Otto spoke, he guided the land dragon with the reins as it raced across the ground.

The dragon carriage Otto owned was a large, canopied vehicle for hauling freight, so his land dragon was correspondingly huge and powerful. Subaru was concerned that such an apparently heavy beast would lack in speed, but Otto had explained, "It makes up for that with endurance. This is an especially hardy species even among long-distance land dragons. It could run for three days straight without getting worn out."

"You'd think running for three days straight would wear out the people riding it instead."

"Two years ago, I had to do that to not let a particular business opportunity slip. Humans can go through a lot if they're ready to risk death to achieve it. Having said that, I keeled over just after trade negotiations were over, and I hovered between life and death for about a week afterward..."

"Like you're ready to risk death, huh."

As Subaru watched the side of the merchant's face, Otto looked toward him with a look that seemed to say, "What?" Subaru silently waved him off, averting his eyes to face forward as he put his elbows on his knees and his chin on his hands.

"I'm quite sorry, I never imagined I'd be carrying a passenger, so I never prepared proper seating for one," Otto said.

"Hey, I'm the one who pushed for this, and I don't mind a little pain in my butt. That blessing keeping the wind from tossing me around is more than enough for me."

Otto's dragon carriage, meant for the simple objective of hauling cargo from place to place, had no extra space for passengers to ride. Naturally, that left Subaru with no choice but to sit next to the other young man on the driver's seat.

Otto continued, "If you get sleepy, it might be a little rough, but please use the wagon. I have to camp frequently myself, so I have a number of blankets on hand."

"That's very gracious of you... So since I don't have to switch dragon carriages anymore, we can just leave Hanumas aside and keep on going, right?"

"That is correct. As a stopover, Hanumas is more affluent than

Fleur, but I have plenty of food and water as it is. This is an urgent request, after all, so we'll bypass it."

No doubt he was very accustomed to traveling. Though they had set out on their journey without a plan, Otto didn't show a single shred of concern as he kept his grip on the reins.

Otto himself had probably already traveled this route several times over. As Subaru watched the side of his face, he sensed a gravitas that belied the great similarity in their ages.

Subaru bit his tongue as he unwittingly compared the difference in experience and courage between them.

"Hey, why did you agree to this, anyway? I have no idea why you said yes."

"Y-you just came right out and asked a very difficult question, Mr. Natsuki."

From the side, Subaru saw a strained smile on Otto's face, but the amiable atmosphere soon returned.

Since he had arrived here, Subaru had rarely been addressed by his family name.

Feeling a bit strange at being called that for the first time in forever, he realized that he'd thrown a fastball straight at something the other party didn't really want to discuss.

"Well, can't take it back now... Confess, and things will go easier for you."

"Yes, Officer. I didn't mean to do it, honest... Wait, why does this feel like I did something wrong?! I didn't mean to do it; it was an accident!"

Otto followed up his exaggerated reaction to Subaru's joking comment by slowly turning his head with a sullen look.

"The wagon behind us is filled to the brim with my cargo... What do you think is inside?"

"...Now that I'm looking at it, seems like vases or something. What, were you carrying artwork?"

"Close, but not quite. What I'm selling isn't what's outside but what's on the inside. The pots are filled with high-quality oil. Originally, I planned to haul these to the northern nation of Gusteko, but..."

Otto's shoulders slumped, his abject expression making plain that things had not gone as expected.

"I wonder if it is an effect of the royal selection? The path between Gusteko and Lugunica has been temporarily closed. I tried to plead my case that I couldn't get my goods to market... But they ended up chasing me away with swords."

In a country as cold as Gusteko, you should be able to make a killing selling oil, but it was more of a great wasteland than a market. To add insult to injury, Otto had sold off metal wares at fire-sale prices to buy the oil he could no longer trade.

As a result, he'd forfeited an excellent chance to sell metal wares on top of losing access to the market where he would have sold the oil instead. This was apparently why he'd drunk himself into a stupor.

"There's no way I can sell a large amount of oil like this in Lugunica for a fair price, and if I sell it at bargain prices again, I'll be bankrupt. And so, I was halfway to throwing my life away when you appeared, Mr. Natsuki."

"And what I paid you makes up for your losses?"

"I can sell all this oil at any price and stay solvent. It will certainly let me keep working."

Otto clapped his hands together to convey his earnest thanks to Subaru, but Subaru waved off the gesture. "Cut that out."

He was equally grateful to Otto. If anything, Subaru's feelings ran even stronger.

For a while, they went back and forth: "It's all thanks to you," "No, thanks to you," "I'm here only because of you," "Yeah, it's fate that we both met," and so on as their bond deepened.

Finally, their casual praises died off, and silence abruptly fell between them.

Subaru's gaze shifted from the road they were galloping down to the plain, continuing as far as the eye could see, as he murmured, "Hey, Otto. Can't we cut across this plain?"

Hearing Subaru's suggestion, Otto slapped his knee as if it was the best joke he'd ever heard.

"My, my. That's too much, even for a jest. When the fog falls on the plains, that's where the White Whale appears. It is the most famous of all demon beasts... Should we meet it, our lives will be forfeit."

"It's that dangerous? No one tries to put it down?"

"No, because by avoiding the fog, you can also bypass the White Whale, so the damage is minimal. I imagine that is the real reason why it persists to this day."

In other words, people had tried to subdue the beast and failed, with the damage sustained in the process discouraging further expeditions.

Complicated thoughts enveloped Subaru when he heard the words *demon beasts*. To him, a demon beast meant an Urugarum, like those he had encountered fairly recently—the same creatures that had gravely injured Subaru and perished at Roswaal's hands. He had something of a history with them.

Subaru mused aloud, "White Whale...huh. So it's shaped like a whale and white colored, then?"

"According to witnesses, at least. Apparently it is so enormous that no one has ever seen its full size, and those people were tossing anything and everything aside as they fled for their lives while it rampaged. A frightening story," Otto concluded. He shut his mouth and would say nothing more. For a merchant like him, the White Whale was no doubt an odious being indeed, since its loitering on these plains for days on end would throw travel schedules into great disarray. Though he would be grateful if someone got rid of it, he had no intention of encountering it himself.

Perhaps Otto's point of view was common to all merchants.

Subaru changed the subject.

"So how long is it going to take to get to the Mathers dominion at this pace?"

"Hmm, let's see. Though night is coming, my land dragon has excellent night vision, and there's no sign of any fog. Plus, I imagine there are no bandits willing to risk their lives by working near the plains right now, so...if things go well, tomorrow morning perhaps?"

After providing that answer, Otto glanced over at Subaru, who raised his eyebrows in response. Otto quickly played innocent, averting his eyes and going, "Ah, nothing." He soon continued, though. "Our destination is...the mansion of Marquis Roswaal...isn't it?"

"Yeah, that's right."

"The small fortune you paid me... Those clothes must be expensive... This is just between us, but who are you, Mr. Natsuki? Are you...involved with the marquis somehow?"

Subaru understood why Otto harbored such misgivings to the point of meekly raising his doubts. From the merchant's point of view, Subaru's identity was a complete mystery, and yet he'd pushed a small fortune into his hands and proposed they rush to the mansion at a time when the rumors swirling around the place were uniformly bad.

"That's right. I'm involved with Roswaal...the marquis. You might have heard some strange rumors, but I don't know what's true or false yet. And I already told you, I don't intend to cause you any trou—"

"No, no! I'm not worried about that at all! It's just, uh...that... According to rumor, the good marquis is famous for his...eccentric interests... I was wondering if it is true?"

"...If what is true?"

Subaru inferred from Otto's equivocation what he wished to ask. Even so, he concealed the hardness of his voice as best he could while prompting Otto to carry on.

"If the good marquis really is backing a young half-elf lady."

"—"

Figures, thought Subaru, the inside of his chest sinking in dismay. The anxiety in Otto's voice made it clear that he was nervous to learn the truth. Emilia's birth was about to be slandered again. Subaru spoke quickly to head off his prejudice.

"Even if I told you no...you'd find out for yourself soon enough. It's true. The candidate the marquis is supporting is a half-elf. But that girl's nothing like you all think she..."

"Is that so—I'm so relieved."

However, Otto's reaction was not the one Subaru expected.

The merchant lowered his brows and put a hand to his chest in apparent relief. Realizing that Subaru was gaping at him in shock, he smiled awkwardly, visibly embarrassed.

"Ah, ahh… I'm sorry, getting worked up all by myself here. I mean, when I heard those rumors… She seemed an odd person to champion."

"To champion… Emilia, you mean?"

"Ah, Lady Emilia is her name? Yes, well, you know. A half-elf would have had a hard life until now in various ways. For someone to rise from an unpleasant background and stand as a royal candidate… Yes, it's very impressive."

Otto's eyes were distant as he watched the road, his voice quivering faintly.

Listening to the merchant's reply, Subaru realized it had thrown him completely off guard. Complex emotions thrashed around in his chest, leaving him unsure of what to say.

Otto, unaware of the chaos in Subaru's heart, rubbed his nose with a finger as he said, "These might be small concerns compared to those of someone like Lady Emilia, but I know what it's like to be misunderstood… An odd point of sympathy, perhaps. I think becoming king will be very difficult, but if she tries hard, maybe… Well, I just wanted to ask."

Otto cut things off there, since going any further would require him to speak more about himself.

Once again, Subaru found himself unable to say a word to Otto. He folded his arms and continued looking downward.

"—"

Normally, Otto's words would have helped Subaru so much that he'd come right out and thank him.

Emilia had irrational obstacles blocking her path. However, even in a world filled with such problems, it didn't mean that everyone hated her. Some people in that world, like Otto, would cheer for her when they learned about her background. To Emilia, that fact had to be the greatest silver lining of all.

It had to be, and yet…

"—"

For some reason, Subaru was unable either to communicate his gratitude to Otto or to keep down the incomprehensible aching in his own chest as the dragon carriage continued to sway.

3

"—Mr. Natsuki! Please wake up! We are finally entering the Mathers dominion!"

Subaru, curled up under a blanket in the wagon, opened his eyes as Otto called his name.

He hadn't been able to sleep much. His head was still hazy when he poked it out of the curtain, and he was greeted by the rays of the morning sun, a line of mountains, and hope.

The sun had risen once again, pouring sunrays down among the mountains and making Subaru squint. In the half day and change that they had spent in their overnight journey, Subaru had arrived back at the Mathers dominion.

"Good job, Otto. Working like a horse while I was asleep like that…"

"Can you not say that as if I have no professionalism here?! More importantly, there is a village named Earlham near Marquis Mathers's mansion, yes?"

Otto had a map spread across his lap, glaring at it and the road ahead as he asked the question. His eyes were a little bloodshot from the all-nighter, but fortunately, he didn't seem worn out from it.

"It's my second all-nighter in a row with some spirits in me in between, but I feel great! If we head straight forward we'll reach the mansion after all! Fueh-heh-heh!"

"Are you really all right?! You didn't take some weird drug to forget about being tired or something?!"

"Do not be concerned. Lugunica is a law-abiding country that bans medicines of that nature."

Subaru warily watched Otto, who seemed to be straddling the line between lucidity and insanity, as his own heart lightened a little at having returned to the Mathers lands.

"I'd love to run straight there without a break, but we might pass by Rem along the way."

"Nah, I don't think so. She did have over half a day's head start on us, after all. More importantly, Mr. Natsuki, shouldn't you prepare yourself for returning to the mansion? You should comb your hair and so forth."

Otto raised a hand as he spoke in a half-joking manner. Subaru was putting his hair back in order when his breath caught.

Now that the mansion was so close, right in front of his nose, all the things about a prospective reunion that Subaru had tried not to think about came rushing to him with a vengeance.

He thought it unlikely that she'd simply welcome him back with open arms.

After their parting of ways at the royal capital, he'd deliberately abandoned the half-finished treatment for his gate to return. Rem had surely arrived first, and ignoring her admonishments, too, meant he might have no allies at all.

But whatever they might think of him, even so—

"I came back to do what I have to do. I'm not ashamed of that at all. I'm not wrong about anything."

He said it to justify it to himself or, perhaps, to make excuses to someone who wasn't even there. He murmured similar things over and over as if they were the magic words that continued to sustain his spirit.

"—It's for Emilia's sake. She can't get by if I'm not here."

Such were the arguments that kept Subaru's fragile mind from crumbling, somehow suppressing the words that would otherwise be ever-present in his memories.

They entered via the highway between the hills, traveling along the road at a safe speed. The road cut through the mountain forests ahead of them, with increasingly familiar scenery. At that pace, it would be less than an hour before they arrived at Roswaal's mansion.

That was when the carriage's wheels came to a screeching stop, and the land dragon let out a ferocious sound as it violently clawed at the ground.

"—?! H-hey, Otto?!"

The instant Subaru felt the carriage stop, the land dragon's blessing must have cut out, since he keenly felt the full impact as the vehicle rocked to the side. Subaru yelped as he was suddenly jostled around inside.

"Otto! What was that just now?! We haven't gotten there yet, have we? Why'd you stop all of a sudd—?"

Otto held the reins low as he spoke to Subaru without looking at him.

"—Mr. Natsuki. Can we make this as far as I proceed with you?"

For a moment, Subaru couldn't process what had been said to him, but then he immediately grabbed Otto by his lapel and pulled him close.

"What do you mean? That wasn't the deal! Damn you, we've come this far; don't cut and run out on me midway. Stay with me until we get to—"

The end, Subaru was going to shout, but his breath caught when he saw that Otto's face was as white as a ghost. He released the pale-faced merchant, who sat on the driver's seat and hung his head.

"I am...very sorry. I had intended to remain with you until the end, Mr. Natsuki. Even so, I don't have the courage to go any farther."

"What are you going on about? What does this have to do with courage? Just a little farther and we'll reach the mansion. It's not like the road is bad. Otto, please!"

"Even if you beg me...I cannot. I don't need the entire reward. I shall return half to you. Therefore, please allow me to pull out of our deal."

Otto put his hand on the driver's seat with a genuinely apologetic look toward Subaru, though still refusing to get into the details. Subaru couldn't hide his bewilderment at the tragic look in Otto's eyes.

"What is it, all of a sudden? Did something happen...?"

"My land dragon...is afraid. And it's not only that. The area around us seems too quiet to me. This is why traveling merchants use land dragons. A land dragon's instincts tell him about places he mustn't approach!"

Otto's hands trembled on top of his lap as he focused on his land dragon. When Subaru peered closer, the land dragon made quiet, ragged breaths as it awaited its master's command. But the way it was snorting at the direction they were traveling announced loud and clear that it held danger for them. That behavior, and Otto's trust for his own land dragon, explained where the merchant's reaction had come from.

Asking Otto and the land dragon to accompany Subaru when none of them had any idea of what situation awaited them—it would have been too cruel to both.

"…Thanks for everything. Sorry to put you through something scary, Otto."

"—Eh?"

Subaru heard a surprised voice behind him as he hopped off the driver's seat down to the ground. The land dragon beside him looked back up at Otto, moving a foot around as it silently pled its case.

"I'll head to the mansion on foot from here. Hey, I've come this far; it's practically right in front of me. You've brought me far enough. Take all the money and go."

"I cannot do such a… No, more importantly, Mr. Natsuki! You mustn't go! Come back with me! Fog is approaching this place right now!"

"The White Whale's gonna show up?"

"To a traveling merchant this is a black omen! When fog covers our destination, it is a matter of life and death for us… No, that doesn't matter here! Anyway, please reconsi—"

"Sorry."

Subaru wore a pained smile after Otto shouted his concern for him. He was far too much of a softy for the cutthroat, deceptive world of the merchant. He pondered the benevolent Otto's suitability for his chosen trade as he walked away from the dragon carriage.

"Just like you're weighing your life and money on your scales, I'm weighing my life and something I value just as much. Something worth that much to me is waiting just ahead."

"Mr. Natsuki, please wait! L-let's discuss this. We can talk it over!"

"I don't blame you at all for turning back. I mean, if you know there's danger, turning back is the right call. Knowing beforehand is enough for me."

Now Subaru knew that the road ahead, as well as his destination, held enough danger to make even a land dragon afraid. But he had to hurry. He had to run forward.

The chance for Subaru to find the answer he sought surely awaited him there.

"—Mr. Natsuki!"

"Thank you."

Otto's voice held concern for Subaru until the very end. Leaving him behind, Subaru rushed full-tilt down the tree-lined highway. He headed for his destination, casting aside the man who had guided him without trying to overcharge.

The sights seemed almost familiar to him, but it was only a resemblance. Just how far did he have to go before arriving at Roswaal's mansion? One way or another, running down the road would lead him there.

With the danger loud and clear and his destination right before his eyes, Subaru's emotions ran wild inside him.

At any rate, he wanted to get there without a moment to lose. If he did, the painful, lingering emotions inside him would come to a head. He'd settle this, whether it turned out how he wanted it to be or not.

"...? The...hell?"

Subaru was running without a care—or rather, while suppressing his innumerable worldly worries—when he came to a halt.

It wasn't because he'd arrived at his destination. The scenery remained unchanged, and it seemed to stretch on so much that he had to wonder just how far the highway continued, with the thick trees on both sides seeming to block all escape. He was out of breath, but he had yet to run out of endurance.

Why, then, had Subaru stopped? That was because—

"It's…too quiet, isn't it…?"

Subaru had paused because he sensed something was wrong. Unintentionally, he repeated what Otto had said earlier.

When he looked around, there was no change in his surroundings whatsoever. Compared to the rustling of leaves as the wind passed through, his own breath was quite noisy.

But that was all he heard. And to Subaru, who'd spent nearly two months in these lands, it felt wrong. The oppressive silence, without even the sounds of insects, was abnormal.

—And then, something suddenly appeared, slipping neatly into Subaru's consciousness.

"Wh…what?!"

He recoiled a step, his throat tightening from shock. Without a sound, a person had appeared in front of him. Furthermore, the figure's entire body was shrouded in black clothing, with something like a hood on, so that even the face of this complete stranger was concealed.

Furthermore, that wasn't all that shocked him.

"This guy… No, these guys…!"

One after another, black figures emerged all around Subaru, as if they were responding to his confusion and his shifting gaze. In the blink of an eye, they numbered more than ten, surrounding Subaru as if mocking his efforts at caution.

"—"

Particularly abnormal was the insane quiet that continued even after the shadowy group's appearance. They continued to watch Subaru in silence; he didn't even hear any of them breathe.

There was no way they were friendly. That said, they hadn't shown any hostility, either. The eerie figures left him tongue-tied, unable to even move a muscle. How did they stare at each other like that?

Feeling the pressure, Subaru felt like time was moving incredibly slowly. Then, that turbulent silence crumbled just as easily as it had begun.

"—"

All at once, the figures faced Subaru and reverently bowed their heads to him.

"—Ah?"

Subaru's brain was unable to process the scene before him.

The incomprehensible band that had emerged was paying Subaru respect for reasons unknown, and leaving him behind in his confusion, they began sliding out of sight.

The wordless scene before Subaru's eyes left him more dumbfounded than anything. Rather than do something to the frozen boy, the figures departed with silent footsteps.

It was probably the silence of their footsteps that had allowed them to slip through Subaru's mental blind spot. But though he understood that much, he knew absolutely nothing else about them.

Subaru tossed aside any attempt to comprehend the figures, suppressing the worry churning around inside him as he continued to run. He focused on heading back to the mansion, as if doing so would shake off the fear and discomfort.

He didn't understand who the figures were or what they were after, so he stopped trying to understand them. That was why he never noticed it.

Why he never noticed the fact that the unknown figures sliding out of his line of sight were headed in Otto's direction.

Nor would Subaru reflect on this later. Not even once.

—His thoughts had stopped as he ran forward, as if he truly believed that it would save him.

4

Worry. Worry dominated his entire body to the point that he wanted to tear and scratch at it.

His feet moved forward. His heart was set on the future. The destination of his mind was ahead of him, and yet he felt like fear of those unknown figures was stalking him from behind.

His ears were ringing loudly. Nausea was rocking his head. He felt like every drop of blood in his body had turned into muddy water.

The anxiety that tormented him was rapidly eclipsing everything within him, making the physical organ housing his formless heart feel like it was going to burst.

—Why did it have to be like this?

Everything seemed to be going well. Everything seemed to be going in the right direction.

It was just a twist of fate. It was merely the timing that had been thrown off.

He should've been able to do it. It should have been clear so that he could do it without hesitation. The stuff at the royal capital was just a bad dream, the result of simply pressing the buttons in the wrong order.

That was why he wanted to meet Emilia now. He knew what he had to do.

He just had to save her. She was in peril. It was his time, just like it had been before.

That's how it'd always been. It'd be like that this time, too. Everything would turn out all right. Subaru would be redeemed in Emilia's eyes. She'd accept that she was wrong, that it would work out only if Subaru was there with her. She would allow him to be at her side once more.

"Ha...ha...ha!"

He was out of breath. His lungs hurt. His overused limbs creaked. His body was crying out in pain.

But he couldn't just stand there. If he did that, *it* would catch up with him. Something irrational was chasing him from behind.

"Shit... Shit, shit... Shit!"

He wanted to meet Emilia. He wanted her to smile at him. He wanted Rem to be nice to him. He wanted to stroke her head. He missed and adored Beatrice's insults and Ram's put-downs. Roswaal's eccentricities and Puck's making the world revolve around him put Subaru's heart at ease.

—He wished he'd never left.

He'd headed to the royal capital, but the time he'd spent there, and the royal capital itself, was the root of all evil.

Reinhard. Felt. Old Man Rom. Ferris. Wilhelm. Julius. Anastasia. Al. Priscilla. The Council of Elders. The Knights. One after another they rose up in the back of his mind, all of them objects of hatred at that moment.

—Curse you. Suffer and die—painfully.

If it weren't for them, Subaru would have never lost sight of himself. If he'd reconciled with Emilia, returning to live his days in peace, he would have obtained perfect happiness.

All of it had slipped out of his hands. That was why he was there to pick it all back up.

"Just a bit farther…and I'll…be back there…!"

His lungs burned with agony. Subaru averted his eyes from the regrets forming cracks in his heart as he ran.

It was cursing everything, and trusting that what he desired lay beyond those damnable things, that was keeping him alive.

"—Aa."

Subaru had been staring at the ground as he ran for all that time, and when he could hardly breathe anymore, he raised his head.

The scenery lining the road had begun to change from what he'd been seeing as he ran. The gaps between the trees were widening, and the natural traces of human labor appeared among them. When he caught sight of the rising slope of a familiar hill, a raspy voice of joy left Subaru's mouth.

He could see white smoke rising above the tree line coming from the other side of the smoke.

Maybe it was from cooking, or maybe it was from boiling hot bathwater, but either way, steam was rising, produced by human hands.

The village. On the other side of that hill was Earlham Village, the one closest to the mansion.

"—Whe…w."

Until that point, only the faces of the people at the mansion had graced the back of his mind, but now he imagined the villagers he had so dearly missed. They included the very pushy children and the astoundingly unguarded adults. These were the good people who had welcomed the trivial things Subaru had brought into this world without laughing them off as absurdities.

He missed their smiling faces so much that the memory of them almost made him cry.

He didn't know why he had forgotten them. It was living proof that Subaru had been in this world. He had saved them. They might have been wiped out had it not been for him. It was Subaru's feat. Was there any other result of his actions he could take that much pride in?

With the pillar that supported him right before him, Subaru's steps quickened.

The dissipating white smoke nearly vanished in the wind. Subaru pressed on, as if fearful of that very thing. Someone was there. People who knew Subaru, people who knew his worth—they were definitely there.

That moment, it was enough. He wanted proof that someone cared for him, that someone had affection for him.

He ran. He sprinted up the hill. When he neared the crest of the slope, he could finally see the source of the white smoke. Subaru climbed up to the peak, using his sleeve to wipe off the sweat trickling down his brow, and cheerfully looked at the village.

—And then, the nightmare finally caught him.

5

When Subaru ran to the village entrance, his gaze shifted around to find the first citizen he could. That was when he frowned, sensing something was wrong.

The moment his legs stopped, the accumulated stress on his heart and lungs crashed down upon him. He gasped for breath over and over, coughing up spit, and strived to let his body recover as his eyes searched the area.

At first glance, he thought that nothing odd had occurred in the village.

The air that morning was very fresh, enough to snap a sleepy person awake.

It was such a clear and sunny day, and yet he couldn't sense anyone in the village whatsoever.

Having been up so late, Subaru didn't fully appreciate the fact that it was still very early in the morning, enough that people might still be asleep. He slumped his shoulders at the sleepyhead villagers and moved on, searching for the cause of the white smoke.

If he looked for the source, he'd surely stumble across someone.

"—"

But Subaru's hopes were in vain. He didn't come across a single face.

By the time he'd nearly reached whatever was burning, everyone was long gone.

What had once been a fire was still faintly smoldering, causing the smoke, but he couldn't sense anyone's presence.

That was when Subaru was haunted not by vague anxieties but by very tangible ones.

For reasons unrelated to fatigue, his breathing and heartbeat quickened. With his body reacting to that panic, Subaru banged on the door of a nearby house. There was no response.

When he rushed in, it was an empty shell. No one was home.

Maybe the whole family was out doing farm chores— No, he couldn't dismiss the situation with a silly joke.

He rushed into the next house, searching for people. There were none. It, too, was unoccupied.

An amorphous chill came over him. Subaru, realizing that it greatly resembled what he'd felt when he met the figures in the forest, almost lost himself as he desperately kept searching for a human presence.

"—!"

He shouted enough for his voice to go hoarse, pounding on house after house, not caring that it was splitting his fingernails.

The result was nothing but silence. Subaru, all alone in the world, collapsed to the ground, powerless.

No matter how often he might encounter them, he couldn't get accustomed to these incomprehensible situations. Naturally, the same went for senseless developments that he did understand.

Forsaken by all, prospects grim, all avenues of escape cut off. This was always Subaru Natsuki's future.

"—"

Having lost count of how many sighs he'd made, Subaru made one more as he decided that further searching was meaningless. No matter how many times he looked around the village, he wouldn't find anyone. There was no one left.

Subaru rose up, brushed off his butt, and tried not to slip on the muddy ground as he stepped forward. Though there was no trace of rain having fallen, there was mud everywhere. He'd lost his footing and tumbled several times over when he'd been running around the place. So Subaru avoided the mud, bypassed anything that might cause him to trip, and headed to the center of the village, the direction of the white smoke.

The fire that had caused the smoke was already out. The smoldering remnants were nearly extinguished. Subaru gently lowered his gaze, looking absentmindedly at the remains.

There was nothing odd to see, save for the charred corpse of the old man from which the white smoke was rising.

"—"

Subaru scratched his head, averting his mind from the sight as he walked toward the village exit. If there was no one inside the settlement, there was no point staying there. He had to hurry to the mansion.

He stepped around the carelessly strewn corpse of a young man, walking carefully so as not to slip on the bloody mud. He gave the bodies of the young couple, piled on each other, a wide berth, passing right beside the old woman lying faceup as he entered the village square.

Subaru searched for any signs of life among the numerous dead therein, seeking any salvation, anyone who might call his name.

But his hope went unfulfilled, for inactivity was all that remained.

Too many detours. He hadn't fulfilled his original intention, and this was the result. He'd taken too much time, and futility was his reward. Everything in that place was in vain. There was nothing there that wasn't, Subaru included.

"—"

Abandoning everything as futile, he dragged his feet in a daze as he crossed the village square. As he did so, his foot abruptly caught on something, sending the half-aware boy tumbling forward.

Groaning from the pain of landing on his shoulder, Subaru reflexively glared at what had snagged his foot.

—And so, he met Petra's empty, unseeing eyes.

"AAAAaaaaaaa—!!"

6

He couldn't escape.

Subaru cried and screamed until his trembling voice went hoarse, a flood of tears pouring down as he wrapped his arms around Petra's remains, cast aside on the ground.

Warmth had long faded from the girl's body. Rigor mortis had set in. The body of an unconscious person ought to have been heavy, but even considering Petra's youth, her body was far too light.

That was probably because of all the blood that had flowed out of the gaping wound in her chest.

Petra had died with her eyes open and an expression of surprise. The only comfort to be found was that the absence of pain or suffering on her face meant that she'd died instantly when her heart was impaled. After all, there was no reason for her to die with a gaping hole in her chest and then suffer in agony on top of that.

Subaru laid Petra's corpse upon the ground and covered her with his track jacket, the only funeral he could provide her. He'd tried to close her eyes, but with her body already stiff, he couldn't grant her even that small mercy.

Praying that Petra would rest in peace, Subaru trembled as he turned his back to her— He continued to avert his eyes from the hellish scene the familiar village had become.

The cause of the white smoke was Muraosa's charred body. The young men had no doubt fought with the swords they had. There were weapons and farm implements scattered about, with the blood of the slain villagers drenching the bare earth around them.

Death had befallen the village. It had all been over long before Subaru arrived.

Far too late, Subaru was now the only person to bear witness to the results of the tragedy befalling that place. He offered up both his hands, as if pleading for someone, anyone to take them.

What happened?

What had happened? What terrible, horrible thing had occurred? Who had violated the village in a merciless slaughter of its innocent denizens, trampling upon their dignity even in death?

No one still breathed. Not a single person was left alive.

A memory of days long forgotten arose in the form of a carefree voice.

"Oh, Master Subaru. Good morning to you. Here to play with the children again?"

He remembered the brash, noisy, fond, and very pushy voices of the young children.

"Subaru's here!" "Subaru came!" "Subaru's all alone!"

One girl had pretentions of adulthood as she made a cheeky promise about the future.

"Eh-eh-eh, Subaru's the one who saved my life, so when I'm bigger, I'm going to return the favor."

He couldn't see her face anymore. His track jacket now covered it.

No one was left. His memories had been trampled underfoot, shredded, discarded, lost.

It wasn't sinking in. Liquid was pouring from every cavity in his face. Whether it was tears, snot, or drool, he had lost the will to hold it back as it continued to sully his face.

"—Aaa."

Then, as Subaru wallowed disgracefully, practically drowning in tears, he came to grasp something far too late. He finally understood the obvious.

There was no reason for the senseless tragedy to have stopped at the village's edge.

"—"

A chill worse than any that had come before shot through Subaru's entire body.

Since Subaru had fallen into that world, he had overcome mortal crises several times over.

Even then, he had never known fear and despair as he did in that moment.

—The despair that, somewhere beyond his reach, the people precious to him had been taken away.

His teeth chattered to their very roots. His eyes, painful from too much crying, could see little, but he raised his limited field of vision to the sky. The clear blue ether seemed innocent in the face of the tragedy beneath it. And under that sky, the mansion awaited.

That place he'd wanted so much to return to, that he'd yearned for, the place practically right before his eyes, was now too frightening to contemplate.

But whatever had turned the village into hell surely hadn't overlooked the mansion.

"—Ah, ahh."

He was scared. He couldn't help but be scared.

He didn't want to think of the possibility that this "something" had torn through the mansion. He was afraid that if he thought it, let alone spoke it aloud, that would make it real.

He shook his head, casting off the fearful images. But though Subaru tried to drive them to the back of his mind, one of them obstinately held on, whispering in Subaru's ear, refusing to be forgotten.

That was why Subaru clung to it, the lowest means for him to escape. If he could voice even the possibility, the chance that something had happened to *her*, then...

"Rem...? Rem...where are you...?"

It was the name of the girl who ought to have arrived before him, the girl who had cared for him, who had cuddled with him, who had affirmed him, and who had betrayed him in the end.

Subaru instinctively knew what it meant to call her name. And knowing this, Subaru had chosen to do it anyway.

In the name of worrying about Rem's safety, he was fooling his heart with the most sordid of means.

"If Rem came back... She'd never sit back after that happened to the village..."

Excuses.

It was another excuse, spoken in a place where he stood alone, and it didn't even fool him.

He was the worst. He was the lowest of the low.

He didn't want to understand, but he did.

If he could voice the possibility that he'd lost the girl he cared for and the possibility his own heart could break, then why not offer up a sacrifice so that he wouldn't have to?

Subaru told himself such lies so that he could pretend not to see his own overly unscrupulous heart.

He felt like the blue-haired girl's pleasant smile, the warmth of her nestling against him, her voice that called Subaru's name, were growing further, further away.

"That's right... Rem... Rem can... Rem..."

Subaru began listlessly tottering along the road to the mansion. He dragged his feet, leaving Petra's remains and the corpses of the villagers behind, covering his ears to block everything out.

He still didn't know what awaited him. He thought both that he didn't want to know and that he needed to know, but he didn't have the courage to run to find out.

Subaru slowly, slowly climbed the upwardly sloping path, clinging to the girl's name like she was the pillar supporting his heart as he walked toward the mansion.

—Rem was dead in the courtyard.

7

The courtyard he had seen on many a morning had turned into a hell unlike anything he'd ever seen.

The small but vivid flower bed had been trampled awry, and the trees standing around the mansion had been felled, snapped in half.

The green grass had been dyed black with blood, with the prostrate corpse joined by the remains of several black-robed figures. Each showed signs of being subjected to incredible violence, with few remaining relatively whole. The gruesome damage to the remains exceeded what he had seen in Earlham Village, no doubt evidence of the great rage behind the murder weapon that had turned these unfortunate victims into mincemeat.

The deadly tool that had wreaked such havoc upon them, a blood-stained iron ball, lay fallen among the dark figures in the center of the garden. The metal orb, linked to a handle via a chain, had smashed apart a number of foes, but in the midst of battle, its mistress had somehow relinquished her grip; it seemed to regret having been unable to fight alongside her to the very end.

And as for the demon who he presumed had wielded it one-handed in ferocious battle…

"—Rem."

…She was long gone from that place.

In a corner of the courtyard, a short distance removed from the iron weapon, was Rem, her servant's uniform dyed crimson red. The surface of the ground where she had fallen was drenched with a great quantity of blood that spoke of the heroism of her demise.

"—"

Looking at the large number of corpses besides Rem's in the courtyard, he knew. She had fought. The fangs that had slaughtered the villagers had menaced the mansion with ill intent. She had battled hard to defeat a number of them, struggled while heavily wounded, and died.

"—"

What had the group of black figures been thinking in killing Rem? *Why? Why? Why, why, why, why, why?*

What did they know about her? Rem tried her best, always worked hard, always took care of others, jumped to too many conclusions, was kind and gentle and stern to Subaru; when times were tough, she was on his side, but she'd left him behind; she loved her sister and hated herself, but she'd just begun to like herself a little more, and— Just when she'd stopped calling herself a substitute for her older sister, just when she'd begun to walk down her own path in life, she…

"…Rem."

Though he called out to her, she made no response.

Though he shook her, her body had already gone cold and hard. He tried to stroke her soft hair several times over, but it clung to her forehead, sticky with blood.

Subaru didn't even have the courage to turn her over and see the look on her face.

Maybe her expression was bitter, locked in place as she struggled against death to her final breath. Perhaps it was peaceful. He didn't have the right to accept either.

After all, it was Subaru Natsuki who'd as good as killed her.

"—"

He left Rem, fallen with her arms wide to the sides, when he noticed the shed containing gardening tools.

Rem's unnatural location. The shed that she seemed to be protecting. And the blood that had flowed out from under the closed door. Despite the scent of death, Subaru suppressed his nausea as he reached toward the shed.

With a *creak*, the door opened; the next instant, the scent of overflowing blood assaulted Subaru's nostrils. He reflexively covered his mouth with his hands as he beheld the results of Rem's attempt at defense.

—Not a single one of the children inside the shed was still alive.

Subaru fell down and pathetically crawled onto the grass, heaving the contents of his stomach upon the lawn. He thought that his overflowing tears and vomit would stop, but there was no apparent limit.

"Uh, fuggh…"

Rem had died to protect the children and failed.

He thought back to the villagers who'd apparently picked up arms and fought. They hadn't run, either. The adults had stayed in the village so that the children could escape. The little ones had run to the manor, with Rem fighting heroically in the courtyard to protect them as they huddled in the closed shed, praying for salvation.

But their prayers were cruelly, mercilessly trampled on, and then their lives were taken from them as well.

"Hyeek."

Abruptly, a cry in falsetto escaped his throat.

It wasn't that anything had happened. It was simply that the forgotten terror had suddenly reared its ugly head once more.

Subaru had returned to the village and the mansion in the hope of finding someone who knew him. And yet, not a single living soul was left. Only the silent dead greeted Subaru.

He felt like those hollow, empty eyes were saying something to him. He felt like the blood-drenched tongues in their wide, gaping mouths were berating him. He felt like they hated him. He recalled the days they had spent sharing smiles with each other.

"No… No, no, no, no, no…!"

—*Why are you alive?*

—*Why did we have to die instead?*

"No… I didn't… This isn't what I wanted at…"

He'd had an ideal. He had dreamed of a hope.

When Subaru heard that Emilia had fallen into peril, he had thought it a blessing from heaven. Since she had lost all faith in him, he believed this was his chance to get back into her good graces. He'd believed he would save her from peril as he had done before, she would thank him, and they'd put their meager differences behind them to walk side by side, hand in hand.

He had disparaged the suffering, the danger, the tragedy that had occurred as nothing more than a means to that end. He had taken it lightly, believing he could fix anything, no matter what happened.

And if the cost of that was a vast number of dead bodies—

"It's…not my fault… I-I didn't…!"

Subaru shook his head, rose to his feet, averted his eyes from the shed, turned his back on Rem's corpse, and ran toward the mansion. He cut through the courtyard, kicking in a window on the terrace and climbing through to intrude into the mansion. The dimly lit manor seemed to treat Subaru like an outsider as the soles of his shoes crushed fragments of glass. He began to run around the building, clinging obsessively to the search for another living soul.

"Someone, anyone, anyone, anyone, anyone, anyone, anyone, anyone, anyone…"

Just as when he had run from the village—no, even baser hopes continued flowing from him.

"It's not my fault… It's not my fault… It's not my…fault…!"

—I didn't want this to happen. So it's not my fault.

He wanted someone to be alive so that they could agree. Or perhaps, the fact that someone had survived at all would be enough to affirm his claim. So Subaru kept searching for survivors.

He had to find one. If he couldn't, he'd never be able to live with himself.

Now faced with the notion that his own, flippant thoughts had brought this tragedy about, there was no way that he could stay composed. To stop his mind from shattering, and to not have to bear the burden of the multitude of dead, he required a more tangible defense.

He violently thrust open the door of the nearest room, peering in to find it empty. Dejected, he moved to the next chamber. Checking whatever room was closest at hand, Subaru continued his search for the four people who ought to have been at the mansion: for Ram, for Beatrice, for Roswaal, and above all, for Emilia.

Subaru's half-crying voice carried a heavy imprint of despair.

"Come on… Come on… I'm begging you… Help me… Help me, please…!!"

Normally, Subaru would have been able to easily reach Beatrice's archive of forbidden books, even without trying. Yet when he needed to most, he was unable to find it no matter how hard he looked.

He wanted to hear invective from her sharp tongue almost more than air itself.

Subaru, dragging his feet along in unmanly fashion, still had tears rolling down his cheeks.

Distracted by sobbing breaths, Subaru continued to walk in search of the living, his own eyes like those of the dead.

—He found Ram's body in the room at the end of the second floor.

Having seen so much death in such a short time, Subaru knew immediately that she was not asleep as she lay on the bed.

Her light skin had grown so pale that you could almost see through her. In contrast, her tongue stood out for being redder than normal. Unlike how her identical younger sister had passed away, Ram, adorned by the cosmetics of death, was lovely even after her passing. Subaru had always glibly said that she'd be cute if she only kept her mouth shut.

—But he'd never said that out of a desire to see her like this.

"Hgheee."

Subaru felt like he heard a curse. The same curse upon Subaru's life spoken by the dead in the village and the courtyard.

Subaru stumbled clumsily out of Ram's bedroom and fled. He put his hands on the wall, slapping his uncooperative knees, and distanced himself as fast as he humanly could.

Closing his ears, shaking his head, Subaru arrived at the dance hall on that floor. He crawled on hands and knees, stumbling several times midway, and pathetically climbed up the stairs.

Ram was dead. That left three survivors. As if they had a mind of their own, his feet avoided the floor where Emilia's room was and climbed to the top level toward the chamber at the center of the main wing.

This was Roswaal's study. The thick double doors remained shut in silence, their formidable solemnity making them seem removed from the wickedness that had infested the rest of the mansion.

The doors weren't locked. He stepped inside and looked all around, feeling half resigned to the possibility of finding Roswaal's corpse slumped over the desk.

Rem was dead. Ram had passed away in the mansion. Subaru himself was no longer certain if he was really looking for survivors or to find the despair that would eradicate his last hope.

"—"

There was no one in the study.

There was no sign of anyone having broken into the room. The desk and the writing supplies on it were just like he remembered.

A slight feeling of relief took hold of Subaru, not only because he was unable to confirm that Roswaal was dead or alive but also because there would not be another casualty to weigh upon his battered conscience any further.

"—?"

No, he realized that his earlier feeling, that the room looked just like he'd remembered it, was off. There was actually one thing that was significantly different from his memory. Namely, the bookshelf wasn't in the same location as usual.

"A secret…passage…?"

The bookshelf on the wall had slid well to the right, revealing the entrance to a dark corridor behind it. He timidly drew close and peered within, finding stairs spiraling downward.

A thought rose up in the back of Subaru's mind. *An emergency escape route.*

As a marquis and lord of the land, it was no surprise that Roswaal had such measures in place for his own protection. It was the sort of thing he'd gleefully arrange beforehand.

The cold wind blowing through the secret passage suggested that it continued for quite a way down. He naturally imagined that the route was for safely escaping from the mansion itself.

"If so, then Emilia…"

Subaru took several deep breaths, hardened his resolve, and stepped into the escape route. When he touched the rather cold wall, he wondered what it must be made of; as he did so, it gave off a pale-blue glow that allowed him to see several meters ahead. Relying on the light, he kept one hand touching the wall as he carefully followed the steps downward, making sure not to slip.

Apparently the hidden passage went underground. When he reached the end of the stairs, the tunnel stretched forward in a straight line. The source of light didn't change, leaving him relying solely on the radiance from the walls. But the feeling that he was really chasing after survivors was enough to support Subaru for the moment.

Whether he himself was dead or alive seemed ambiguous to him now.

"—Nn, oh?"

The wall he had been touching suddenly ended, leaving him abruptly groping into thin air.

Subaru unwittingly flailed forward and was greeted by a hall in the middle of the passage.

Really, it was more the size of a lounge than a hall. Smaller than a guest room, the space was supported by unevenly distributed pillars, so haphazard that he felt like the architect had a twisted mind.

Slipping past the annoying supports, Subaru sluggishly advanced. Ever since he'd gone underground, he'd felt like his limbs were stuffed with lead as languor dulled his movements. Even his thoughts were clouding; even his memories from mere seconds before seemed vague.

It was a hard battle to take even a single step at a time. His eyelids were heavy; both his shoulders felt like millstones holding him still. Even so, a combination of tenacity, hatred, sense of duty, and madness pushed Subaru's body forward.

Threading between the pillars, he headed straight forward to see an iron door at the back of the room. When he reached it, the breeze slipping between the split at the center told him that the path continued ahead.

—*What was I looking for, anyway?*

He reached out with bloodless fingertips before his stagnant thoughts could produce an answer. Subaru opened and shut his mouth as he breathed hard, grasping the door for no reason other than his sense of responsibility.

"—Agauaa!"

Screaming in fierce pain, Subaru shook his right arm as if trying to tear it off. Touching the doorknob had left his entire hand in scalding pain. Subaru anticipated further agony as he lowered his eyes onto his right hand.

—He saw that it was missing its index finger.

"—Huh?"

Dumbfounded and astounded, Subaru lifted his hand before his eyes and spread it out. Now colored white, with cracked skin, it was missing its index finger from the knuckle. The middle finger and thumb were also missing their tips.

"—"

Slowly, his gaze returned to the door. Subaru's finger was stuck to the door where he'd grabbed it.

More precisely, it had ripped his finger right off.

—*Gotta get it back on, quick.*

With only that incoherent thought in his head, Subaru reached out once more to take back the finger he'd lost. But lethargy afflicted his body even more than before; his thoughts reached his shoulder and elbow but not any further than that. Impatient that his arm would not move, Subaru tried to step toward the door, but the instant he did, his right foot shattered from the ankle down.

"—aaa!"

Subaru fell on his side, his voice trickling out of his throat though he was unable to form words. He didn't know if he was screaming out of pain or in a futile struggle to live.

The instant he drew in breath to scream more, white frost filled the inside of his chest, and he could move no more.

His lungs convulsed. In a single moment, his ability to breathe came to an end. He made short, shallow gasps, but his lungs could not expand nor take in oxygen anymore. In that perilous state, Subaru's eyes alone desperately shifted about.

He had very little feeling anywhere in his body. It was the second time he'd lost a leg, but the pain and sense of loss from its shattering were on a different level than mere severing. The right side of his torso, now the underside of him, was cracked in several places.

His tongue stopped trembling as white breath came over it. Only then did Subaru realize the truth.

His cheek was now in contact with the ground. If he moved his head, his flesh would probably crack and tear right off. He no longer felt any pain. He moved violently, tearing his right cheek and ear right off, but he didn't care. He spent some time repositioning his body so that he was lying faceup. When he looked back at the upside down view of the little room, he understood.

Of course the pillars were in irregular locations. They weren't pillars at all. No, they were pillars, but their function wasn't to hold up a structure.

These were human pillars, men who had frozen over and died.

Subaru had wandered into the same white apocalypse, and his body would become a frozen statue like the other victims'. And it would happen very soon.

His breathing had already stopped.

His limited oxygen flowed to his brain, but in the world of absolute cold, which would end sooner, his brain functions or his life?

He understood nothing. He saw nothing.

From the tips of his fingers, the being called Subaru Natsuki was coming to an end, replaced by a fragment of ice.

Or perhaps it would have been more accurate to say it was no longer Subaru Natsuki there but a madman wearing his flesh?

Perhaps his mind had died long before, the moment he arrived in the village.

He lost all feeling in his lower body. He couldn't see his arm anymore. It was strange that his brain was functioning at all. Where did one's life reside? The brain or the heart?

There was no way that he would find the answer in that freezing world.

In the realm ruled by nothing but white, there was a frigid murmur.

"—You are far too late."

And then…

—Subaru Natsuki shattered into tiny pieces, into white crystals, and vanished from the world.

CHAPTER 4
ON THE PERIPHERY OF MADNESS

1

—When the darkness split apart and he awoke, it began with the pain of sunlight burning his eyes.

"—id?"

Warm blood flowed through his limbs. His shattered lower body was firmly standing upon the ground.

Right after the first blink, all his lost mental functions seemed to return at once. His brain instantly restarted and then short-circuited from information overload, making his eyes literally spin.

Where the ringing in his ears had dominated his world, the sounds of thronging humans going about their lives came rushing in. Various people mingled along the dusty road, burying his field of vision in the living souls he had so craved.

Subaru stood rooted in place as the human wave parted around him. The beating of his cracked heart grew fiercer.

"Hey! Hey there! You listening?!"

Along with a click of the tongue, the rough voice reached him from right beside him. Subaru slowly shifted his gaze toward it and saw a stern, scowling face with a vertical scar on it.

The man rubbed the white streak with a finger.

"Gimme a break, kid. Don't just stare into space like that."

"Eh, ah?"

The very faint reply drew a sigh out of the man.

"What's with that weak reply? Well, whatever. More importantly, something happen to you?"

The speaker held out his hand with a nice, shiny red fruit sitting on top of it. Subaru came to the conclusion that the man's appearance was a truly terrible match for the person inside. It seemed surreal.

Subaru remained silent as he gazed absentmindedly at the fruit. His situational awareness was badly lacking.

However, the man didn't suspect that something was wrong with Subaru, instead leaning forward as he said, "Hey, enough fooling around here. I asked, how many abbles? Don't make me say it over and over."

The man reached over the counter and grabbed hold of Subaru's shoulder. He roughly pulled him closer, and Subaru's defenseless body pitched forward and crashed against the shelf. The man let go with a surprised look on his face.

"Wh-what are you doing?! Stand up properly. Your legs are all wobbly, damn it…"

"L-l-legs?"

The man pointed to Subaru's lower body with an exasperated look on his face.

"You've got two good ones attached to your hips. What, day-dreamed you'd lost them or something?"

When Subaru looked down, he did have legs, trembling and shaking though they were. Since they were unreliable and unable to support his body, he was leaning on the shelves at the moment.

With an annoyed voice, the man said, "I'm begging you, quit the bad jokes. This ain't normal conversation, and it's messin' with me."

But Subaru's body did not respond.

Reality didn't register as real. He felt detached somehow, like some sort of discord had developed in the connection between his body and his soul.

What was he doing there?

What had happened to him?

He felt like something had happened to him, but what?

—*What am I doing here? What, what, what...?*

Suddenly, a girl's voice sounded in his ears.

"—Subaru?"

"—"

Unable to speak a word, Subaru felt his eyes go wide as he lifted up his face.

Behind the counter, there was a tiny silhouette standing near the stern, tall man, cleaning things up. She wore an apron dress that was mostly black, with a white apron and white headdress. She stood straight with a small stature and an elegant body. With the counter between them, she turned her lovely face toward Subaru. Her shoulder-length blue hair fluttered in the wind, drawing attention to her refreshing, gentle image.

Tears formed in his eyes.

"Ahh?"

"Subaru?"

Sobs poured out of him as his field of vision blurred. He earnestly rubbed both eyes, fearful that the clear, distinct image of the girl would fade.

And yet, she grew more and more distant as the murmurs loudened.

Before he realized it, he'd lost the support of the counter and fallen onto the street. Unable to send strength and will to his feet, he lay there amid the pedestrians coming and going, tears flowing as he gasped with disjointed breaths.

No, it was not breathing...

"Hu-hee... Hi-hi, ha-ha... He-hi, hi-ha-ha-ha...!"

—It was laughter.

The murmurs broadened. He could tell that more and more people were shifting their gazes to him.

Someone was watching him. Someone saw him. He wasn't by

himself. He wasn't isolated. From this alone, he knew he was accepted, even lying there in the street like a marionette with cut strings.

Rather than run around the counter, the girl leaped right over it to move to his side.

"Subaru, what's wrong?! Are you all right? Get a grip on…"

The girl wrapped her arms around the fallen Subaru to sit him up. As she did…

"Eh?"

She felt so defenseless, and he hugged her back with all his strength.

The girl accepted the embrace with astonishment. Her breath was so close, and her warmth was so comforting as he buried his nose into her shoulder and hugged her tight.

Perplexed, she tried to say something.

"Er… Um, Subaru? Umm…"

Each word, each syllable, each character, each breath, was a hymn to Subaru.

He embraced her firmly, his arms refusing to let go. Nor did the girl stir even an inch, quietly accepting the embrace, making no move to brush him off.

The warmth of her body, the heartbeats of life, made him feel that others were alive like nothing else could.

"Hi-ha… Uhi-ha, hi-hi-hi-hi."

—The madman named Subaru Natsuki continued to simply laugh.

2

Ferris, sitting in a leather-covered chair, put a finger to his cheek and solemnly declared, "To be frank, Ferri can only say that it is all over now, *meow*…"

His ears twitched, and he swept back his flaxen hair as he shifted his gaze away from Subaru, sleeping in a feminine-looking bed. He looked instead to Rem with a pitying look in his eyes. He continued,

"Ferri can only do something about physical wounds, you see. Issues with the body are workable, whether within or without...but there is nothing Ferri can do for the mind, *meow*."

After Ferris's apology for his powerlessness, Rem bowed in a show of respect.

"...No, thank you very much for exhausting all your efforts."

But somehow, her flat voice sounded devoid of emotion. This was not like her normal suppression of her opinions. Rem's inner turmoil was simply too great and had turned into profound sadness.

Ferris closed one eye in a pained look. Rem did not notice his reaction and gently leaned her head forward, shifting her attention to Subaru where he lay on the bed.

They had Subaru in bed to tend to him, but that didn't mean he was asleep. Both his eyes were wide open as he stared straight at the ceiling. From time to time, he'd make a fragmented laugh, like he'd just remembered something, and when that passed, he would suddenly break into tears.

In his unstable state, Subaru's torment continued apace.

—Truly, the change in the boy had been a sudden one.

Until that morning—no, the entire time he'd been walking with Rem through the royal capital that morning—he had been his normal self. Certainly the incident the day before weighed on him, and his behavior showed some signs that he was stressed, but Subaru was striving as he normally did. Rem deeply respected his wishes and sought to be close to him without changing his behavior.

She didn't think anything had happened that could trigger this.

Rem painfully regretted that the instant Subaru had abruptly changed was when she'd taken her eyes off him. Even so, she was right there at the shop, listening to the shopkeeper converse with him.

Thanks to Rem's tireless efforts, the store had sold its merchandise nicely, and the shopkeeper, in quite high spirits, seemed inclined to give them a souvenir. He was asking how many abbles Subaru wanted to take with him, and she remembered him answering, "How 'bout all of 'em?"

The very next moment, his demeanor abruptly changed, and he

fell limply onto the street. When Rem sat him up, he seemed so overcome by sadness and tears of joy that he kept laughing.

Deeming he wasn't well, Rem carried Subaru back to the Crusch villa, accepting all the trouble it might cause. Suspecting it was some kind of magical interference, she politely insisted that Ferris examine Subaru.

However, it had all come to naught. Even Ferris, the most accomplished healer in all of the royal capital, could not identify the cause of his sudden change. If Ferris could do nothing, it might well mean that gathering all the great magic users in the entire royal capital would still not be enough to heal him.

Subaru's present condition was unrelated to magic. But his mind had suddenly become unbalanced.

Ferris asked, "Ferri doesn't really want to ask, *meow*, but what will you do?"

"Without understanding the cause, dealing with it is difficult... I am sorry to have troubled you, Master Felix."

"Mmm, don't worry ameowt it. As a matter of fact, it's better for Ferri's treatment now that he's not making a weird fuss, in a meownner of speaking."

Subaru hated Ferris's treatment and often voiced his complaints. On that level, Rem could understand how he was easier to deal with lying down and listless. The words were still highly insensitive.

Ferris continued, "But...but is it really good to continue treatment meow?"

Rem, who was watching Subaru, lifted up her head and shifted her gaze toward Ferris.

"...What do you mean?"

"Don't be upset by my asking, *meow*, but the treatment for Subaru's gate is to make life easier for him, yes?"

"Yes."

"If he can no longer live a normal life, treating him is meaningless, isn't it?"

"—Subaru is...!"

The even more insensitive remark drove Rem to forget Ferris's status as she yelled. But even faced with the maid's emotions, Ferris's look of doubt did not falter.

"Are you saying don't stop now, *meow*? Seeing him like this? Are you serious? It's true some things happened to him, but if that's enough to break him, he's not likely to ever recover!"

Ferris looked down at Subaru with undiluted scorn. To Rem, who knew that this was the man to whom Lugunica had granted the title of "Blue," the archetype for all water magic users, his behavior was all too callous.

If someone couldn't be healed, throw the person away. That was the judgment of the kingdom's foremost healer? What did he understand about the individual named Subaru to judge that he had no prospects for healing?

"Oh my, what a stare mew have... Subawu's a lucky man. Not that he ever realized it."

"Subaru's current situation is unrelated to the royal selection. He is not a person who would lose his mind over minor failures."

"Believe that all you want. As far as Ferri is concerned, keeping his sanity after everything that's happened presents problems of its own, *meow*. And besiiides..."

Ferris set aside his flippant tone as he looked frostily at Rem.

"Don't misunderstand. Ferri doesn't hate Subawu, so this isn't meowt of some kind of special grudge against him."

"..."

"This isn't particular to Subawu as a person. Ferri just *hates* people who lose their will to live, pure and simple."

Ferris pointed at Subaru, and then he touched his finger to his own chin. "Even for someone with my meowgic specialty, there's no way to use that power besides healing. Ferri helps all kinds of people day after day to be of service to Lady Crusch. *Meow*, everyone struggles hard to live, so thanks doesn't matter, but Ferri hates wasting this power on anyone."

"I think that is admirable."

"Thank you— But it's not right to save people who don't want to live. Even if you heal the body, isn't it just saving an unused life? If that's the case, end it before it causes other people trouble. Well, in this case it already has, *meow*."

Ferris delivered his blunt assessment with a stern face.

Behind that hard demeanor, Rem keenly felt Ferris's sincerity concerning the many lives he had no doubt saved. His way of saying it was dismissive, but it was what Ferris had learned from watching life and death in all that time. That had informed his views on life itself.

"Even so, Subaru is…"

Rem, battered by Ferris's words, looked at the boy with pure regret. Subaru was unaware that he was the subject of the conversation as he made faint, intermittent, warped giggles, as if hearing these things had stirred the wounds remaining in his mind.

Deep inside, Rem wanted nothing more than to lose her grip on herself, cling to Subaru, and cry aloud. But that would bring dishonor to him and tarnish the good name of Roswaal, her benefactor. More than anything else, it would be a betrayal of the feelings she herself had carried while watching over him all this time.

A clear voice flowed into the room, abruptly breaking the awkward silence within.

"—Ferris, I believe your view is just a little too strict."

Rem reflexively raised her head at the voice. When Ferris noticed the visitor, his expression brightened. After all, his eyes were always full of zealous devotion when they gazed upon her.

"Lady Crusch," said Rem.

"I do not go as far as to say weakness is a crime. I do believe, however, that condoning that weakness and wallowing in it while leaving the situation uncorrected is very much a vice."

When Rem hastily lowered her head at Crusch's arrival, the duchess checked her with a hand.

With a shake of her long green hair, she moved to the edge of the bed. Her eyes narrowed as she looked down at Subaru, who had a wicked smile on his face even then.

"I see. This certainly is an alarming state. Do you know the cause?"

Hearing Crusch's question, Ferris raised both his hands up as he replied, "No. According to Rem, he suddenly fell over, so Ferri examined him from head to toe. But there's no sign of any interference with his mana, *meow*."

"Is it possible this is some kind of curse? It is difficult to imagine, but I can think of someone taking measures against those with knowledge of the royal candidates. Or one could suspect that this is a show of force by another camp. However..."

"Neither is very likely, is it, *meow*? There's not much time to set something up, and who'd go after Subawu in the first place? Anyone involved would know he's powerless, and there is no meowgical interference anyway, curses included. Ferri's positive. And besides..."

As Ferris's words trailed off, he tilted his head and gently leaned into Crusch, who stood there with her arms folded.

"Lady Crusch, do you doubt Ferri's abilities?"

"Of course not. I could never question your ability, personality, or loyalty. Even if you were to hold a dagger in front of me, ready to run me through, that thought is set in stone."

"Oh my, Lady Crusch, what a meowgnificent line... Ahh, Ferri's falling to pieces."

Crusch left Ferris to squirm and wallow as she shifted her penetrating gaze toward Rem.

"Ferris has spoken. And if Ferris's power will not suffice, none in my house is capable of treating Subaru Natsuki. I'm sorry we can be of no assistance."

Crusch's apology, despite doing nothing wrong herself, sent Rem into another low bow.

"—Not at all. Your deep consideration leaves me speechless."

In truth, beyond the reach of words and pleasantries, Crusch had conveyed warmth to her that she could never return. The finest healer in all the kingdom had rendered his diagnosis, and the head of a rival political camp had conveyed sympathy nonetheless. What more could Rem hope for from them?

Crusch and Ferris had done nothing wrong. Rem knew that.

—After all, she had her own suspicions about how Subaru had ended up in that state.

"—The Witch."

The presence, the "miasma" of the Witch enveloping Subaru's entire body had become denser still. What linked that miasma to Subaru's abnormal state was unclear, but it was a fact that she'd sensed an outpouring of it just before he had collapsed.

If the cause was the Witch's poison, she could not criticize Ferris's judgment that there was nothing he could do. Very few beings were able to sense the presence of that substance in the first place. Not even Ram could catch the scent the way Rem could.

Nothing good came with such pall. Those who planned wicked things were rich with it. Her physiological distaste for it, and the hateful memories that accompanied it, made her deeply prejudiced against those who bore it.

Although the actions of the boy with the strongest Witch smell she'd ever met had melted her hard heart and swept those prejudices aside…

Even so. Yes, even so.

Rem knew that nothing good came from that miasma.

—The demon in her knew this.

3

Rem bowed and conveyed her deepest gratitude.

"—You have gone through great trouble for us. On behalf of my master, I thank you for your benevolence until this day."

Crusch and Ferris stood before her. Rem and the others were meeting in the Crusch villa's reception hall—in other words, Rem was bidding them farewell.

"I am sorry we could be of no help. By rights, it is presumptuous to receive compensation for such a thing…"

Seeing Crusch's eyes fall slightly, Rem lifted her face and firmly replied, "Not at all. Ending our request before it was finished is due to our own circumstances. You have given us your utmost consideration until now, Lady Crusch. It is only right that we pay compensation as promised."

Receiving her reply, Crusch made one final apology: "I am sorry." She would say nothing more.

With his master's lips closed, Ferris followed up.

"To be honest, it does leave things half-done, but it can't be helped, *meow*? Rem, be in good health. As for Subawu...get well soon, is what Ferri should probably say?"

With one eye closed and one finger raised, Ferris indicated Subaru, standing behind Rem, leaning against the door in a slovenly state.

His condition had not improved. His reactions were as dull as before, with his consciousness stranded somewhere between dream and reality. In spite of that, he followed like a child when they led him around by the hand, and he could at least manage not to fall over. Though he still suddenly broke into little fits of laughter and tears from time to time.

Rem replied, "My words are insufficient to apologize for the rudeness caused by a member of our house. I thank you from the bottom of my heart for treating him with benevolence."

Crusch replied, "We had a contract, and at the very least, I have exchanged words with him. I could never treat him in an uncouth manner. I believe things will be difficult from here, however..."

Rem glanced at the faintly smiling Subaru, grasping the hem of her apron in a display of resolve.

"I am...prepared for that."

Just as Crusch had gloomily pointed out, she knew there were many hardships to come. Even so, Rem had appointed herself to be the one who would walk with Subaru through thick and thin.

After all, she'd never forgotten what he had said to her long ago.

Let's laugh, hug each other, and talk about tomorrow. I've always dreamed of laughing with a demon and talking about the future.

She'd remembered that scene in her head many times, tens of times, hundreds of times over.

That was why she could give Subaru no less than what he had given to her. For what she had received was too precious for any sum of money to ever repay.

Crusch lowered her eyes and shook her head.

"I regret that I was unable to fulfill your request."

Rem smiled a little. She was grateful for Crusch's considerate words, especially then, when she felt ready to crumble.

"It is all because of our shortcomings— Though this chapter has reached an unfortunate result, I pray that you will do many great things, now and in the future, Lady Crusch."

"And you as well. Tell Emilia, 'Let us both fight to bring no disgrace to our souls.'"

With that exchange, Rem keenly felt that her duty in that place had come to an end. Subaru's treatment had been abandoned before it was over, and she wasn't able to fulfill Roswaal's secret command.

She would no doubt be sternly scolded for scurrying back. Even so, she had to return to the mansion…for Subaru's sake.

"Ferri understands you're returning to the mansion, but do mew have any leads for treatment?"

Rem held back the regret in her voice and replied to Ferris's question with her single ray of hope.

"At the very least, if he can meet Lady Emilia…"

No matter how much she spoke to him, how much she touched him, how much she continued in vain, the boy never responded to Rem with his usual Subaru-like reactions. But even in this state, sometimes words rich with meaning would tumble out of Subaru's mouth.

"Names…"

"Mmm?"

"From time to time, he says names. My name, Sister's. And…"

She was happy that her own name was among those he whispered. On the other hand, the fact that he didn't respond when she called his made her sad.

Though much of his behavior was meaningless, the name he murmured with the most frequency was…

"—Lady Emilia's. If he is able to meet her, perhaps it will change him somehow."

"But Ferri heard they parted on really bad terms. It hasn't even been four days since then; is that enough time for her to calm down, *meow*? If you could wait a little longer… Ah, you really can't, huh?"

"I am well aware that Lady Emilia has a poor understanding of her own heart. However, this is no longer something I can decide on my own. I must return and receive instructions…"

Rem's words, full of concern for her lord and master, were for the purpose of deceiving her own heart. She was hiding what she truly desired, burying it under her duties as a servant. After all, it pained her to the point of tears that she was not enough to save his heart and mind.

Abruptly, Crusch lifted her face and narrowed her eyes.

"—Wilhelm has arrived."

Following Crusch's gaze, Rem saw that a dragon carriage was entering the courtyard of the villa from the iron gates. A familiar aged gentleman was sitting in the driver's seat.

Crusch continued, "At the moment, this is the only long-distance dragon carriage that my house is able to lend. I cannot reveal the details, but a large number of these vehicles have been required for another matter of late."

Ferris followed up, "You're in luck, *meow*. If you head along the Liphas Highway, you should get back to the mansion before tomeowrrow. It might take you half a day's travel, give or take."

Rem, watching the dragon carriage's arrival, thought that the rays of the sun high above were dazzling indeed.

Since it was around noon now, an all-out carriage ride would mean arriving back at the mansion around midnight. If they were close to the manor, her shared consciousness with Ram would no doubt inform her sister of their return.

"Thank you very much for your kindheartedness."

Crusch replied, without a single hint of false pleasantries, "I do not mind. It is still a far cry from what I would normally be able to provide, so I can only hope that this modest offering nonetheless accommodates your needs."

Rem thought that getting to know Crusch as a person might have been one of the few happy things she'd gained from the time she had spent there.

"Then this time I must excuse mys—"

As Rem was stating her final farewell, Crusch interrupted her.

"Rem."

When Rem stopped, she saw indecision in Crusch's eyes for the very first time. The duchess continued, "This is extremely inelegant of me…but there is something I wish to ask."

"Yes, what is it?"

"Why do you strive for Subaru Natsuki so?"

Watching Rem and the boy leaning against her, emotion vanished from Crusch's amber eyes. She continued, "The relationship between you and Subaru Natsuki is not the master-retainer relationship Ferris and I share. I simply find it distasteful to judge men and women by appearances alone."

"—"

With Rem falling into silence, the tone of Crusch's voice dropped, as if she was apologizing for her own lack of clarity.

"I do not mind if you do not wish to answer. I am embarrassed to even ask."

Ferris silently watched his master as Rem shook her head at both of them.

"No, I am not hesitating to answer. I am simply unsure about what words I should use— It is a difficult thing to explain."

When she was on the verge of putting it into words, she felt it change into something else entirely.

It was natural for Crusch to have doubts. What existed inside Rem didn't stay the same for even a second. Its size, strength, and heat shifted from moment to moment, putting down its roots inside Rem.

She didn't want to come out and say it. She couldn't come out and say it. How, then, to describe something formless inside Rem to another person?

"I suppose it is because…Subaru is special?"

"—"

Rem didn't really understand if that qualified as an answer or not. However, she felt like that response best exemplified what was at the bottom of her own heart.

"Did something…happen to both of you?"

As she supported Subaru, putting a hand to her chest, she inclined her head at the lack of a reaction.

When she looked, both Crusch and Ferris were standing there, gaping with somewhat surprised expressions. Rem had a gnawing feeling that their reactions might indicate she'd said something rude.

Master and servant traded gazes, nodding to each other.

"I am sorry. I am somewhat astounded at what I was doing."

"No, nooo, it was unavoidable. Ferri was surprised, too. Like… Rem, you weren't even there for the talks at the royal palace…"

Rem didn't really understand what they were saying. However, Crusch seemed satisfied with her reply as she stated, "I apologize for my impolite and unrefined question. I'm very sorry—Subaru Natsuki is a lucky man."

Crusch was smiling a little. Ferris followed up teasingly, "He really is. If he ever gets his senses back, Ferri has to tease him about it, *meow*."

They had conveyed, by fairly undiplomatic means, that they wished for Subaru's recovery, so Rem gave them a small smile rich in gratitude.

The two sent her off.

"Be in good health."

"Good luck, *meow*!"

Rem gave them both one deep, final bow before leading Subaru by the hand out of the Crusch villa. Wilhelm, waiting at the gates, greeted her with a nod as he offered her the reins. She accepted them, bowing to the aged gentleman in return.

"You have also been exceptionally benevolent to us, Master Wilhelm."

"Not at all. Words wasted on these old bones. Besides, I feel as powerless as my master. It never occurred to me to do something before this happened."

Wilhelm narrowed his eyes as he watched Subaru, his pupils filled with complex emotions.

Now that Rem thought about it, the old man was probably the person at the Crusch villa who'd had the most contact with Subaru. Though it had been for a mere four days, one might say that the sword training had given the two a relationship as master and pupil. Perhaps Wilhelm felt regret that he could not save Subaru, either.

He commented, "It would seem I have indeed not advanced a single step since that time…"

Wilhelm murmured to himself, apparently gazing through Subaru at something off in the distance.

"Master Wilhelm?"

When Rem called out to the older man, he blinked and shook his head.

"Pardon me. There is nothing I can do, but I shall at least pray for Sir Subaru's convalescence. Miss Rem, take due care while traveling that path."

Rem did her best to ignore the faint, fleeting anxiety in the aged gentleman's eyes at the end.

"Thank you very much. Be in good health, Master Wilhelm."

Even at the best of times, Rem was more awkward than other people. She could only reach out with both hands and do one thing at a time. And now, she'd decided just what her hands would support.

"Subaru, this way."

"…U, aa?"

Supporting his wobbly body, she hoisted Subaru up from behind and sat him in the driver's seat. Rem took her place beside him, accepting Subaru's presence atop the cramped-feeling seat. She sat right up against him, wrapping her left arm around his hip and firmly grasping the reins with her right hand.

"It might be a little cramped, but please bear with it."

They would have to race in this posture for a long, long time. Rem was worried about the strain on Subaru, but she would also need to protect him after they arrived back at the mansion. Roswaal and the others were unlikely to give him a warm welcome.

If Subaru would be without other allies, Rem had to be the one he could count on.

"Because...I will always be by your side, Subaru. Always."

Rem, deeply hardening her resolve, snapped the reins, and the land dragon began to race along the ground. As the mansion receded behind them, the elderly gentleman watched them go.

Slowly, the carriage's wheels gradually turned faster and faster. Rem felt the sensation through the reins, as if the wheels themselves were expressing the state of her heart.

4

—Setting out from the royal capital, the journey to the Mathers dominion was a comparatively quiet one.

Rem had been concerned about Subaru acting up, but fortunately there was nearly no sign of that while atop the dragon carriage. Yes, Rem was right at his side, limiting his movements, but he spent the majority of the time quietly in his seat, gazing absentmindedly at the scrolling landscape.

So far as she could tell, the mental issues that caused his laughter and tears had also lessened. Perhaps the change in scenery had produced some small change in Subaru's heart as well. Hope sprouted in Rem's chest that Subaru really might be able to recover. However, the scent of the miasma tickling her nose dashed cold water on her heart's expectations.

"—"

Gradually, having Subaru's head resting on her own shoulder brought a faint smile to Rem's lips. In truth, she was happy that he was defenseless, guileless, completely entrusting his whole body to her.

Rem knew that this Subaru was not his normal self and that what he was doing was not of his actual will. Even so, having him rely on her like that was the pinnacle of joy.

"Subaru, this way, a little farther."

"...Mm, u."

Close enough feel his breath, Rem pulled Subaru's body even deeper into her own. Atop the narrow driver's seat, they had half-melted into each other already, but Rem instead rested Subaru upon her own left knee. Her right hand firmly re-gripped the reins as she secured his body in place.

Rem was thoughtfully doing as much as she could to prevent Subaru from pushing himself during the drive. She let him occupy most of the cramped driver's seat; when Subaru's snoring seemed troubled, she lent him a reassuring hand; sometimes she would stop the dragon carriage to get Subaru to drink some water and assist him with physical necessities.

Moving by dragon carriage put a not-insignificant burden upon the driver. Paying close attention for over half a day at a time, a normal person would collapse from exhaustion before the journey was over as often as not. However, Rem's physical body was made of sterner stuff than a normal person's. Her mental endurance was also strong, and more than that, the fact that her labors were for Subaru's sake was the best match to light a fire under her.

"By rights, I really shouldn't put my personal feelings into it, though..."

Subaru, embracing her, made no reply. From the look of his profile, he was still hovering between dream and reality. Rem's murmur was more for her own benefit than his.

"Perhaps remaining in the royal capital was not what you really wanted, but...in truth, I was just a little happy. I cannot have you to myself at the mansion, after all."

At Roswaal Manor, the time that Rem could spend together with Subaru every day was fairly limited. After all, she had her hands full with work at the mansion while he was always off with someone or other.

"During work hours it is with Sister, in your free time, with Lady Emilia...and you even spend some of your limited time teasing Miss Beatrice... I had to put up with all that."

"...Nn, hu."

"You were always so busy; you never had time to stand still... At the mansion, you worked for the villagers and for me... In the royal capital, for Lady Emilia... Always, always so busy."

So far as Rem knew, Subaru was always running and running,

never at a standstill. Perhaps it was for someone else, perhaps it was for himself; there was no single reason. But seeing Subaru run to and fro like that put a single emotion into Rem's heart.

"That's why I was…just a tiny bit happy that I was able to have you all to myself at Lady Crusch's mansion, even though I knew you had many worries. I'm sorry, Subaru."

Subaru snored on, grimacing as Rem apologized with a faint smile. She softly caressed the forehead under his bangs, barely a tickle, and sighed slightly.

"Even though I heard that you had an argument with Lady Emilia. I'm sorry, Subaru."

She apologized again. She was thinking back to the day of the royal selection assembly at the palace. Rem hadn't actually been there, so she didn't know exactly what Subaru and Emilia had said to each other when their relationship ruptured.

"After all, neither Lady Emilia nor Master Roswaal spoke to me in detail about it. The gist was, 'Subaru is at the castle, go get him, he will be in the care of Lady Crusch…' I was truly surprised when I met you at the castle after that, though."

Nothing could make her forget the blow to her chest when she found Subaru's haggard state in the waiting room at the castle. She was both concerned at his condition and convinced that he must not be left alone.

"That is why I am at your side as much as I can, Subaru. But half of it is out of worry, and the other half is for my own sake… Being around you has made me into a naughty girl, Subaru."

Even though she ought to be thinking of him, it was there that she discovered her own joy.

It was always like that when she was with Subaru. She always discovered parts of herself that she didn't know existed. Rem counted off on her fingers things that she had come to realize about her old self.

"I have discovered many unpleasant things about myself. I discovered that I am lonely when you are getting along well with Sister, I am annoyed when you speak to Lady Emilia with your face all red, and I think it most unfair when I see you playing with Miss Beatrice."

But her present self hadn't discovered only bad things by any measure.

"I am happy when you are getting along well with Sister. I think it is adorable when you speak to Lady Emilia with your face all red. When I see you playing with Miss Beatrice, I think, *He's so gentle...* I have those kinds of warm feelings in me as well."

She continued whimsically confessing things to herself as if the lack of a reply was a good thing. Rem's words wouldn't stop, with feelings flowing out of her that she could never have said to his face. That moment, the things normally trapped in her heart were pouring out all at once.

"I would never have discovered these feelings, both good and bad, if I were not with you, Subaru. That is why I have thought of my time with you as happy... That makes it difficult right now."

Having expressed those warm thoughts, Rem bit her lip, lowering her head at her own meekness.

Even though such gloom had enveloped Subaru, Rem had been prepared for whenever he would spit it out. Had her passive stance not brought the current situation about? If they had grown so close, shouldn't she have asked Subaru about his worries? And wasn't her own weakness, her own desire to monopolize him, the reason why she had not done so?

As Rem brooded, Subaru turned in her arms, sleeping uneasily.

"Subaru, it is all right. Relax and go to sleep..."

Rem spoke in a gentle voice, breaking the train of thought that was devolving into self-hatred.

The forced march had indeed put quite a strain on his body. She'd meant to ride right through the night to reach the mansion, but it seemed better to camp somewhere for a short while. Since it would be midnight in another two to three hours, that pace would have them arriving at the mansion before the crack of dawn.

"In that case, it will be difficult to convey matters to Sister through our mental connection..."

It worked only for a given range, and only on the condition that both their minds were awake. The limitations of range and willpower were particularly strict when Rem was transmitting to Ram. It was not possible to link to Ram at the present range, and even if range were not an issue, it would soon be late at night.

"...Yes, we should camp."

Having made that decision, Rem directed the land dragon to come to a stop through the reins. The creature gently halted, breathing through its nostrils as it looked up at Rem. She left Subaru in the driver's seat, leaping down to the ground to confirm that the area was safe.

Night had already fallen over the Liphas Highway. For illumination, Rem had only the light of the moon and a lagmite crystal attached to the dragon carriage to rely on. Fortunately, there was little cloud cover that night, so the light of the moon was plenty to see by. There was probably little chance of being attacked by some kind of highwaymen.

"Pardon me, Subaru."

Rem picked up the boy sleeping on the driver's seat bridal-style, resting him upon a blanket inside the carriage.

After watching Subaru's relaxed breathing and his sleeping face, Rem exited the carriage and proceeded to stand watch over the campsite. She had little concern about bandits, but more than a few wild-dog and demon-beast packs were known to roam the highway at night. Rem knew that wild animals and demon beasts hungry for the taste of flesh and blood were far more dangerous than human beings.

"But you are here, too, tonight, so perhaps I have little need to worry about that."

Rem reached out with her hand, stroking the head of the land dragon as it lowered the tip of its snout toward her.

This was the wise and prudent creature that had stuck with her throughout the reckless forced march. Though he and Rem were first-time acquaintances, he had shown no sign of rebelling against her commands. She imagined the duchess's family ought to be praised for the scrupulous training of its beasts of burden.

It was not unrelated, however, to the fact the land dragon's instincts told it that a demon occupied a higher place on the food chain.

Among the various species of dragons, land dragons were

conspicuous for their friendly relations with the humanoid races. They often occupied crucial roles in the lives of mankind and were beloved for their gentle personalities.

Flying dragons and water dragons required special training, and many of them were ill-tempered. Thanks to that, they had relatively little place in the daily lives of humanoids.

At any rate, land dragons were well known among dragon-kind for their gentleness and intimacy with people, but as a species, they drew the line when it came to all other beasts.

There were virtually no wild animals so ignorant that they would willingly attack a land dragon. Plus, the land dragons themselves possessed an unusually keen nose for any kind of danger.

Nothing short of a sizable band of highwaymen or a particularly large pack of demon beasts would attack them, and land dragons could sniff out such a large gathering before it ever arrived. This was the greatest reason that they were prized treasures for merchants and other travelers.

Rem whispered toward the dragon carriage, "Rest well, Subaru."

She continued to pet the nearby beast as she sat on the ground. As she did, she leaned against its tough hide, covered herself with a blanket, and she spread her attention to the surrounding area.

If they departed the next morning with the rising sun, they'd surely arrive back at the mansion before noon.

She would return without having fulfilled her objectives. She had to take her scolding without a single word of complaint. Even so, she at least had to work to keep Subaru from being hurt in the process.

"And to get him back to his old self…"

Surely only Emilia could do that. Rem could not help but be irritated by that.

In the first place, Emilia was a very difficult person for Rem to get close to.

Even Roswaal, who had welcomed her as a guest, treated her as a superior now that she was a royal selection candidate.

In fact, he had also ordered both Rem and Ram to get close to her.

Her master, Roswaal, treating Emilia more highly than himself did not particularly bother Rem. Ram seemed displeased with Roswaal's adherence to hierarchy, but Rem's regard for such things was not as strong as her older sister's.

Of course, Ram was not such a fool as to openly air her opinion on the matter. Nonetheless, Rem frequently picked up hints of deep dissatisfaction over their telepathy, whereas normally she would sense very little.

The complicated feelings Rem felt toward Emilia had nothing to do with Roswaal. It was terribly vulgar, but Rem's conflicted thoughts toward Emilia were the product of the circumstances of her birth—the fact that she was a half-elf. In other words, because she was a half-demon.

In her head, Rem understood that Emilia herself had done nothing wrong. However, the emotional part of herself just couldn't accept it. Emilia was not in the wrong. However, half-demons had affected Rem's life, their influence far too large to lightly dismiss.

She still remembered how the Witch Cult had laid waste to her birthplace. That fact pricked terribly at Rem's heart.

As a result, she had firmly maintained her position of "guest and servant" where Emilia was concerned. Rem disregarded her emotions and responded to Emilia's instructions like an automaton. If no special occasion demanded it, Rem avoided coming into contact with her so that she would not pick up on her demeanor. Their tacit relationship was to never encounter the other by choice, whether their intentions were fair or foul.

Time passed, and Rem had thought their weak relationship would continue unaffected by the royal selection. Based on her position, she thought it highly unlikely she would be involved with the matter at all. When thinking of her own role to play, she decided that going out of her way to support Emilia went beyond her duties.

—And yet, Rem's feelings toward her had changed since back then.

She wondered if it was herself who had changed or Emilia? It was probably both, set in motion by a common cause—Subaru. Since the moment he wedged himself into her daily life, Rem's world had undergone great changes. When how you feel about the world changes, everything looks different, like black and white bursting into vivid color.

Her work at the mansion felt more rewarding than before. No longer afraid of standing by her sister's side, she gained the confidence to approach Roswaal and Beatrice more. In spite of her decision not to lend her support, she'd found herself exchanging words with Emilia more often. After all, she knew that they shared a common interest.

And though she held the boy in her own fleeting thoughts, she knew just who was the apple of his eye.

That was why Emilia remained a source of irritation for Rem.

"I cannot bring myself to love, or hate, Lady Emilia. I am indecisive, aren't I…?"

It was a quiet night. The only things she heard were the faint sounds of insects and the breathing of the land dragon at her side. Relying only on the light of the moon, the boundary between dream and reality was indistinct. Her thoughts shifted from place to place of their own volition.

Time seemed to flow slowly. She felt like she'd looked up at the moon numerous times, only to find its position unchanged.

The night was long. That time alone was a deep, cold eternity.

Abruptly, Rem was seized by the urge to sneak back inside the carriage behind her, which she was protecting. There, Subaru was sleeping with a gentle expression, too deeply to be dreaming. How good would it feel to slide under the blankets at his side, to share that warmth between them?

"Even though I was touching him so closely until just earlier… It is a luxury I cannot afford."

Rem rebuked herself for being affected by the urge, but her heart would not stop picturing the fantasy.

—A temptation arose, the temptation to throw anything and everything to the winds.

At this rate, harsh realities far removed from Subaru's ideals awaited him upon his return to the mansion. She could still run off with the dragon carriage somewhere, with nothing but her own conscience to chide her. The funds Roswaal had granted her for traveling expenses were considerable. With that, she and Subaru could no doubt head somewhere and live in seclusion together.

With time and continued contact with people, Subaru could move past his present childlike state and regain himself. Even if it was different from before, they might be able to share the same moments together.

Surrounded by people who had no idea that they had fled there, she and a recovered Subaru could begin brand-new lives together. It would be a quiet life with the one she cared about, with no one to get in her way—

"Tee-hee, now that's a fantasy..."

Rem shook her head and, holding her knees, pressed her forehead against them, smiling weakly at her own imagination.

There was no way that she could choose to turn her back on everything. To even have the thought was a sin. She could never simply abandon Sister, abandon Ram, back at the mansion. Sister and Rem were two halves of a single whole. On top of that, she couldn't even imagine what burdens Ram would have to carry in her absence.

She was a kind older sister who indulged Rem, so no doubt she would forgive even this. That was why she could never betray Sister.

Roswaal had entrusted Rem with such a fortune precisely because he had faith in her loyalty. Her diligent personality would not permit her to betray such trust, either.

"More than that... I cannot leave Subaru in this state after all."

To begin with, Rem was well aware of her strong personal desire to have things to herself. If at all possible, she wanted everyone precious to her to be right at her fingertips. Doing her utmost for others helped her feel the worth of her existence deep down. It was no exaggeration to say that she was born predisposed to be a maid.

That was why the effort required to care for Subaru in this state was not really a hardship from her perspective. Indeed, she would feel fulfilled if Subaru was unable to live day to day without her.

But this wasn't the real Subaru.

The words she had used to reply to Crusch when they parted ways came to mind.

I suppose it is…because Subaru is special?

Yes. That was everything.

She remembered his smile. She remembered his voice. She remembered his words. Rem remembered what he had said to her and the warmth of his hand reaching out to her back when everything in her life was stagnant, when she was drowning in resignation. It was Subaru who had rescued Rem from the mistaken path of despair that she walked. Rem had made an error in judgment and planned to abandon those children, and it was Subaru who had saved them.

Even though he was bathed in demon-beast curses, walking his own tightrope between life and death, Subaru had abandoned no one. Not Ram and not Rem.

It was enough. It was plenty. Nothing more was required.

What more did Rem need than to devote herself to Subaru Natsuki, body and soul?

What more was required than the feelings burning in her chest?

She would do whatever was necessary so that he could regain his true self, so that she might know his company once more.

And why? Because the person known as Subaru Natsuki—

"…Is a bedeviled, incredible person."

5

Rem stroked her hair back, moist from the foggy morning air, and gently raised her head.

Perhaps it was accurate to call her half awake. Rem felt a little woozy, hovering somewhere between sleep and waking as her internal clock told her it was time to finally rise to her feet.

There had been no changes of note during the night. No demon beast or highwayman had appeared; she hadn't even sensed any.

All that said, Rem seemed to have been fairly worn out as well. Certain of her comparative safety, her body had strived to recover while she was half-awake.

She rose to her feet, stretching up high as she felt the cool morning breeze.

It was a lazy, unladylike gesture. She would never do such a thing where others could see, but she had no concern about that at the moment. The only one around was Subaru, sleeping soundly beside h—

"S-Subaru?!"

Rem jumped in surprise when she noticed Subaru was right beside her, curled up under a blanket.

Since he'd been leaning on Rem for support, the young man gently flopped onto the grass, scowling as he turned his body a little.

"H-he came out of the carriage while I was sleeping and cuddled up next to me…?"

Rem hastily looked between the boy and the dragon carriage behind him. Even putting the truth into words sent her into quite a panic.

On the one hand, she was shocked that she hadn't noticed him moving; on the other, she blushed hard as she realized just how tolerant her heart had become where Subaru was concerned.

In other words, even if Subaru had assaulted her in her sleep, she would never have resisted.

"…I have been too careless."

Even as she made that maidenly lament, Rem thought deep down that Subaru's action might be a good omen, the next step after he behaved himself so well during the dragon carriage ride.

Subaru made no response except laughing or crying. Yet even in that state, he had performed a voluntary action, getting out of the dragon carriage under his own power. Rem held onto the hope that his broken heart was beginning to mend and his personality beginning to reform.

"—All right. Let us go back, Subaru."

If a change had been initiated, things would probably head in a good direction thereafter. Such optimistic thoughts were not like her, but this, too, was no doubt the influence of the young man before her eyes. And that internal shift was something Rem considered very dear to her.

She believed that the thoughts rising into her head the night before had been a bad dream caused by her timid mind and tired body.

She'd completely forgotten it, a cheerful future having overwritten it as if it had never existed.

She lifted up the still sleeping Subaru, resting him upon the driver's seat as she roused the land dragon. She brought water for the awakened beast to drink, rewarding him for his long hours standing watch, and prepared for their departure.

With one hand embracing Subaru over her knees and the other holding the reins, they departed once again. The carriage wheels turned, and the scenery moved.

They were about halfway there. It would probably take another seven to eight hours of travel.

Her mental and physical endurance was far stronger than on the day of their departure, with its tragic circumstances. Subaru was deeply asleep, and Rem gazed at the side of his face, conveying her impatient feelings through the reins so as to pick up the pace.

A faint vibration ran through the dragon carriage. Rem adjusted her embrace of the curled-up Subaru, intertwining her own fingers with his.

"It looks so slender...but this is indeed a boy's hand."

Resigning herself to her weakness in fleeing to that hand, she hoped her meek desire to touch him could be forgiven. It was a little ritual for forgetting about a bad dream.

"This warmth, having you so close... If I have that, it is enough."

After all, hoping for more was simply her own selfishness.

Her feelings from sensing that warmth, and the fact he needed her, had been carved into Rem's heart. She would give him her utmost efforts.

—She would give him everything she had.

6

—There was something amiss in the air.

As the dragon carriage raced onward, Subaru seemed to be sleeping poorly, so Rem had rested him atop her knees, using her supporting arm to stroke his black hair when she finally realized it.

Maybe it was the fact she'd had a lot of time to think things over the night before. Rem, having accepted to a certain extent the complicated feelings within her, was jubilant on the inside when she saw that Subaru had gotten out of the dragon carriage in the dead of night to snuggle up against her.

If that was the reason she had failed to notice the change sooner, she was a great fool indeed.

"It is…too quiet…"

In all that time on the Liphas Highway, Rem had not come across another land dragon even once. This was an offshoot from the main highway, but seeing none at all, even on the distant horizon, was clearly unnatural. Normally, traveling merchants en route to the royal capital and peasants returning with new farm implements were here and there all over the highway.

And yet, the road had been deserted since the day before.

She had not taken any special measures to avoid farms, but she hadn't seen a single person, man or child. What was particularly wrong was that the cries of birds and insects had vanished from her ears a short while earlier.

A bad feeling rushed into the back of Rem's mind.

Such silence meant that the creatures of the wild were in hiding. It was a sure omen of something beyond the ken of man. As they cut through the hills and entered the mountain road, drawing closer to the mansion, that malaise had only increased.

With unease, Rem snapped the reins to spur the land dragon, already running at a desperate speed, to hurry even faster. She knew she was pushing it too far, but she had no time to spare to locate the cause of that unease. She didn't mind if it turned out to be a baseless fear. She would apologize to both Subaru and the land dragon for accompanying her on the reckless journey. She would face them just as she had faced her own anxieties the night before.

And just after she had that thought…

"—Sister?"

Suddenly, thoughts that were not her own threw her mind into chaos. Nearly unbearable levels of anxiety, anger, and fury flooded her, and then it all immediately vanished, leaving Rem on her own.

It had been Ram. Those feelings had flowed into her from her sister through their shared link.

Ram was always a model of self-control on the outside, but in truth, she was built of stern stuff on the inside, too. Normally, the only things that could shake her were related to Rem or their master.

And yet, Ram had been possessed by such fury that she'd communicated it to even Rem via their shared connection.

Furthermore, the fact it had cut out immediately meant that she was controlling herself so that Rem would not pick it up.

Rem guessed that her sister assumed she was in the royal capital, not able to make it in time as her older sister fell into peril. But Rem was close enough to do something, even if that was not Ram's wish. That was why...

"I must hurry back—!"

With a concrete reason to make haste, she gripped the reins so hard that her hand went white. In an instant, Rem's sense of urgency and impatience cast all her misgivings about her surroundings to the winds.

On the surface, Rem was normally emotionless, always striving to maintain her inner calm, but when lives were on the line, she lost sight of everything around her. It was Rem's defining flaw, one that Ram had pointed out to her many times and one a former colleague had pointed out to her as well.

And now that flaw was rearing its ugly head once again.

—When the land dragon's head sailed before her eyes, Rem saw it in slow motion.

CHAPTER 5

ACEDIA

1

—The head of the running land dragon flew from the base of its neck. Without a conscious creature to pull it, the large frame of the carriage tumbled accordingly, leaping off the road and turning onto its side.

The overturned vehicle made a spectacular gash in the ground, kicking up a dust cloud with a great roar. In an instant, they formed a disastrous picture with the carriage wrecked and the fallen land dragon's body tangled in one of the wheels.

They were in a tranquil, forested area in the mountains, surrounded by trees on all sides. The dragon carriage had already entered the Mathers dominion; it was probably about two hours of running from reaching its destination. But the dragon carriage had been cruelly destroyed along the way, with only the sound of a free-spinning wheel resounding through that hollow place. With the land dragon a corpse and the vehicle nothing more than a wreck, the scent of blood began to hover over the area.

"…Uu, uua."

And there, a young man lay, raising a voice of lament after being thrown from the dragon carriage.

He had fallen into a cluster of bushes a short distance away from the half-destroyed dragon carriage. Mosses and vines had likely cushioned his fall.

Miraculously, the youth's injuries were quite light. But his defenseless state didn't mean that he didn't feel the pain of his wounds.

He was scratched and bruised in several places. Fortunately, he had no broken bones, nor any major blood loss from his wounds. But the pain was more than enough to make him cower like a little child in shock.

"A, huu… Gu, hi…!"

The dark-haired young man cried and moaned in pain as he lay upon the grass.

The ground had scratched his forehead, and the soil was stained with red. His tears and mucus were especially unsightly. The disgraceful picture of a grown man splayed on the ground, along with the wrecked carriage, formed an unbearable scene that told of the tragedy of the crash.

"__"

And yet, the shadowy black-robed figures continued to stand in place and watch, as if they were part of the background.

Over ten such figures stood encircling the young man and the dragon carriage. Having ascertained that the headless corpse of the land dragon was indeed good and dead, their attention was focused on the young man.

The figures wore hooded black outfits from head to toe, leaving their faces and even their genders impossible to fathom. They wavered, seemingly gliding along the ground as the circle closed in on the teen.

Then, one of the figures, walking soundlessly, mumbled something. "—la."

As soon as one had voiced it, the next murmured something similar. The low murmurs continued like this as a ceaseless chain, a cascading chant as the shadows enveloped the young man.

The world was composed of two things alone—the sound of leaves in the wind and the black figures' murmurs.

Eventually, the young man heard those whispers, and they sparked a change in him.

"—Agaa, aa! Aa, aaa!"

The young man's injured, pain-filled body thrashed around, flopping on his back, wriggling like a fish suffocating out of the water. His anguish was clearly of a different nature than before. It was as if his distress came not from without but from within his own flesh. He agonized as if there were something running amok inside his body, chewing away at his heart.

From all appearances, he had noticed the muttering of the figures around him and reacted to them.

The shadows looked down at the suffering boy, making no move to halt their chant. But one of their number seemed to come to some kind of conclusion about the writhing young man and extended a hand toward his body.

"—Don't touch Subaru!"

The next moment, an iron ball howled as it sailed through the air, shattering the head of the figure who had tried to touch Subaru, the young man on the ground.

Skull fragments flew around the area as the figure fell and the chain clinked lightly. The weapon danced toward the others like a ferocious silver snake in search of further prey.

However, the group made its decision quickly.

Instantly abandoning their dead comrade, they scattered voicelessly to evade the chain's pursuit. As if by reflex, they drew cross-like daggers from their flanks and gripped their weapons of poor taste with both hands, together keeping watch over north, south, east, and west.

The figures numbered eleven. The way they had instantly responded to a surprise attack by taking up a formation to eliminate blind spots was nothing short of commendable.

However, that mattered against only an attacker whose options were limited to two dimensions: front, back, left, and right.

"—Shii!"

Above the group, someone sprang from among the trees, her

apron dress fluttering. With enough power in her legs to leave shoe marks in the trunk of a tree, her body shot forward at an angle. The girl leaped down with incredible speed, moving just a moment before her prey could detect the sound above them.

What descended was the end of the deadly weapon's handle, driving into an unfortunate figure's skull. With a sharp sound, a cavity opened in its cranium; blood spilled out of the victim as they wobbled and collapsed.

The girl kicked the body toward another figure standing to the side to obstruct its vision as she leaped behind it. However, this one did not hesitate to strike its comrade's corpse. With a swing of two blades, the figure sliced its comrade-turned-corpse apart, regaining its field of vision— The next moment, a twisting iron ball fell upon the menace in black, turning it into bloody fog.

Having hurled her weapon out in front of her, the small girl froze in position. Seeing that she had stopped, the figures took the brief opening to hurl their cross-like swords in unison. The girl, apparently defenseless as blades rushed toward her from all sides, drew a miniature version of her weapon from her side with her left hand and batted down all the daggers in one swing.

After the girl's incredible feat, it was her attackers who were open now. They paused for less than a second, but before the opponent they now faced, that time was lethal.

"Roaaaaa!"

The girl shouted, howling as she bared her teeth.

With a great backhand swing of the flail, she mowed down every tree in its path, tracing a semicircle of utter destruction. Another enemy was caught in the iron mass's advance, slain as blunt trauma ripped their limbs right off.

The beautiful blue-haired girl who had taken their lives had an ivory white horn protruding from her forehead. That truth was enough to identify her as a monster in a girl's flesh.

"You shall not lay one finger on Subaru."

The adorable demon's lovely face was stained with blood; her eyes were brimming with ferocity and aggression. But the position she had taken made clear that she was protecting Subaru from the figures surrounding him.

Having spoken her warning, Rem ignored her own bloody left shoulder and swung the iron ball around above her head. She had sustained the wound to her shoulder when the dragon carriage went on its side, unable to completely evade the carriage as it bounced. If she had been by herself, she would most likely have escaped uninjured, but that wasn't possible with Subaru in her arms.

It was all she could do to use her own body to shield Subaru and throw him to a safe place.

She had seen him fall on the bush as she intended while she shared the same fate as the wrecked dragon carriage.

As a result, her forehead had been lacerated, and a branch had stabbed her left shoulder fairly deeply. She seemed to have a fracture in her left femur close to her hip; moving sent a shot of ferocious pain through her that made her white cheeks go numb.

But Rem stepped forward with a gait that betrayed none of that pain. She glared at the group in black, spewing in a voice filled with hatred, "Witch Cult—!"

Rem spat blood as she called out to them, but as before, the figures made no sign of a human response. Unchanged, they faced off against Rem, almost as if they weren't even conscious of what they were doing.

They were at an impasse—the instant Rem made that judgment, she moved first to break the stalemate.

"—Yaa!"

She altered the course of the iron ball she was swinging above her head, lengthening the chain to its full extent. The single blow snapped the trees along the side of the road, smashing wood and soil together and sending them flying toward the figures. Her opponents variously leaped and ducked to evade, then rushed at Rem to seize the opening she had given them.

Rem, her arm extended, twisted her body so that she could draw her limb and distant weapon back to her. However, a blade would to tear into her chest before the iron ball could arrive—

"—Raa!"

A moment before the tip of the figure's knife reached Rem, her demon foot rose from below to send its jaw flying. No, this was not a metaphor for its head being kicked aloft—the blow was so powerful that her enemy's jaw literally sailed away.

The figure's face was covered in fresh blood. Even so, it did not hesitate out of pain as it thrust the blade forward. The action, made in complete disregard for the attacker's own life, was wrong for any living thing.

"—"

The head of the figure who had failed such a basic biological test was shattered from behind as Rem's iron ball returned.

Showered in blood and pieces of flesh, Rem gripped the iron ball with her left hand. Holding it such that the iron spikes posed no danger to her, she used what was now an iron fist to flatten the face of the enemy rushing right at her flank.

Where there had once been twelve, now there were six. Rem breathed raggedly as her demon gaze pierced the assassins, now half their original number.

A rock tapered and sharpened at one end like a lance sailed into that gaze. With a tilt of her head, she dodged it just before impact. Her hair, moving a fraction slower, was ripped from the side of her head; the pain and surprise turned her vision pure red.

As the shock to her head robbed her of her decision-making ability, Rem went by the sudden slushy feeling beneath her feet and leaped. The moment after she jumped, her delayed thought process told her just what a mistake she had made.

—She had sprung into the air, rendered herself unable to move, against an enemy capable of long-range attacks.

A fireball appeared and burned its way through the great treetops, charging at Rem as she sailed through the air. She felt like the high temperature was setting her flesh alight as she instantly thrust her left hand in front of her.

"*Hyuma!!*"

Rem deployed a thin layer of ice in front of her. The instant the fireball slammed into it, white steam erupted, and the dying hiss of the vaporizing ice clawed in her ears. She had managed to reduce the force of the flames, but she was unable to nullify it completely.

Her decision was instant.

She plunged her left fist, still in motion, into the inferno, sacrificing it to break the flames apart.

"—Uaaa!"

Withstanding the explosion in midair, Rem's body spun as it was blown away, and her back collided with the trunk of a tree. The thick trunk broke and crashed to the ground with Rem on top.

When she got up, she groaned in agony at the dull pain in her left arm.

When she looked at the scorched remnants of her limb, she couldn't even feel pain past the elbow. Without the services of a healer on Ferris's level, no doubt she'd never have use of that hand again.

Even with a grave wound like that, Rem bit her lip and dragged her mind back to reality. She grit her teeth against the pain, using her aggression and rage to light a fire in her belly and drive the anguish out of her mind. She roared, asserting her own existence, and tried to draw even a little of the figures' attention to her.

She prayed only that Subaru had vanished from their awareness.

But.

"—"

One of the group had approached without a sound, and it drove a hand into Rem's torso with incredible force, slamming her into the great tree behind her.

The force, enough to crack Rem's sternum and crush her internal organs, left her spitting out a copious amount of blood.

Coughing up the sticky liquid burned her throat. Her body sank in the agony that coursed through every corner of it. When the hand lashed out again, by sheer luck, she fell to her knees and escaped having her skull crushed. The palm thrust into the great tree behind her, sending it sailing away with unbelievable ease.

The unarmed figure, able to form craters in the ground's surface with a single stomp, was clearly different from the others.

When it leaped sideways in pursuit, Rem rolled to evade it, spat out the blood remaining in her mouth, and searched for the iron ball she had dropped.

"Ah, uh?!"

The instant she dodged a stone lance, which still grazed the side of her face, a rock slammed right into her body from behind. Her spine creaked ferociously, and her small form crashed into the ground and bounced into the air.

The unarmed figure was waiting for Rem at the end of her arc. They were holding in their hand the iron ball Rem had released, and they swung the deadly spiked weapon up to meet her mid-bounce.

"—El Hyuma!"

The chant she'd built up burst out of her lungs. Mana combined with the blood she spat out, freezing it over. A blade of crimson ice sliced off the arm of the one holding the iron ball, forcing his thick limb to drop the weapon.

"Gaurururu!"

Crashing into the ground, Rem regained control of her body and snatched up the handle of the fallen iron ball into her right hand. Simultaneously, she kicked the weapon itself at the figure from behind, using the weight of the ball to tightly wrap the chain around its thick neck.

A dull sound echoed as she snapped its spine. Seeing her foe's head turn at a 180-degree angle back at her, Rem relaxed slightly after felling a powerful foe. That instant…

"—!!"

The figure's body, which should have been powerless, lashed out with a ferocious kick that devastated Rem's torso.

The blow connected with her left side, fracturing every bone in that half of her rib cage and completely snapping her fractured left thigh. After that one blow, the figure expired for good this time, but the damage Rem suffered was severe.

"Uu, aaa…!"

Moaning and coughing up blood, she cursed her now-useless left side as she stood back up. She'd likely just taken care of the best that the enemy group had. There were five left. The fact that they hadn't approached her meant that close combat wasn't their specialty. She could still do this.

—She could get close and snap their necks.

But could she really do that when only her right side could move properly?

"What a weak thing I am…!"

Rem shook her head, suppressed her frail musings, and roused her despairing self. Whether she could didn't matter. She had to do it. She *had* to.

So her left side was dead to her. What of it? She could still move her right side. If her right arm became useless to her, she'd stomp them with her foot. If her right leg became unusable, she'd tear out their throats with her teeth.

If she killed the last one, and Subaru was still alive, Rem would have won.

"—"

The moment she thought of why she fought, Rem's heart sought the sight of the young man dear to her. She looked toward where he had fallen to suppress the last of the hesitation within her. She would burn that final image in her eyes, and it would be the kindling to set her heart ablaze.

"—Subaru?!"

He was gone.

Subaru ought to have been there, gasping from pain, from agony, from fear…but he was not.

Rem hastily scanned the whole area. She wondered if he'd been caught up in the battle and knocked away somewhere. But search as she might, she couldn't see him anywhere.

Then Rem finally realized: "They're one short…?"

There were five figures left among the group. But Rem could make out only four.

The figures had shifted to stand side by side, blocking the road, arms lowered with crosses in both hands. It was as if they had moved to conceal their comrade from Rem's field of vision.

To keep her away from their ally as they fled with Subaru.

"Why…you…"

Her shaking voice fell from trembling lips.

Her lips, which felt bloodless due to all she had lost, were dyed crimson from the great amount she had coughed up. Such violent war paint transformed Rem's adorable face into that of a veritable demon.

"You weren't content with Sister's horn…so you had to take away my reason for living…?!"

The iron ball danced around as her right hand gripped its handle. Her good leg was filled with explosive energy. The figures before her thrust their crosses forward in some kind of pose, rushing at her all at once. That instant… ·

"Do you wish to take even my reason for dying here away from me—?!!"

Rem's roar rent the air as her leg pushed her up, as if the ground itself had launched her.

To the front, an enormous wall of flame spread out before Rem as she leaped. She broke through that barrier, smashing in the face of an enemy standing beside it. The moment after, a fireball bore down on her, large enough to bury her entire field of vision.

"—!!"

A thunderous shout. An orange glow rose up amid the trees bathed in the morning sun, then another and another.

The inferno surged wildly, burning away the trees, with the very world groaning as the high temperature turned the area to ash.

—On that scorched plain, the charred remnants of a white apron dress fluttered and vanished into the wind.

2

Subaru drooled as he swayed on the figure's shoulder, not offering any resistance.

He no longer felt most of the pain from the wounds he'd suffered from falling out of the dragon carriage. It wasn't that he couldn't feel them, but other pain blotted out anything external, so it didn't matter.

He moaned, the agony tearing at his heart robbing him of all will to put up a fight.

Back where the dragon carriage had fallen on its side, the figures surrounding Subaru had begun some kind of chant. As he listened to that sound, Subaru felt something alien well up inside his body, wriggling and eating at him from the inside, as if the ringing in his skull wasn't enough to drive him into raging madness all by itself.

Over and over, he heard someone's voice over the chant. It sounded different, like the whisper of a woman's voice—a whisper like a curse.

In her kind, gentle way, she berated the agonized Subaru and drove him mad.

If it went on a little more, just a little more, he thought and then shuddered.

That pain broke the hearts of men. It bent them into unrecognizable shapes. It changed them. It made people into not-people. That was the kind of curse that it was.

"Hu-he, hi-hi-hi, he-hi-hi-hi…"

Suddenly, the corners of his lips curled into a crazed smile, drooling as he seemed to remember something.

The reverberation of the wriggling black thing grew distant, and his attention began to shift from his internal agony to his external once again. Accordingly, he forgot the eerie feeling that had threatened to shatter his heart and began to cry plaintively in response to the more immediate pain.

"U, higu, a, uu…"

Subaru's body hurt all over. He sought a hand to console him. A voice. Warmth.

But the figure running through the woods, seemingly rushing along a game trail, paid Subaru no heed. It gripped Subaru with such incredible strength that he could not move an inch, and yet the delicate body possessed unimaginable agility, running through the forest like the wind itself.

The depths of the woods had no markings, yet the figure's steps held the certainty of one with a guide. How many tens of minutes had they been running like that? Gradually, the speed eased, and they finally came to a complete stop.

In front of them was a prominent wall of rock, bare except for the lichens covering its surface. The wall, stretching up above eye level, was a natural fortress that could not be easily overcome without the aid of appropriate tools.

Perhaps he'd taken a wrong turn. However, the figure showed no hint of confusion as he stood before the rock face. Gently, he stepped forward and pressed a hand to one section of the stone.

"—"

The faint goose bumps on Subaru's flesh were similar to the ones he felt when someone used magic right next to him.

Where his abductor touched the wall before him, the mass of rock blocking his path vanished instantly, as if truly by magic. It was a stupefying supernatural phenomenon. Apparently the hole left by the vanished rock now belonged to a cave. The figure adjusted its hold on Subaru and carried him gracefully into the hole.

The air in the cave was cold and chilly, but the figure's gait was calm. From time to time, Subaru's moans seemed to spoil that tranquility, but his kidnapper showed no sign of caring. After advancing several dozen yards, even the light filtering in through the entrance faded. Likely, the rock had been restored, hiding the cave again.

They could see within the hollow space even without the light from the entrance. The narrow, rocky corridor had white crystals at regular intervals, and their glowing light guided the figure down the path. Following that light, the black-robed being went deeper and deeper into the cave, carrying Subaru farther and farther into darkness.

The deeper they went, the more the black wriggling thing inside Subaru's body began to stir. This time, instead of tearing at Subaru's internal organs, it licked at every corner of his being, as if showing its affection.

The unceasing pain and accelerating, increasing uncanny feeling made Subaru quiver on his captor's shoulder. Tears flowed from the corners of his eyes as he continued his frivolous laughter.

Finally, the seemingly interminable corridor of rock came to an end.

The glow of the crystals was a little stronger. He was able to make things out more clearly than in the corridor, and this was an especially large natural cavern.

There, Subaru would come face-to-face with the true "malice" of that world.

"Oh my?"

—There was a thin man.

The man in the cavern, surrounded by shadows, wore black robes like the others. He was a slight bit taller than Subaru, but his physique was skin and bones, as frail as a corpse. His deep-green hair was lifeless; he looked weak and unhealthy.

—Were it not for the madness in his eyes.

The figure carrying Subaru bound his unresisting body to the cavern wall. With iron chains and shackles attached to his limbs, Subaru's mind appeared absent as he was tossed onto the hard ground.

The man opened his eyes, eyeing Subaru with deep interest. He leaned forward a fair ways, with his hips bent at a ninety-degree angle and his head bent perpendicular to his neck. His gaze, as cold as a reptile's, shot through Subaru.

"I seeee… Certainly, certainly, this is of great interest."

He stared at Subaru, taking him all in, and nodded as if he understood something. The one who had brought Subaru knelt earnestly on the spot, awaiting the man's next words with great reverence.

As the first knelt, the others followed suit. However, the man in the center did not react to the show of respect around him, instead sticking his right thumb into his mouth as he sank into thought alone. It seemed like he might bite his nail for fun; instead, his back molars crushed the digit itself.

Drawing the red flesh from the corner of his mouth, the man paid no heed to the bleeding from his mangled finger as he tossed out a question.

"Could you... possibly be 'Pride,' by any chance?"

But even with an insane man calling out to him, Subaru was not in his right mind, either. Subaru watched the self-mutilation, seeming like he wanted to look away but continuing to frivolously laugh all the while. The two men, neither in his right mind, stared at each other. The madness in the eyes of each one seemed to startle the other.

"Hmm... That doesn't seem to be a reply."

The man roused his own body, their rivalry disintegrating with a whimper.

The man pulled his thumb out of his lips as he seemed to remember something, with no sign of a dampening mood. He touched his blood-smeared hand to his own forehead.

"Ahh, I see. It occurs to me that I have been rude. My goodness, I have yet to introduce myself, yes?"

A wry, malevolent smile came over him as he acted with wholly incongruous courtesy. Subaru's insane smile seemed to strike him as proof positive of some kind of intimacy between them.

"I am Petelgeuse Romanée-Conti—"

The man politely bowed at the waist as he stated his name. After that, he turned his head alone forward and stated his title...

"...Archbishop of Sin of the Witch Cult... Entrusted with the duties of Slooooth!"

The man—Petelgeuse—pointed at Subaru with the fingers of both hands and cackled.

His obnoxiously loud laughter ripped through the tranquility of the cave with a gloomy echo.

3

The guffaws echoed off the walls of the cold, dark cavern.

It was unclear what struck Petelgeuse as so funny he would laugh, but he shook with joy as he bared his bloodstained teeth.

Faced with the man's amusement, Subaru's cheeks were stretched from his own dry laughs.

The iron manacles were fastened to him so tightly that his hands and feet had changed color; numbness spread through him thanks to his constricted arteries. It seemed that his welcome was in no way a warm one.

"Ahh, what a comedy! What a very, very, very, very interesting scene. Truly, truly, truly, truly, truly!! My brain trembles…!"

Wild laughter came over Petelgeuse as he traced some kind of symbol on the wall with the drops of blood from his hand. The shape's lack of meaning made the makeshift mural a reflection of the man's state of mind.

As the two men with a diminished appreciation of reality faced off against each other, one of the kneeling figures intervened. It was the tall one who had carried Subaru there. The figure murmured something to Petelgeuse.

"—"

It was a whisper like the sound of an insect's wings, reaching only Petelgeuse. Once he listened to it, Petelgeuse's wild laughter vanished. He set aside all jest and tilted his head to form a right angle.

"Iiis that so… Ahh, that makes my heart leap; it makes my heart shiver, yes!"

The tone of his voice and his expression were completely different. With a serious look, he changed his tone instantly; this time, Petelgeuse crunched down on the hitherto undamaged fingers of his left hand, one by one, without the slightest hesitation. The sounds of cracked bones and crushed flesh resounded.

"Ow… Ow, ow, ow, ow, ow, ow, ow, ow, ow, ow! Ahh, I am full of liiife!"

Petelgeuse shook the crushed fingers of his left hand, splattering blood as he looked up at the ceiling.

Unmoved, the shadow watched him, remaining on its knees as it whispered again to Petelgeuse.

"My left ring finger, destroyed! Ahh, what a sweet ordeal this is! For our diligence to have been so richly rewarded… Today, we have shown this uncertain world what love truly is!"

"—"

"Ahh, that is just fine. The remaining bones of the left ring finger have fused with the middle and index. There are still, still, still, still nine fingers left, many, many more opportunities to prove my devotion."

He stretched out his hand, dripping with blood, and placed it on the kneeling figure's head as if in thanks. Subaru could not see into their mind as their entire body shook, but they seemed deeply moved by Petelgeuse's action.

"Yes! An ordeal! An ordeal! This is an ordeal! A test of faithhhh, all to convey our affection! Illuminate! Guide! Ahh, my brain treeeeembles!"

As Petelgeuse laughed in delight, spraying saliva, the figures clapped their hands together in apparent adulation. It was a strange, eerie gathering, one only they comprehended.

The figure's report became more detailed, but within the tranquil cavern, it was quieter than a mouse's paws. Furthermore, it was almost as if its purpose was to provide vile material for Petelgeuse's one-man comedy routine.

Petelgeuse twisted his hips, lowered his body, and leaned forward to bring his face close to Subaru's.

"Setting that aside, him! Ahh, himmmm! Just what is this man?"

With stinky breath blowing on him at close range, Subaru's crazed eyes looked up, unmoved.

"Certainly, certainly, certainly, certainly-ly-ly, this is straaange. Turbulent, unfathomable… What is someone like you, not recorded in the Gospel, doing in this situation, on the eve of the ordeal?"

"—"

"Dragon carriage! Ahh, land dragons are looovely! Adorably loyal, diligent in obedience, diligent in work, a marvelous species striving for diligence in all things!"

"—"

"You killed one! Ahh, that too iss good! It drew the carriage, so it could not be helped! Ahh, you have been industrious once again! As long as there are still fingers on my hands, diligence is the most crucial thing of all! Ahh, love! Life! People! Diligence in all things!"

Petelgeuse was so worked up, he bent his body so far back that he almost touched the ground.

He sprang back to his feet like a drawn bow with a look of ecstasy.

"My fingers are so diligent, they brought down a land dragon, a living symbol of diligence! Ahh, my brain trembles. Trembles, trembles, treeeeeeeeeeeembles!"

Petelgeuse, his madness rising to heights unknowable to normal men, had blood trickling out of his nose. As it reached his lips, Petelgeuse licked it with his tongue, his cheeks relaxing with an intoxicated look about him. He closed his eyes, his body shuddering as his fervor reached its peak.

Petelgeuse wildly wiped away the nosebleed with the sleeve of his religious habit and let out a long sigh.

"Ahh... The land dragon that died was slothful, was it not?"

With that, the previous excitement was nowhere to be found as he pointed toward the entrance of the cavern and spoke with a calm demeanor and a deliberate voice.

"Here on the eve of the day of the coming ordeal, the immediate disposal of the wrecked dragon carriage will keep from revealing our existence. We have eliminated all human presence, so there is no concern about witnesses from...others on board? You did take care of them, didn't you?"

"—"

Petelgeuse, listening to the figure's report, shook his head. The bones in his neck creaked.

"One other in the vehicle... A blue-haired girl. The left ring finger engaged, demolishing the dragon carriage, and entered combat while the boy was being secured. The girl destroyed the ring finger in the process... It is unclear whether the girl is dead or alive."

For a while he sank into thought, his head turning left and right like the pendulum of a clock, tilting, twisting, turning, swaying, and finally, leaning forward.

"Unclear…whether…she is dead…or alive?"

Petelgeuse murmured with a hint of darkness in his voice as he raised his face up and looked at the figure's hollow eyes.

"Are you *sloth*…?"

As the figure's eyes snapped wide, Petelgeuse ferociously grabbed both sides of its face. His crushed fingers on both hands smeared its cheeks with blood, but Petelgeuse didn't care as he yelled, "You left an element of uncertainty here, on the eve of the trial?! That! That, that, thaaat! Is how you faaaaithfully repay the Gospel?! Ahh, such sloths! Sloths, sloths, sloths, sloths!"

It was unclear where a man of skin and bones held such power, but Petelgeuse easily shook the head in his hands, shoving the figure's back to the ground and straddling it. Then he looked up toward the sky, tears flowing down his cheeks.

"And! My finger's laziness is my own! Ahh, please forgive the indolence in this flesh, filled with affection for thee! Living solely to work diligently for body and soul of the Gospel! For how things must be! Forgive that I have wasted my time in idleness!"

As tears poured down from Petelgeuse, the figure on the ground let out a sob of its own. Making a humanlike reaction for the first time, it looked up at the sky and prayed, just like Petelgeuse.

"Love! This is love! One must sacrifice for love! Laziness cannot be permitted! I must obey the Gospel! I must return the love granted to me with my own!"

"—"

In a shrieking voice, Petelgeuse gave a command to the black robes.

"The girl whose death is uncertain… Find her! If she is alive, wring her neck. If she is dead, cut her head off her corpse and bring her here! Reward her with love!"

In response, the figures seemingly melted into the darkness of the cavern and vanished.

As they departed, Petelgeuse was gazed off absently, breathing raggedly on his knees for a while before turning toward Subaru.

"Now then, then, then, then, then, then, then, then."

Still kneeling, Petelgeuse drew close to Subaru, who was in a crouch.

"So in the end, what *are* you?"

"Uh, aah..."

"The Gospel does not seem to have guided you here, but Her affection hovers thickly all around you. Truly, truly, truuuly a most interessting thing!"

Petelgeuse stuck out his tongue, drawing near enough to lick Subaru's eyeballs. The green-haired man clapped his hands, unable to conceal his delight at the boy who was staring at things that weren't there.

"I should know the faces of all except 'Pride,' but having said that, I don't think the affection you have received is unrelated to the Gospel."

With that murmur, Petelgeuse reached within his habit and pulled out a single tome. It was a book with a black cover, about as large and heavy as a dictionary. At first glance, he looked like he was simply carrying his favorite book with him, but that was too normal an act for a madman.

"Ahh... I feel the love of the Gospel. My brain, it shivers..."

Petelgeuse rested the book without a title in his hands, calmly and reverently turning the pages.

"You are not recorded within the Gospel. Of course, there is also nothing here about any problems occurring here today, on the eve of the Great Ordeal! In other words!!"

Petelgeuse slammed the book shut, spit spraying as he lifted up the closed book.

"It means you are nothing to get seriously worked up about! Even though you have received such deep, deep, deep, deeeep affection... It is quite an inconsistency!"

He poked a finger at his temple, clawing at it with the nail as if he were trying to dig a hole. He tore the skin, yet the bloody, violent sight right before Subaru's eyes elicited no reaction. The boy merely continued his frivolous laughter, watching idly as Petelgeuse harmed himself.

"Ah, ah, ah, ahh... It is so lonely to be ignored! Even though! Even though! I have been soooo warm and friendly to you, you, you, youuuuuuu..."

His words trailed off, and the next moment, Petelgeuse's hands grasped Subaru's face.

The boy's expression was frozen, his mind off somewhere else as Petelgeuse forced Subaru to look at him. Unsurprisingly, even in his stupefied state, Subaru scowled and resisted the rough treatment.

Petelgeuse's voice was quiet, but there was a power in his eyes that would not take no for an answer.

"—Look into my eyes."

Startled, Subaru shuddered. His face was blank as he looked at Petelgeuse like he was told. Those gray eyes, giving off the glow of madness, evaluated Subaru's mind.

"You will respond. Your mind will respond. I demand answers to my questions. What are you doing here? Why have you been granted such affection? Why do you not have a Gospel? Does that mean she whispers directly to your heart?"

"Uu, a, uaaa..."

"It seems we are at an impasse. Therefore, I shall rearrange my questions."

After his string of questions was rebuffed, Petelgeuse tilted his head ninety degrees to the right. With his head horizontal, he glared up at Subaru from below.

"Do you hearrr me?"

"—Auu!"

Petelgeuse stretched out his tongue, licking Subaru's left eyeball.

Subaru's chains clinked as he tried to get away from Petelgeuse after the extremely creepy gesture.

However, that lasted only until he heard the next sentence.

"—Why, might I ask, are you preteeending to be crazy?"

4

"Aa! Aaaa!"

Gross, no, I'm scared, forgive me, save me, scared, scared, scared, scared.

He didn't know what was being said to him.

The ghastliness of someone licking his eyeball, the discomfort of being stared at like that, and his urge to flee the madness of the eyes looking at him, all made his body freeze.

With his mouth gaping absently, his open eye having been licked, Subaru was asked again, "Why are you pretennnding to be crazy?"

Subaru tried to slam him with a manacled arm. The chain went taut, denying his freedom. His arm flailed in the air a little before falling back to the ground on its side.

"Guu! Auaaa! Aiii!"

"No, no, no, no, it is a very important question. Why, for what purpose, with what meaning, are you acting like you are seized with such madness?"

He mustn't listen. He mustn't let the words into his ears. He mustn't know.

He shook his head, yelling as he struggled against the manacles. His consciousness was somewhere far away. He had to blot from his ears the words of the man in front of him, for he was forbidden to listen, to know, to realize.

"The subconscious does not prepare such convenient escape routes. You consciously, and with full knowledge, wrapped yourself in such madness, yes?"

"Aaa! Gauaa! Guruaaa!"

"Your madness is too lucid. The crafty, deliberate way you seek sympathy and beg for love, it is quite rude to those who are actually insane."

Subaru raised his voice, shouting enough to tear his throat apart, trying to make the man's words go away. But the man seemed to mock his resistance, and his voice drove into Subaru's eardrum like a needle.

"Your pretense of being a madman is quite lacking. If you were truly insane, if you were drenched in lunacy in a true sense, you would never recognize the eyes of another. For you would not understand anyone exists beyond your mad self, a world of one person, trapped in the desolate wasteland of his own mind!"

"—Baa! Baaa! Baaaaaa!"

"Ahh, what a comedy, what a farce indeed! Why, why are you pretennnding to be a madman?! If you were truly a deviant, the pretense would not fall away so quickly! I can't stop laughing!"

It hurt to breathe. He felt horrible. Something was pushing its way up inside him, trying to assert its own existence. No, it had been there from the start. He'd simply sealed it away and pretended not to look at it.

It was because he knew of its presence that he absolutely could not allow it to surface.

"Pitiable! Pathetic! You, such a lowly and deep sinner, drunk on your own pathos—I pity you from the heart! You are loved so much; why do you need to deny it?! Do you desire to remain in stagnation as the wind whittles you away, without drowning in the love you have been granted freely, without returning their devotion?! Ahh, how can this, how can this beee!"

The gray-colored man grabbed Subaru's head and violently tossed him toward the wall. The powerful motion slammed his upper body against the rock, sending sparks scattering as his head began to bleed profusely.

"Ah, ah, ah, you…are indeed slothful!"

There was a *clang*, and Subaru felt like something in his head had split in two.

I don't hear you. I'm not listening. It's all the ravings of a madman. None of it hit the mark. None of it arrived at any truth. I still don't get anything. That's as it should be. That's as it ought to be. It has to be like that. If it's not, I'll—

"Ahh, that's quite far enough."

The black thing inside him reached its peak, ready to explode at any moment. Just before it did, the man pulled him back from the brink with a calm murmur, as if the previous madness was a distant memory.

Bereft of the world of thick madness, the sense of danger Subaru felt from the man redoubled, raising goose bumps on his skin. The man said to him, "Yes, backing you into a corner will cause a trifle, yes, a trifle, trifle, trifle too much trouble later. Take your time, slowly face up to the truth of your devotion, and you shall surely find your own answer."

"Aa... Uguu...!"

What was the man trying to say to him...?

From beginning to end, the words out of his mouth had been a string of insults. Subaru didn't get it. The man was acting like he understood something about him. One moment, he was like an adult kindly leading a little boy by the hand; another, he acted like a monster tempting lost people while they tried to cross a bridge.

He was a monster beyond fathom. The distance between them could stay as it was, forever.

Before he crossed the divide into the land of no return.

The man said, "Ahh, in other words... You are not a sloth. You are diligent."

5

Subaru's eyes bore a lack of understanding as the madman's perceptive words pressed upon him.

Petelgeuse folded his arms, gazing up at the heavens, murmuring as if he was praying. This was the only action that made his title of archbishop seem not to be a farce.

After praying for a while, Petelgeuse seemed to notice something and looked back.

"—Oh my?"

He was gazing at the figures emerging one after another within the cavern, the ones that had vanished and gone outside.

The black robes seemed to sprout right out of the ground, their numbers exceeding ten. They knelt in reverence to Petelgeuse, bowing their heads low as they awaited instructions.

"What is the meaning of thisss?"

"—"

"What, the girl is coming here? Ahh, that is why you have returned? That is good! That is very good! By all, all, all, all, all means, let us welcome her. I must welcome her with my very own handsss!"

Petelgeuse was bursting with joy. The meaning of his words did not reach Subaru. However, the boy was panting as if he had a fever. Nothing trickled out of his mouth but a moaning voice, but on the inside, an inexplicable feeling was guiding something inside him to the surface.

But, "—!"

His mouth felt like some invisible object was blocking it, leaving his voice trapped within.

What he felt shutting his throat was different from fear or his other emotions. It was like something tangible, something physical was keeping his lips sealed. Subaru opened his eyes, sensing something like an unseen hand was constricting his throat. When he looked over, he saw Petelgeuse cackle.

"Now, no need to be hasty... We have plenty of time."

Petelgeuse's dry, cackling laughter reverberated throughout the cavern.

Even if the invisible gag disappeared, Subaru would have no way to stop the eerie rumble from echoing against his eardrums. Forbidden to even laugh or cry, all he could do was wait in silence.

—It was a bit under an hour when the change he waited hopefully for finally arrived.

The figures remained on their knees, keeping their silence was their custom. Between them, Petelgeuse paced around without speaking a word, leaving only his footsteps and Subaru's ragged breaths to disturb the air of the chamber.

The first figure to raise his head was the one closest to the corridor connecting to the chamber.

Following that individual's movements, the other fanatics lifted their faces one after another. Petelgeuse, noticing their movements, looked toward the cavern's entrance just as they did and laughed.

An expression of glee came over his face, wide enough to split the corners of his mouth.

"It seems she has arriiiived."

The echo of a great roar drowned out Petelgeuse's delighted murmur. An incredibly heavy-sounding explosion shattered it, and the sound of destruction sent fierce vibrations through the cavern's cold air. The successive sounds reached Subaru through the hard ground as well, and all present were able to sense that the entrance had been smashed by a most violent knock.

The figures swayed and stood up, drawing their crosses from their flanks and posing with their hands held low.

Though they were in a chamber, when ten-odd people moved together it was impossible to claim they had plenty of room. They deployed with the urgency of a school classroom fire drill, readying themselves to respond to the assailant.

There wasn't anywhere near enough space to leap and run around. It was a favorable condition for an intruder at a numerical disadvantage.

"—I've found you."

Her roaring iron ball sailed and mowed down the shadowy figures, creating several red smears against the wall. The flail, butchering three figures with the first blow, was an unstoppable murder weapon that robbed life from everything it touched. There was no option but to dodge it, but the confined cavern made that a difficult proposition.

Falling to the ground, the iron ball shattered the rocky surface, and its barbs, smeared with blood and flesh, made a dull sound as they split the earth. The blue hair of the girl walking ahead of it was dyed completely black as her brilliantly glowing eyes surveyed the chamber. They landed on the boy lying on the ground. Her lips quivered as she made a shallow breath.

"Subaru. I'm so glad…"

The demon—Rem—relaxed her shoulders as she called the boy by name with relief.

Her appearance was ghastly, with the cuts all over her expressing the heroism involved in her arrival. There was not a single part of her body not drenched in blood. Her blue hair was now pitch-black; there was no visible trace of the apron dress that had been burned to a crisp. Her legs, poking out of her ripped and shredded skirt, were lacerated. Her left arm had been burned so cruelly that Subaru wanted to avert his eyes.

With her entire body covered in the perfume of blood and death, Rem smiled reassuringly toward him even so.

And with Rem looming so violently before him, Petelgeuse raised his voice in acclaim.

"Ahh—oh my, how marvelouss!"

He had forgotten that Rem had slain his subordinates before his very eyes; to the contrary, it seemed to have stirred him all the more, with his excited voice bursting with praise.

"A girl! A single girl! Bearing all these wounds yet moving forward! And for what? For this young man! You have gone to these lengths to rescue this beloved boy! You are possessed by love; you *live* for love!"

"You may save your sermon, devotee of the Witch…"

Petelgeuse was standing between Subaru and Rem, practically frothing at the mouth as he shouted in joy. Rem gazed coldly at his crazed state as she continued, "You are a band of fools to enter the dominion of Master Roswaal, lord of the Mathers territory, and commit illegal acts. With my master absent, I, Rem, sentence you to death in his place."

"As tattered as you appear? You should not make promises you cannot keep. To begin with, you have come only to take this young man away from here, so enough with your convenient excuses."

Petelgeuse crouched and clutched Subaru's head, lifting it up. Enjoying himself, he grabbed Subaru by the hair, nodding it up and down against his will.

"…ch him."

"What was that?"

"I said, don't touch him!!"

Rem's face contorted in fury at Petelgeuse's antics. Seeing the demon girl lose her composure, he laughed in satisfaction.

"Yes, very good. Bare your true desires, bare your heart, bare your love! Love! Love! This is love! Love is what guided you here! To deny that love, to conceal it, to disguise it with falsehoods, all are betrayals of that love! Insults! Ahh, and so *slothful*!"

"One insult after another…!"

"I am so glad for that shout. That is your true desire, devoid of all unnecessary impurities, for you rushed here purely out of your feelings for this young man!"

Rem, still enraged, was cowed into silence as Petelgeuse pressed his point. His mad eyes gazed at her with a glint of compassion; then his gaze fell upon the boy at his fingertips.

"It is deeply regrettable. A devotee of love to such an extent as thee… Why are your eyes firmly locked on one such as this? An effete, ignorant, disgraceful, shameless sight such as this… Truly the product of sloth!"

"What do you know about Subaru?! Do not speak out of turn, devotee of the Witch!"

"You are upset because you do not accept this, are you not? That this young man, the object of your love…is already finished, long lost to you."

"He isn't finished! I am here. I have not forgotten Subaru's words. I will take him by the hand and lead him away. So long as I am here, he is not finished!"

—These were not mere words of consolation. They were words conveying a firm truth inside Rem.

As Rem shouted, Petelgeuse laughed, slowly lifting up Subaru's head while leaning him against the wall.

"—"

Some kind of voice came up from inside Subaru. He didn't know what was being said or why.

Rem saw the partial change in the boy drowning in a sea of rejection. She leaped with her wounded body.

As Rem sprang into the air, the figures that had maintained their silence so far did the same in pursuit of her. Two figures kicked off the wall to approach. Their cross-shaped swords, melting into the darkness, stabbed at the small girl.

She yelled back, "Don't get between Subaru and me!!"

She swung her right arm with the chain for the iron ball wrapped around her forearm. With a high-pitched sound, she deflected the crucifixes, following through to gouge out large parts of one figure's face. Another tried to grapple with her after its blade was deflected, but the iron ball, trailing behind, easily caved in the back of its skull.

The two corpses fell to the ground as Rem landed in the center of the chamber—right in the middle of the fanatics.

Just before the blades around her were about to slice her apart, Rem spat out blood as she shouted, "—El Hyuma!"

The incantation surged cold, making the corpses at Rem's feet bounce. No—the fresh blood flowing from the corpses froze, forming sharp-tipped blades of red ice that turned on the enemies around her.

The black robes leaped in hard, but it was they who were impaled. When they came to a stop, their torsos run through, Rem's fist and flail mercilessly smashed them to pieces.

Petelgeuse exclaimed, "Splendid. Splendid indeed! It is no exaggeration to say that you are splendid! And yet, why! Ahh, why! I cannot accept love! I do not acknowledge this! I do not understand! Without the words, there is no salvation, no more than you can grasp a cloud! And yet, why is it?!"

"Do not speak such words so cheaply! I already have my salvation! After that night when I should have lost all, there is no greater than what I had that morning! That is why!"

Rem brushed aside the madman's voice, her eyes staring straight at Subaru.

"I will repay everything I have received with everything I am. I have no intention of labeling the feelings behind my actions, behind my desire to take those actions, as cheaply as you do!"

The figures in the chamber once numbered around fifteen. Already, nearly half of them had perished from Rem's attacks. The remainder seemed incapable of halting her fury. Her superiority was beyond question. The might of the demon race was very real.

And yet, why?

Petelgeuse clutched his head, letting out hot breaths as he surveyed the cruelty inflicted on his faithful.

"Aa, aa, aa…"

He didn't seem shaken by grief, fear, or anxiety. Her anxiety only grew as it became clear to her that his reaction was one of pure excitement.

At Petelgeuse's side, Subaru watched Rem's rampaging battle.

Slowly, the meaning of the scene, and the girl's reason for fighting, seeped into his brain.

He didn't understand. He didn't want to understand. He wasn't trying to understand. And yet, it reached him all the same. The sight of her bleeding, wounded, and yet continuing to fight stirred something inside his chest, bringing it to the surface.

Perhaps he had to put into words what troubled him. Yet if he did, he could no longer remain in a stupefied state. It meant facing up to what was right, what was wrong, and why he was there.

For Subaru, to fear this, to prioritize his love of himself over all else, was just—

Petelgeuse rose to his feet as he said, "My brain trembles."

The sleeves of his black habit swayed as he calmly stepped forward.

Unlike his adherents, his hands held nothing in them. Indeed, the relaxed way his open hands swung before him held not a single smidgeon of visible hostility. His body was skin and bones; his behavior betrayed no suggestion he was strong.

Noticing Petelgeuse's advance, Rem knocked down yet another of the black robes and leaped. Hanging upside down from the ceiling, she glared as Petelgeuse advanced beneath her. An instant later, she would shoot out like an arrow with an attack that would surely smash Petelgeuse's thin body to pieces.

And yet, why?

Why was a terrible feeling clawing at her heart even so?

"Get away from Suba—"

Rem's voice cut off. The rest of his name never reached Subaru's ears.

But the echo of her voice delivered a decisive tremor to Subaru's heart.

Rem herself had surely not intended any such thing. But the girl's repeated, earnest cries thawed Subaru's frozen heart.

"—m."

He made a faint sound from the back of his throat and crawled.

It was a meaningless fragment of a word, carrying not even an iota of the feelings he wished to convey. And yet, as he gasped for breath, Subaru lifted his face and put all his emotions into one short word...

"...Rem."

His voice was as frail as a whisper. He didn't know how long it had been since he had spoken that name on his lips. And yet his voice was so weak, threatening to disappear completely.

"—Ah."

His feeble voice seemed to die on the wind. He wondered if she could even hear it.

As the blood-drenched girl grasped the ceiling, a faintly soft look came over her face. Her lips slackened just a little, her eyes radiating with joy as they beheld Subaru.

"Subaru—"

As the boy returned from stupefaction to reality, he clearly heard Rem call out his name.

And then...

—In an instant, her entire body was torn to pieces that audibly fell onto the cold, hard floor.

Subaru lost his voice as he beheld the blood spreading from Rem's fallen body.

"...aa?"

Her corpse, fallen to the ground, had been cruelly destroyed for all to see.

When she had intruded into the cavern, she was wounded all over yet lovely. Now, each of her limbs was bent in a different direction; the wounds to her front and back looked as if the fingertips of a giant had gouged out her torso. And what had wreaked such violence upon her body was...

"The authority of 'Sloth'—"

As Petelgeuse murmured, Rem's body, limbs destroyed, floated up before his eyes. There was no visible sign of magical interference, yet neither had anyone lifted her up. Even so, Rem's body hovered. It was as if hands had stretched up from beneath her to raise her overhead.

"—Unseen Hands."

Petelgeuse looked back, raising both hands before his own face while Rem's body floated behind him. There was no one in her vicinity with hands to place on her. No one was touching her.

It was a bizarre spectacle.

"The power to reach places the hand cannot and do anything without moving one's body. Utmost diligence while being a sloth of the flesh— Ahh, such slothful feelings make...my... brain...shiver."

Subaru watched Rem's final moments, dumbfounded. She would never move again. His voice wouldn't come out. His eyes widened as he forgot to breathe and his grip on the world around him felt less real, slipping into stupefaction once more. His mind was wrapped in darkness, as if he were falling and falling down a bottomless pit—

As he tried to flee from reality, Petelgeuse stopped him, roughly grabbing hold of his bangs and using them to lift his head.

"You are not permitted to run from this."

The shock of the pain made Subaru grimace as he thrashed around, trying to thrust Petelgeuse back. Petelgeuse did not allow him to do any such thing, though the boy stretched his chains to their limit. The metallic bonds tore at Subaru's flesh to the point of drawing blood, but Subaru's eyes were forced to face forward.

"Look. Go ahead, look. Look, please. The girl is dead. She died for love. She fought while injured, struggled against her fears as she stepped forward, and died with her desires unfulfilled."

"Ua, aa..."

"Look, please. Look at her burns. This is the result of *your* actions."

"—aa?"

Rem's body floated as Subaru's head was thrust forward as far as the chains around him would permit. Even so, Subaru writhed and stomped on the ground as a pair of hands held him in place.

The madman's putrid breath washed over him; Subaru panted with the bloodstained Rem before his eyes.

"It is the result of your actions. You were slothful and did nothing. And because of that, she is dead! Because you killed her!"

"...You."

"It was by my hand! It was by my fingers! It was by my flesh! But it was you, you, you, you, you, you who, who, who...killed her, yes!"

Petelgeuse's abnormal power toyed with Rem's body as he chirped, almost like he was singing.

Rem's body, lying down in midair, shifted like a marionette on a string as her arms and legs dangled. Her twisted limbs danced according to the madman's whims.

"...op it."

There came a *scrish* of something ripping apart.

Unable to handle the manipulation, Rem's body broke...and so did something within Subaru.

"Owww, ow it hurts, it hurts, the pain, the pain, save me, save me... Ahh, Subaru?"

It was a cheap taunt, the lowest of base humor. The madman violated Rem with his antics. With easy enjoyment, he debased the girl Subaru revered directly in front of him.

That spectacle was so ugly that he dearly wanted to avert his eyes and make himself forget it.

"—Petelgeuuuuuse!!"

Subaru was afraid of seeing reality, but the rotting stench hovering around him had been enough to pull him back to his senses. He stretched his neck, trying to bite at the windpipe that was tantalizingly close. But the manacles intervened and his canines fell just a little short. He stumbled forward, tumbling hard onto his face.

His nose was bleeding and he had chipped a front tooth. Petelgeuse laughed in delight as he looked down at Subaru.

"I'll kill you, I'll kill you...kill, kill, I'll kill you. I'll kill you. I'll kill you! Kill, kill...die, I'll have you killed, die, die, dieeeee!"

"To hate another so that you may live, that fierce passion toward others is the opposite side of the coin of love! Ahh, how splendidly warped this is! This spurs both my fingers and me to greater heights of diligence!"

"Kill... I'll kill you. You...killed...Rem. I'll...kill, kill, kill. I'll have you killed. Yeah! I'll kill you! Kill, kill! Die, damn you! Damn you, aah! Die, damn you!"

He spewed saliva as he spat out curses and raised a resentful howl.

He didn't care if his arms tore off. He didn't care if his legs tore off. If he could get free of those manacles and kill the man before his eyes then and there, it was enough. He hated, hated, hated the man to no end. The man had to die. He could not be suffered to live.

He had to make very sure that the man died then, that moment, that very instant.

Subaru thrashed his entire body around in rage as Petelgeuse stood beside him. Abruptly, the latter's crazed laughter faded, and he murmured, "This has been a rather untidy affair, but it is finally time that we must part."

With a hand, he assembled the surviving figures together and pointed toward the cavern's wrecked entrance.

"We shall abandon this place. You will disregard the number of fingers remaining, continue the role of the left hand, and join with the other five fingers— The ordeal shall be conducted as planned."

"Die! Die, damn you! Die, die, dieeee!"

Having issued his brief orders, Petelgeuse clapped his hands. On that signal, the black robes vanished, melting into the gloomy darkness of the cavern. And one by one, all trace of life vanished from the hollow, with Petelgeuse himself finally departing, walking leisurely toward the entrance. The loud clicks of his shoes echoed off the rock walls of the cavern, with Subaru howling, cursing him with death over and over as his back grew distant.

"Wait, you piece of shit! Kill! I'll kill you! Die here! Die here, now! Die right now! Die! Die! Die!!"

"Ohh, I forgot one thing, it would seem."

Even with the bloodthirsty shouts directed at him, the madman stopped and called back as lighthearted as ever. As Subaru glared at Petelgeuse, the latter looked back, nodded to the former, and crossed both hands over his own chest.

"You truly do not understand your position. In spite of this, I would have you make a decision here and now."

The madman's head tilted into a perfect right angle with enough force to break his neck, or so it seemed. A dark smile appeared.

"I will leave your arms and legs bound. All that awaits you is death. And yet…if you were to take up the Gospel in this place, you can still be saved."

"Go to hell! Die here, right now! I'll tear you apart! Blow you away! Blast you to pieces!"

"You can be saved if you become one of us. If not, you are a mere stranger. It is clear and simple, yes?"

Petelgeuse, stating what seemed to him like a most wise plan, proceeded to turn his back on Subaru. He treated the foul curses flowing out of the boy's mouth like nothing more than a breeze, with his feet regarding the pool of blood like a puddle of water left by an early afternoon shower, his casual demeanor wholly unaffected.

By rights, Petelgeuse would have departed without taking any further notice of Subaru.

However, he did not, for a heavy, watery sound drew his attention to the side.

"—Aaah."

Petelgeuse looked toward the sound, nodding as he stared at the blue-haired girl who had fallen there. Having lost all interest in playing with her as a doll, he was just about to leave when he noticed her tossed by the wayside.

—It was no exaggeration to say that this, too, was treating her like a toy.

"You, too, are a devotee of love. Yes, yes. You tried very hard."

Petelgeuse stood still and corrected the posture of Rem's corpse, making a sign of the cross over her. He seemed to praise and acknowledge the girl's actions up until several minutes prior. However...

"You died for love, defying your destiny with all your might. However, you lie ruined and unfulfilled, having lost the object of your love, unable to fulfill your desire with emptiness hovering all about you..."

His acclamation turned on a dime, lamenting the futility of Rem's actions as his cheeks twisted into a mocking smile.

"Because...you were slothful!"

There was no greater way to belittle the existence of the lone girl Rem.

"—!!"

Howls and shouts fiercely echoed throughout the cave. Subaru Natsuki raised an inhuman cry, his anger great enough to fill his entire throat, his rage enough that he couldn't form words, his regret enough to produce tears of blood.

Hearing this, Petelgeuse laughed, as if it were a shower of the highest possible praise.

He cackled and cackled.

"—"

He did not stop walking.

Of course, Subaru could hope neither to stop him from behind nor wring his neck.

He kept hearing that cackling voice for long after.

Even with Petelgeuse himself gone, even though his own curses couldn't reach the man, even though the light inside the cave dimmed all at once and left him alone with the corpse in the darkness, it wouldn't stop.

Cackle, cackle.

Cackle, cackle.

—*Cackle, cackle, cackle, cackle, cackle.*

6

"Kill, kill, kill, kill, kill, kill."

Amid the darkness, dead to the world, he spewed enough blood-lust and hatred to burn a man alive.

He murmured and spat over and over, forgetting how many times it had been, yet his scorching hatred did not subside.

"—"

He had never hated anyone, not a person, not any living being, as much as he did then.

Since arriving in that world, he had experienced hatred of the formless thing called Fate several times over. He had been beaten down into the ground, with reality pitilessly thrust in his face, with that callous world making him pay for bad decisions with his life—but the times he had hated and cursed were fewer than the number of his fingers.

But to this point in his life, he had never hated another individual to that extent.

"Petelgeuse...Romanée-Conti...!"

Voicing the name on his lips, he recalled the man behind his eyes. His eardrums wallowed in his own shout. When his brain thought about that man, a fire raged inside him that made every drop of his blood boil.

—What the hell was with that man, anyway?

Subaru understood nothing about his identity. All he knew was that Petelgeuse walked far from the path of sanity, that he was a demon in human flesh who could not be reasoned with, and that he was a despicable person, the foulest of villains. He was the most awful of men who'd hurt Rem, the girl who'd sacrificed her own body in an attempt to rescue Subaru, and went on to humiliate and dishonor her life. He couldn't even imagine the damage that letting that man live would wreak.

That was why Subaru had to kill him. Subaru needed to kill him with his own hands, not letting anyone else do the deed. He had to kill Petelgeuse with his own hands. If he couldn't do that, how could he pay him back for Rem's death?

"Kill, kill, I will…kill you with my own hands…"

Subaru embraced the bloodlust pouring from his own mouth and earnestly twisted his own body, clinking his shackles.

He'd tried to force his arms out of the manacles or kick them off his legs several times over.

The manacles were clasped tightly and rather painfully on Subaru's limbs, to begin with.

He felt the pain. His fury would not permit him to forget it. But even as that discomfort clawed at his nerves, he bit it back with thoughts of what Rem had undergone.

Even if the manacles tore off his hands and wrists, he didn't really care. As long as he could escape, as long as he could move a single finger, as long as he had a single tooth left, he'd snuff out Petelgeuse's life.

—Several hours had already passed since his foe had departed the cave.

The lagmite ore had lost most of its power, so the cavern fell into darkness. Subaru wondered if it was some kind of mistake. He was inside a natural cavern, yet not even a single insect lived within it. He was the only living being there.

"—! Petelgeuse!!"

A moment before Subaru noticed the darkness and silence, he wrung the hateful man's name from his throat to keep his thoughts intact.

Within the gloom, unable to see a thing, Subaru could sense nothing beyond himself in the whole world. His ragged breaths, the beats of his heart, the sounds of the chains chafing, the *drip-drops* of water—isolation and solitude quickly weakened the human heart.

If he remained in this place like that much longer, with no change whatsoever…

"Woaaaaa! Petelgeuse! Petelgeuse!!"

Subaru abandoned his body to hatred, as if rejecting the image of his mental balance crumbling away.

A human mind walled off from the outside world was well on its way to decay, to collapse, to a final end.

Subaru screamed as if trying to avert his eyes from reality, trying to shake off the fear of being left behind.

As long as he could shout his hatred, he would remain sane.

As long as he was enveloped in bloodlust like a madman, he would not go mad.

To keep his sanity, Subaru needed hatred.

—Subaru did not know how many more hours passed after that.

"Hff, hff... Kuh...ll."

Subaru's consciousness hovered somewhere between alertness and unconsciousness. Fatigue, debilitation, the abrasions on his body—all these dragged down Subaru's body and spirit.

Still bound by the manacles, his limbs, abused beyond their limits, no longer accepted the brain's instructions. The metal scraped his flesh and even wore down the bones of his wrists and ankles. Just moving around sent him into convulsions from the ferocious pain.

—*Kill, kill, kill, kill, kill.*

In spite of that, even then, bloodlust welled up from the very bottom of his heart. That moment, with both body and head no longer listening, it was the heart alone that kept Subaru going.

It had been dozens of hours since he had been abandoned in that world of solitude. His body and spirit had reached their limits, but Subaru's consciousness had not shut down.

Archbishop of Sin. Petelgeuse of "Sloth." Witch Cult. Right hand. Left hand. Unseen Hands. Index finger. Ring finger. Little finger. Diligence. Sloth. Sloth. Sloth—

These were the keywords Subaru had gleaned from Petelgeuse's high-pitched, shouted ramblings. With his head dying on him, he recalled these terms, wondering what they meant, thinking about Petelgeuse to keep his consciousness together even a little bit and to keep his hatred astir.

He needed to remember a fresher, firmer, clearer image of the man's face. He reflected along the same lines—the man's voice, his appearance, his way of walking, his manner of speaking—exactly as if thinking about one's dearly beloved. The direction of Subaru's sentiments was the only thing that had changed. He was still using it as fuel to ignite his soul and keep himself awake.

From afar, it seemed Subaru's spirit had already arrived at the dimension of madness.

Perhaps the mind would wear down and vanish first. Perhaps his body, unable to keep up with his active mind, would expire first. He was on a path where the end was nigh; it was simply a choice between one dead end or the other. Surely keeping his mind intact no longer had any meaning other than that.

Subaru continued his futile struggle, but he was truly alone in all the world.

"—aa?"

His panting within the darkness had been frail, but his breath abruptly caught when he felt that something was off.

It was troublesome to even move his head, but Subaru looked in the direction of the disturbance. Of course, his field of vision displayed nothing but the darkness of the cavern.

But he felt something from that darkness nonetheless.

Slowly, truly slowly, he felt a presence rising. It moved at only a snail's pace, bit by bit, but inexorably drew closer to Subaru.

"—"

Somehow, even within complete darkness, it seemed to know where he was.

Subaru shuddered with urgency and unease at the individual. But that feeling immediately fell away as a different feeling rose up in the back of his mind.

—Where is this feeling coming from in the first place?

He heard a sound like clothes rustling and extremely faint breath. The distance was rather close, no more than several yards away from Subaru. Having thought that far, he suddenly realized: it was at close range, not from the entrance, that the presence had abruptly appeared—

No, what if *she* had started breathing again…?

"R-Rem…?"

He called out the name of the girl to whom the sounds and presence were likeliest to belong.

That can't be right, Subaru's logical mind denied. Though he couldn't endure looking straight at her, the last thing he had seen while the cave still had light was the horrific state of Rem's body, to the point that he thought one of her fallen foes was far more likely to rise from the dead.

She couldn't be alive. She was dead. Of course she was dead.

Yet in spite of that, he half believed that the presence in front of his own eyes was alive, and it must be Rem. And if she were dead, it was probably her just the same, coming to take him away. It had to be Rem either way. Therefore, there was no reason to be worried about the presence at all.

"Rem, Rem…?"

"—"

He addressed her, clinging to hope, but the silence returned with a vengeance.

Even so, perhaps Subaru's voice made the other being certain of its goal, because it felt like it started crawling just a little faster. Yet it was truly only a very slight change.

Slowly, slowly, he heard something pulling closer across the cold, rocky surface of the ground.

Subaru pulled himself up, with the chains attached to his hands and feet ringing as he moved as close to her as he could. He'd advanced such a short distance, and the tormenting shame summoned tears once again, though he had thought they were dry.

He kept himself from sobbing. He didn't want Rem to hear that.

Within the darkness, only the sound of crawling continued, with the distance closing and closing. And then—

Subaru felt the struggling presence reach his body. The instant he felt something graze his upper arm, he instantly tried to take her hand and call out her name.

"Re…"

His throat froze over.

The grasp on his arm was so light, so cold, that none would think it came from a living person.

"R-Rem...?"

Rem's body lay facedown beneath the kneeling Subaru. The girl's slender arm was shaking a little, but it was as cold as could be, devoid of warmth-giving blood.

She was as icy as a corpse. She could no longer be here in this world. Yet though she should have been finished, she had dragged her body over and clung to Subaru. She touched his arms, his shoulders, his chest, his head, as if to make sure they were there; she pressed everything against him in a hug from the front.

"—"

Subaru, silently accepting the embrace of the dead, had no idea what would happen.

A breath away from each other, Subaru was certain that it was Rem hugging his body. However, her flesh felt dead to the touch, unreal, as if she were animated solely by the dying embers of her life.

But it was not unpleasant. Subaru meekly returned her continuing embrace. When he thought about it, they'd been close against each other many times, but that might have been the first time they'd touched like that.

Perhaps that was how Rem wanted the final moment of her life to be. If so, the least he could do was to respond to her wishes.

Even with Rem already dying and Subaru having already given up, perhaps his arms could transmit his feelings to her.

It was Rem who brought the continuing cold, silent embrace to an end.

"Rem?"

As Subaru hugged her, her body surrendered its strength, collapsing onto his lap. He hastily moved to support her, but the next motion made that impossible. After all...

"—Uuu?!"

...Rem grabbed his outstretched arms and smashed them to the ground.

Subaru, pulled forward and down, was shocked at the sudden violence achieved with strength far beyond his imagination. Hence, he was slow to react to Rem's next action. Subaru's arms, pressed to the floor, were bathed in a large amount of liquid.

It was a cold, viscous substance with a rusty scent. The fact that Subaru had become so used to the smell made him rather slow to realize that Rem had coughed up blood.

A chill ran up his spine at the discomfort of so much of another person's blood pouring over him. But the bad feeling vanished in an instant.

"—ma."

The whisper vibrated faintly in the air as the intervention of mana achieved its result.

"—Dwaa!"

Pain, like something sharp digging into his wrists, seized Subaru. The unexpected numbing ache shot from his wrists straight through his forearms, all the way to his shoulders.

He didn't know what was going on. He shuddered at the thought that Rem was doing this, coughing blood on him, sending sudden jolts of pain through him, and proceeding to turn both arms into useless appendages. But the next moment...

—The wrist manacles, unable to bear the pressure pushing out from the inside, noisily blew apart.

"—Oh."

The destruction sent metal fragments flying, and a tinkling sound echoed throughout the cavern.

Subaru breathed raggedly as his pain radically eased, and his entire arms felt incredibly free despite the scalding sensation. He opened and closed both of his now-unfettered hands, confirming that they could still move.

Then he understood.

"Rem, you..."

Rem had used magic to freeze the blood from her mouth, utilizing the pressure to destroy the manacles from within.

Of course, both of Subaru's arms, having directly endured the effects of magic, hadn't emerged unscathed. That said, he could rotate his wrists and get his fingers to do as he asked. If he disregarded the pain, he could move them normally again.

In other words, Rem had succeeded.

"Re...?"

Subaru was about to voice his thanks when he felt a very light body bump against his chest.

Light. So very, very light. She'd lost so much blood, the last of her consciousness was a candle in the wind, ready to be snuffed out.

In other words, her life would soon expire.

"Rem...wait, Rem. Wait...don't..."

Don't leave me, he might have meant to say.

Do you hate me? he might have wanted to ask.

Subaru despaired at the true thoughts and feelings behind both.

That once again, she had protected a weak, miserable creature such as him.

She'd literally come back from the dead to save him, yet he...

"...Nn."

"Rem?"

Rem's tongue, as cold as a corpse's, tried to form words with some kind of meaning behind them.

She barely had the strength to speak a single syllable, yet she'd wrung magical energy out of her immobile body and hazy mind. She'd worked herself past the point of death to accomplish her objective, but she wanted to leave one last thing behind.

Subaru, not wanting to let such a message slip by, embraced her body and drew it close. He brought his ear near her quivering lips so that he could carve each word, each syllable, upon his very soul.

The girl's last words were...

"L...ive."

"—!"

"I l...o..."

She died.

That moment, Rem died.

Within Subaru's arms, her light body grew heavy. Her form, both light and so, so heavy, her frame completely bereft of her soul, burdened Subaru's entire being with its excessive weightlessness.

—In the end, haltingly, haltingly, Rem had told Subaru, "Live."

—His wails resounded throughout the dark cave.

7

By the time Subaru removed his leg shackles and exited the cave, it had been several hours since Rem had died.

His hands, free from the wrist manacles, had snatched a cross sword from the nearest figure's corpse. Using that, he'd unfettered his legs over a period of long hours.

"...Light, huh."

Subaru rotated his scraped ankles. Each step sent pain running through him fierce enough to make his mind go blank. If he ignored that, not a problem. His legs were more than enough to support him while he carried Rem's remains.

He tossed the broken crucifix sword against a wall. The impact made the lagmite ore in the wall glow, bathing the cavern in pale light. Subaru felt like his eyes were burning. With Rem in his arms, he gazed at her face, not having seen it in the light for over a day.

Tears gently fell from his eyes.

—Subaru would never be able to forget the cruel state of the girl in his arms.

"Let's go, Rem."

Subaru relied on the light as he made his way through the dark cave, following the narrow corridor to the entrance. From inside the passage, the rock blocking the entrance was transparent. Subaru passed right through it.

It was probably some kind of magic trick to obstruct vision. It was probably closer to a hologram than a mirage. Subaru had neither the determination nor a compelling reason to consider the matter further.

When Subaru exited the cave, it was not the light created by lagmite ore that greeted him but the orange rays from the sun. The light pouring from the sunset scorched the world beneath it.

The sun was sinking past the horizon of the forest and hills beyond it, giving its final greeting before retiring from its daily duty and dyeing the world in the same color as its own flames.

Subaru, greeted by that scene, stood with the rock wall behind him and unfamiliar trees standing everywhere he looked. A quick glance around the area revealed no trace of a road, forest trail, or anything else that resembled a path. He should have expected as much. A group infiltrating an area would logically set up far from human habitation.

"But I'll walk..."

His destination was the same as before: Roswaal's mansion in the Mathers dominion.

Subaru was sure that Rem had been heading to the mansion with him when his mind was a hazy abyss. He rummaged through his memories of the dragon coach rocking him as he rested peacefully on Rem's lap.

Thinking of Rem made his heart tighten painfully. He wanted to thank her and tell her he was sorry.

When he remembered Petelgeuse, his body creaked with hatred, almost as if it would snap. Rage. Sadness. Hatred. Love. These supported Subaru. These kept Subaru alive.

His path was uncertain, and there was nothing to guide him. Even so, Subaru's mind rebelled, and his feet stepped forward to search for an uncertain destination.

—Perhaps it might be said that what happened to him was nothing short of a miracle. Without anyone's aid, with nothing to rely on, Subaru arrived at his destination. The one desire of his shriveled mind was granted—surely it could be called nothing else.

It was the first miracle that world had bestowed upon Subaru since his arrival. If there was indeed a deity that governed fate, that god was finally smiling upon Subaru.

And then, Subaru knew.

"——Ha."

*   *   *

If there was a deity that governed fate, its manner of laughter was surely the same as Petelgeuse's.

—The village had been violated in exactly the same hellish manner he had seen before.

The houses had been burned down; the villagers were covered in blood. The remains of those who had futilely struggled against the theft of their lives had been carelessly gathered in the center of the community, piled into a mountain of corpses.

He looked right; he looked left. There were only smoldering embers and the stench of death. He could not hope for any survivors.

Looking over the corpses of the villagers, Subaru realized that this world held one difference from the one before it.

"Petra. Mildo. Luca. Meyna. Cain. Dyne…"

The cruel sight of the children's corpses was a part of the mountain of corpses and the river of blood.

"—"

With Rem still in his arms, Subaru's knees let go. He fell on the spot, clutching tight the cold body in his arms, and wept.

What had he been doing all that time…?

Knowing what would happen, why did he sit back and watch…?

Until he slipped through the game trail and saw the smoke rising from the direction of the village, Subaru had completely banished from his own brain the hellish sight that had shattered his mind.

No, he'd averted his eyes. He'd wrapped himself in grief over Rem's death and used it and his limitless hatred of Petelgeuse as excuses to deny his memories of that hell.

Once again, Subaru Natsuki had fled from reality due to his selfishness. The result was the sight before his eyes.

The children had died there because Rem, who would have protected the children like last time, had been unable to arrive at the village. The adults were not able to let the children escape.

The sight of their own children being murdered, as if for sport, had been burned into their eyes before they, too, died in agony.

Not a single one had been spared. Subaru had stood by and done nothing, and this tragedy was the end result, leaving only despair and resentment in its wake.

That contemptible reality ate at Subaru's heart.

I get it now. I get all of it.

—*Petelgeuse.*

The man who had killed the villagers, the children, and Rem.

He, the madman, had committed those unforgivable acts not once, but twice.

"—Ha."

His plan was set in stone. He knew what he needed to do.

"Petelgeuse…"

He had to kill Petelgeuse. Murder him, kill him, keep killing until the last cell of his body was burned away, his entire being erased from that world.

Nothing short of that could even begin to make up for these deaths.

His thoughts were dyed with nothing but hatred. His field of vision turned crimson red. He knew that what was left of the blood he'd lost had mostly gone to his head—it was even bleeding out of his nose. He roughly wiped away the nosebleed, re-gripped Rem so that she would not be stained, and rose to his feet. His knees shook, his ankles quivered; whether he could stand, let alone walk, was an open question.

"Kill, kill, kill, kill, I'll kill you…"

But if he could walk, if he could move forward, then he could surely tear out the man's windpipe with his teeth.

Dragged forward by his hardened, bloodlust-dyed mind, Subaru headed toward the mansion.

He'd seen the hell at the village. Next was the mansion. What was it that awaited him there?

Right before his death, right before he started things over, something had happened, but his memories were broken, unclear.

He thought that he'd arrived at the mansion and seen something that decisively cracked his psyche. He desperately lit up the neurons in his head trying to remember what it was.

He'd found Rem dead.

And this time, that experience had already run its course.

"Khah."

Spontaneously, laughter spilled out of him.

Really, really, nothing has changed at all, has it?

Only the order had been altered. Nothing had changed in terms of what had happened. Had he ever before spent his relived time in such idleness as he had then?

Before, no matter what had happened, Subaru gained something over the course of death. But trapped in his own cage, he hadn't been able to salvage anything. Now that he'd encountered the same hell once again, was there anything he could gain from it? Having wasted his Return by Death, did he have any value at all?

"—"

At some point, he'd begun to lose sight of the target of his bloodlust.

Petelgeuse. That name was all that kept Subaru going. That was a good thing. He was who Subaru wanted to kill, right? *So kill him already.*

After he'd been killed, "—" could die for all he cared.

Who is "—," anyway? Just kill them, too, then? Yeah, if everyone dies, all the better.

When such static began to invade Subaru's thoughts, his mind flickered on and off, over and over.

Subaru looked ahead of him with bloodshot eyes as he once again straddled the fence between sanity and madness. Having already decided to head to the mansion, come what may, he chose to postpone dealing with the immediate problem, like he always did. Then…

"—!!"

The instant he crested the hill, Subaru witnessed the destruction of Roswaal Manor.

A ferocious sound erupted, and smoke rose all around. The roof collapsed; the terrace fell to pieces. All at once, the glass windows cracked and shattered into glistening shards, the cracked white walls wailing like a maiden as they were rent asunder.

When he arrived, Subaru stared up at the front gate, dumbfounded at the overpowering devastation. The mansion had lost its shape in a single instant, just as if someone had demolished it with explosives.

The familiar building had lost all integrity, its meticulously arranged garden was buried in rubble, and the ruin that had once been the mansion was falling to pieces.

"Wh-what the…"

He groped through his memories. But he had no memory of this experience. Something had happened that he didn't remember. Or perhaps the shock of being on the verge of death was so vivid that he'd forgotten the destruction surrounding him as he died.

Having lost his bearings, an all-too-thin man's crazed laughter rose in the back of his trembling mind.

If the slaughter of the village had been that madman's deeds, he'd surely directed his vile actions at the mansion as well. If that was the case, was this destruction Petelgeuse's?

"What in the world is he doing…?"

Faced with a spectacle beyond his understanding, Subaru continued to carry Rem as he exhaled white breaths. Discouraged, he craved a stronger sensation within his arms, but it was cold that flowed through his hands and turned to sadness in his chest. His body shivered; he coughed at the cold pain in his lungs.

—Far too late, Subaru finally realized that his own ragged breaths looked like white clouds.

"—?!"

The moment he realized it, pain enveloped his body, stabbing at his skin. His exhalations were white, and the air he inhaled was freezing his internal organs, like he was breathing blowing snow. He felt like his body was dying from the inside out. Subaru's instincts screamed to him that his life was in jeopardy.

I…don't…know…what's…going…on.

His entire body robbed of its warmth, it became hard to even stand, and so he buckled.

He squatted down on the spot, leaning forward before he hit the ground, and fell on his side, still carrying Rem. That was his final act of resistance. His fallen body froze to the very core, his limbs no longer able to even tremble.

Unable to convey his thoughts to his limbs, Subaru knew that his mind had been severed from his body. Subaru had already experienced it several times, but he'd never get used to that feeling of desolate helplessness.

His nervous system sent commands to his entire body to resist the impending end even a little, to somewhere, anywhere that could move. Behind his closed right eyelid, his eye was barely functional.

With all his spirit, Subaru moved his eyelid, using his barely functional eye to look up at an angle, in the direction of the mansion. Once it reached that position, it would probably never move again. Before the view faded, he saw something…

"…a."

—He saw a beast standing on the wreckage of the collapsed mansion.

It was a holy beast, with gray fur all over its body, with glowing golden eyes.

The sight of it standing on all fours, calmly swaying its long, long tail, was most mysterious.

More than anything, the beast was enormous, rivaling the mansion itself.

"—"

Beholding the sight from afar, Subaru understood what had caused the mansion's collapse: the sudden appearance of that beast from inside it. Of course the building couldn't withstand the pressure of something that huge emerging from inside.

"—"

The gray beast swayed, surveying the area with its eyes. Its face most resembled that of a great feline predator. Sharp fangs poked out of its mouth; the giant being exhaled breaths like blowing white snow, repainted the world into a frozen hell with the white powder to freeze all that lived.

What was that?

As he thought about it, his vision whited out. He realized then that he'd stopped breathing. At some point, he'd stopped feeling the bitter cold. Warmth, though, he could feel.

That warmth tempted Subaru to give himself entirely to it, to forget the burning hatred, to forget sadness enough to tear his soul asunder, to forget anything and everything.

Forget, forget. Let your mind wander to oblivion and the frozen warmth within.

Just before he fell asleep, he felt like he heard someone's voice.

"Sleep…together with my daughter."

It was a low, ferocious voice. Yet it somehow sounded forlorn and sad. He didn't understand. He didn't understand. Not within the meaningless serenity.

Subaru Natsuki melted. He melted, he melted, he melted, and then disappeared.

8

—He realized that his mind was in deep, deep darkness.

His consciousness, dead to the world within the expanding, eternal darkness, shifted its gaze in search of any change. It wondered just how long the pitch-black world of the end would continue. It felt as if it had been locked away, completely beyond the world's reach.

What is this place? What am I doing here?

It was odd for him to have such questions. To begin with, he didn't understand who he was to be thinking in such a manner.

His mind was all that hung in emptiness, lacking any body to support it or receive its thoughts.

He stood. His legs were on the ground. But what he thought was beneath his feet blended with the darkness covering his vision, and so his footing was uncertain.

—Abruptly, there was a change in the vast world of nothing but darkness.

A shadow warped and flattened out, and a crack emerged in the nothingness. Without a sound, the rip in space rent apart the world of eternal darkness, connecting the interior of that void to another void.

Just after the momentary anomaly, a lone human silhouette emerged from the widening crack.

"—"

He thought that the figure was a woman.

The instant he recognized it, emotions he could not put into words nearly took over his mind.

He felt fierce, explosive emotions well up. He wanted to run to the figure, embrace her slender body, put his lips to her nape, to drive home that he was himself.

And yet, he lacked the legs with which to rush to her, the arms with which to embrace her, the lips with which to kiss her and prove that he existed.

Even though his chagrin made him want to cry, he didn't understand why these emotions manifested.

He didn't know. He didn't understand. He comprehended nothing.

But the figure seemed to understand how he felt, slowly reaching out with her arms, somehow closing the unchanging distance on her own. Those two hands gently came close enough to firmly embrace him.

As the fingertips touched him, great happiness flooded into him, as if joy was gushing from every cell in her body, filling every nook and cranny of his consciousness.

And then she said…

"—I love you."

9

The moment Subaru's consciousness went back in time and inhabited his body once more, the boy spectacularly tumbled to the ground.

Cadmon, standing behind the counter as he watched him fall onto the road without any forewarning, leaned over in a rush.

"Whoa! Wh-what's wrong, kid?!"

Subaru scowled, having fallen right over without softening the blow and earned himself meaningless injury.

"Er... I just slipped a bit."

"That 'slip' was so bad, I wondered if you'd lost a leg or something. Can you stand and walk? I can't associate with you if you don't quit all this crazy stuff."

"What do you mean, 'crazy'? You're making me sound like some sort of scoundrel with no common sense."

"A mischief-maker either way, and that goes for how you come and go without proper clothes on, too. I get the sense you're a trouble-some sort who's hard to deal with, to be honest."

Having said those terrible things, Cadmon *tut-tut*ted in a show of dissatisfaction.

And when Subaru abruptly felt a tug on his sleeve, he looked back. He couldn't help but gasp.

"Subaru, are you all right?"

He saw a girl standing there, setting her hand on his wounds.

When she began to heal him with magic, she noticed Subaru staring at her and tilted her head a little. Her pretty blue hair swayed above her shoulders. Seeing her stirred fierce emotions in Subaru's chest.

Memories, memories, memories flooded in, rushing to the back of his mind. He silently widened his eyes as he felt the raging torrent wash over his freshly returned consciousness.

What should I say? What can I say? he thought, his mouth agape as answers escaped him.

"—"

He tried instantly to call out her name, but his parched tongue wouldn't immediately form the sounds. His consciousness whirled in the air as the welling emotions weighed upon his chest enough to crush it.

Biting his tongue in his impatience, Subaru's lips quivered as he spoke the girl's name.

"Re...m..."

The word was formed so softly within his mouth and was so faint and halting, he didn't know if it reached her. Concerned she hadn't heard it, he breathed in to immediately speak her name again.

"—Yes, I am Rem."

And yet, a reply came. A moment before he repeated her name, the girl—Rem—smiled in response to Subaru's clumsy address.

He had called out to Rem, and she had answered.

"Rem."

"Subaru?"

"Rem, Rem...Rem."

Rem raised her eyebrows, looking conflicted at hearing her name so many times.

Subaru, too, thought it was strange and bizarre. Yet even knowing this, he couldn't stop the word from pouring out.

He'd called her name, and Rem had answered, right before his eyes. That was enough to make him happy. After she died so brutally, he was happy just to have her before his eyes again. He had never been that happy in his life.

"What is wrong? You are making an expression like you have just seen a ghost. I assure you, I am right here. I am your Rem, Subaru."

Rem smiled pleasantly, joking for once.

It surely hurt her to see Subaru as haggard as he was. And the phrase she had used, that he had "just seen a ghost," was not one he could laugh away.

Really, truly, he couldn't laugh off those words at all.

"Rem, I... I..."

"You are a difficult audience. I think that a smile suits you far better than that dark expression, Subaru. Therefore, I thought I would make you smile, but..."

Rem lowered her eyes in disappointment. During that time, she'd finished neatly healing Subaru's wound. After a visual confirmation, she declared, "I am finished," and began withdrawing her fingertips.

"Subaru?"

As her fingers began to move, Subaru caught them with his hand to keep that warmth from slipping away.

Rem's face registered surprise at his bold action, but she immediately noticed the keen emotions thickly covering Subaru's face.

"Really, what is it? I mean… I am happy to have you be the one doing this, but it is rather sudden and took me by surprise."

"Thin. Small… Warm, huh."

He felt Rem's small fingers as they rested snugly in his own hand. That soft warmth was proof that she was alive. Her body with blood flowing through it felt so different than her stiff, bloodless flesh.

She lived. She was alive. She'd come back to life.

Such an obvious thing consoled Subaru's heart, once shattered.

"Subaru, I somewhat mind being called small, so I do not wish to hear it often, but it is fine if it's you. As for warm, that goes without saying. I am alive, after all."

That last phrase made Subaru gasp and look up at Rem. Face-to-face, their eyes met, with deep compassion in Rem's pale-blue irises.

"Are you anxious? But I am here. I will save you, Subaru, even at the cost of my life, so it's all right."

—No. She was wrong.

Subaru had let Rem die. He'd killed her. Twice. Ruthlessly. Mercilessly.

The first time, one could claim he had nothing to do with it. But the second time was different. The second time, he could make no excuses whatsoever: Rem had died for Subaru's sake.

To protect him, to save him, for his sake, she had used her life and wrung it out to the last, dying for Subaru's sake.

The Rem before his eyes didn't know this. Subaru alone knew.

"—"

Before he realized it, he was gripping Rem's small hand, bowing his face so that she would not see it.

Seeing his behavior, Rem felt her fingers tremble in anxiety, wondering if she had done something to inconvenience him. But that was only for a single moment.

"It's all right. It's all right. Everything is fine."

Rem realized through her fingers that Subaru was afraid. So she used her free hand to pat his back, gently consoling him like a child.

And this she did, stroking him, showing him affection, until Subaru raised his head. Always gentle, always loving.

10

"Sorry to interrupt your touching moment, but I can't do any business like this."

Cadmon gazed at the episode in front of his shop and waved both away as he spoke. Normally, that would have rubbed Subaru the wrong way, prompting him to say something like, "It's not like you were gonna get any business done whether we were here or not," but here, Subaru followed the lead of Rem's hand, gently departing from that place.

If Cadmon had really wanted to get in the way, he would've done something five minutes earlier. He was a fundamentally good person, and that was why he'd waited for Subaru to calm down before breaking out his capitalist spirit.

For his part, Subaru did not have any room to notice such benevolence. That moment, the inside of his chest was governed by one emotion alone.

—*Kill. Kill. Kill. Kill. Kill. Kill. Kill. Kill. Kill. Kill.*

Even though Return by Death had remade the world, that hatred was the one thing that had not been erased.

This time, Subaru had a mortal enemy. And that enemy had a name.

Petelgeuse Romanée-Conti.

He was the worst of all madmen and had committed the great, unforgivable crime of slaughtering Rem and the villagers.

It was Subaru's duty to use the power of Return by Death to kill that man.

As Rem led Subaru away from the front of the shop by the hand, she stopped.

"...Subaru, if you have a moment?"

When Rem looked back, Subaru replied, "What is it?" with a casual shrug of his shoulders, making light of the dark emotions inside his heart. She stared at him, making a small sound through her well-shaped nose.

"No... I might be mistaken. It is simply that...I feel like the bad odor coming from you has grown stronger."

"A bad odor, huh?"

When she pointed it out, Subaru gave his own arm a sniff, but he couldn't make out anything.

Coming from Rem, those words likely meant that she smelled the scent of the Witch. Thinking back, he felt that Petelgeuse had ranted about Subaru's nature in some capacity.

"So my Return by Death does have to do with the Witch...?"

The more he Returned by Death, the stronger the Witch's presence became around Subaru.

He'd used that to strike back at the demon beasts in the forest, and afterward, he'd been too busy to look into the matter deeply so had dropped it.

Maybe that subconscious urge to make that conclusion was part of the Witch's power.

As Subaru pondered these thoughts, Rem watched him with a look of concern. Subaru hadn't meant to cause her any trouble. He pushed those thoughts off for later.

"Don't make that face, Rem. Your lovely features will go to waste, and that would make for a dark future."

"I'm sorry. I'm quite a worrywart, really..."

As Rem babbled, Subaru thought of what he might say to put her at ease. Promptly, he lightly lifted their still-intertwined hands.

"Well, if you're worried about my running off somewhere, just keep a hold of me like this, okay?"

"Eh?"

"There's no way I can out-muscle you, so you should feel safer that way, right?"

As he made the statement, hiding the unexpected blush that came with it, Rem looked between Subaru and their joined hands.

"Yes."

With a pleasant smile, she nodded, standing neither before Subaru nor behind him but right at his side.

From there, the two walked abreast. Rem stared at the hand she was holding, firmly shut her mouth, and matched her pace to Subaru's.

As he walked with that adorable girl, smiling softly from the warmth she felt through the touch of his palm... Subaru continued to seethe with bloodlust and hatred.

Even though their hands were together, their hearts were at opposite poles.

Subaru Natsuki's heart was tempted far into that deep, deep, dark abyss—

AFTERWORD

Good day! Good evening! Good morning!

Thank you for buying Volume 5! This is Tappei Nagatsuki aka Gray-Colored Mouse!

Greetings are more important than anything. Incidentally, at my workplace, we greet people with "Good morning," no matter if it's morning, noon, or night. Beyond that, "I'm heading to the john for a bit" carries the hidden meaning of "I'm going to number Five." No particular relation to Volume 5, mind you.

And so, we quickly plunge into *Re:ZERO -Starting Life in Another World-*'s fifth volume.

As the fifth in the series, the story is finally plunging into its heart. You can expect many more twists and turns, with shocking details concerning the tantalizing romance between our main character and our heroine.

But! I'm sorry about the storyline! Here we are, just charging into the center of the tale as the wrapping paper is starting to come off, and the main character and heroine clash and go their separate ways just before they can fall in love, with no calm in the fifth volume to be had.

In the first place, even though the author lives a busy personal life with no time for calm whatsoever, I have nothing in my psyche for granting heartwarming lives to the characters in my story.

I write these afterwords at the end of each volume, but the writing conditions for the work on Volume 5 were particularly severe.

First, it's summer. Midsummer, to be exact.

Just looking at the word makes most grown men go limp. That's true for me as well. It's not as if my efficiency goes up when my computer cries out in the heat. Who was it who got my hopes up for a cool summer this year? Nostradamus? Granny, perchance?

There were factors beyond summer that provided a severe jolt to my system. Very severe.

As is long-established practice in Japan, I set out to involve myself in various events before I meet my honored ancestors, such as my first signing event, my first TRPG, and my first online purchase, all involving a different mix of pleasures and troubles that threatened to make *me* into an honored ancestor.

The signing event was really fun! It's probably an author's greatest joy. If I do another one, I pledge to bring some kind of spoiler to bring me and everyone at the event together.

Please don't ask about the online purchase. It is the result of a life of love. I regret nothing.

Now then, after expending all those lines on things that have nothing to do with the work's contents, let me engage in the usual words of thanks.

To Mr. Ikemoto the editor, this goes for every time, but sorry for all the trouble. I will never forget the completely unproductive e-mailing we did past each other at four thirty AM. It never occurred to me to say, "Hey, just call me on the phone," and I'm sorry for not answering your last e-mail for a whole half a day! I got to taste pork cutlet and taco rice! It was delicious!

To the illustrator, Otsuka-sensei, I have no words sufficient to thank you for responding to your absurd, off-the-wall author with such speed. I'm very satisfied with the two new characters, and I'm deeply moved by how Lady Crusch looks on the cover. I look forward to your work going forward.

To the designer, Kusano-sensei, this volume's cover is really incredible, too, completely blowing away my meager authorly concerns about where we'll put the logo... As expected of you.

Once again, there is Matsuse Daichi-sensei, who has begun serializing the first arc of the comic version of *Re:ZERO* in *Monthly Comic Alive*. Makoto Fuugetsu-sensei is serializing the second arc in *Big Gangan*. I am a very lucky author to have you drawing this girl and that girl with such rich facial expressions. Thank you very much!

As with every volume, I am truly grateful to everyone who participated in publishing this work. To the MF Bunko editorial staff, executives, proofreaders, and everyone at each and every bookstore, you have truly done much for me.

And even more, it's the support of all the readers sending in those warm messages of support and fan letters that give authors the strength to write. Truly, thank you very much.

Well then, I hope to see you again next time for Volume 6—the most important volume to date.

August 2014
Tappei Nagatsuki
(As he listens to elementary schoolers' voices
wail over summer break coming to an end)

OTTO

"Now then, I've finally arrived in the free space known as the Review Pages…! So many things happened in the main story that this is the only place I can actually do something!"

"On top of that, the worst thing is that I haven't had a proper role in the story yet. Is it too much to say everyone's going, 'So who is that guy?'?!"

"Well, so much information came out this time around that a commercially minded guy like you with a minor role in the story didn't stand out! Let's show everyone what a great pair we are, Otto!"

"You say that, but… Er, no, enthusiasm is very important! And I have an announcement! Err, first, Volume 1 of the very popular serialized comic version of *Re:ZERO* in *Monthly Comic Alive* is going on sale. Limited first-edition copies contain a bonus short story, with wickedly designed, all-new illustrations!"

"Now that you mention comic editions, *Re:ZERO Arc 2* will be serialized in *Monthly Big Gangan* starting in October. So Matsuse Daichi-sensei and Makoto Fuugetsu-sensei are putting two really nice versions of *Re:ZERO* out there."

"In *Alive*, you're getting a short story every month, and that episode is scheduled to go on sale in December, short story included. Barely a chance to breathe here, huh?"

"I'd like a break from announcements about now, but there are still more. Yes, a new development for the *Re:ZERO* project—a joint project with Ministop!"

Subaru

"Wh-what in the…?!"

"Thank you for the expected reaction! Original *Re:ZERO* goods are going on sale at two national convenience store chains, Ministop and Lawson! There'll be fan goods you can't get *anywhere* else! I'll get embarrassed if I talk about this in a loud voice, so go check the details on the next page!"

"That sounds too incredible to just set it aside, but, well, I'm wondering when I can break this stalemate. When's the next volume?"

"Book number six is expected to go on sale March 2015. Sorry for the wait, but the sixth volume is also set to be released with a reverse trap included. It's not only a book but also a comic, and an issue of *Monthly Comic Alive* is included. That combination, with all the various illustrations included, will be marvelous, even invincible!"

"This is all announcements to the very end, but please be advised, the preorder cutoff will come rather soon. As Mr. Natsuki indicated, please refer to the next page for details."

"Man, those words come extra convincing out of the mouth of a merchant on the verge of bankruptcy. I'll take them to heart!"

"Can you please stop putting other people down until the bitter end?!"

IS IT WRONG TO TRY TO PICK UP GIRLS IN A DUNGEON?, VOL. 1–9

A would-be hero turns damsel in distress in this hilarious send-up of sword-and-sorcery tropes.

MANGA ADAPTATION AVAILABLE NOW!

Is It Wrong to Try to Pick Up Girls in a Dungeon? © Fujino Omori / SB Creative Corp.

FUJINO OMORI
ILLUSTRATION BY SUZUHITO YASUDA

ANOTHER

The spine-chilling horror novel that took Japan by storm is now available in print for the first time in English—in a gorgeous hardcover edition.

MANGA ADAPTATION AVAILABLE NOW!

Another © Yukito Ayatsuji 2009/ KADOKAWA CORPORATION, Tokyo

A CERTAIN MAGICAL INDEX, VOL. 1–12

Science and magic collide as Japan's most popular light novel franchise makes its English-language debut.

MANGA ADAPTATION AVAILABLE NOW!

A CERTAIN MAGICAL INDEX © Kazuma Kamachi ILLUSTRATION: Kiyotaka Haimura KADOKAWA CORPORATION ASCII MEDIA WORKS

1

KAZUMA KAMACHI
ILLUSTRATION BY
KIYOTAKA HAIMURA

A Certain Magical Index

Another
yukito ayatsuji

VISIT YENPRESS.COM TO CHECK OUT ALL THE TITLES IN OUR NEW LIGHT NOVEL INITIATIVE AND...

GET YOUR YEN ON!

www.YenPress.com